AN
EXTRA
LIFE

8 Minutes in Heaven

with My Father

Original title
Una vita Extra 8 minuti in Paradiso con mio padre
© St. Petersburg Press, 2023

Published by St. Petersburg Press
St. Petersburg, FL
www.stpetersburgpress.com
Copyright ©2023

Design and composition by Isa Crosta and St. Petersburg Press
Cover design by Fabio Dal Boni

Print ISBN: 978-1-940300-71-9
eBook ISBN: 978-1-940300-72-6

First Edition

AN
EXTRA
LIFE

8 Minutes in Heaven

with My Father

FABIO DAL BONI

I am fortunate to be living the best of lives, with the full and reciprocated love of my wife Alexa, who has always put up with me and given me her constant support in this undertaking, as in all other adventures of mine, both imaginary and real.

I dedicate this book to her, to our children, Matilde and Leonardo, to my older children, Luca and Federica, and, with infinite thanks, to my dear Father, Sergio, and my adored Mother, Erika. I love you with all possible and impossible love.

CONTENTS

AUTHOR'S NOTE

~

An Extra Life is based on a true story, my story, and my recollection of events. It's also a family saga that I tell to the best of my knowledge and how I experienced events. I've spent several years researching dates, locations, names, and historical events, and I've tried to be as accurate as possible.

For narrative reasons some names, characters, places, and incidents are the product of my imagination or are used fictitiously. Any resemblance to actual persons, living or dead, events, or locales is entirely coincidental.

A WELL KEPT SECRET

~

For eight long years, I kept a secret. I didn't do it to protect myself or my family from some unknown danger. Nor because it was something to be ashamed of. I just preferred keeping it to myself, only revealing it to a few, very few people, about ten altogether, chosen almost by chance, either because they showed an open mind and a sensitive soul at the right moment, or because I always felt we were on the same wavelength.

Making it known was far more complicated than simply clicking on the public/private option on one's profile on Facebook, Instagram, or Linkedin. What's so difficult or wrong with publishing a photo showing you with a few extra pounds and somewhat less hair? Not much, it seems to me. A few laughs, then one moves on.

What I am about to tell you in the following pages is still so intimate and unsettling that I found myself crying as my fingers moved on the keyboard to write about it. And when I turned off the computer because "enough is enough for one day," I went to bed with my bones shaking and my breath short.

Some of my acquaintances, perhaps even all of them, will be shocked, and I apologize sincerely for this.

Eight years ago, I died.

My heart stopped suddenly. Time's up. Farewell!

I was dead for eight minutes.

In that fraction of time, perhaps an imperceptible instant over a lifetime, yet one capable of leaving an indelible mark, I found answers, even to those questions for which I have never looked for specific and definitive answers during my earthly life. From the most simple ones, which accompany us from our early years - Who am I? Who are my parents? - to the more spiritual one – What's the meaning of life? – and deeper still – What happens when my soul leaves my body?

During those interminable eight minutes, when my heart stopped beating, I traveled a path of buried memories, those from my first 59 years and those decanted into my subconscious self by the stories of my parents and about their parents.

I walked with the angels that have always been at my side and whom I was finally able to recognize.

I saw before my eyes a hundred years of stories of generations devastated by war, by tyranny. A hundred years of friendships and betrayals, dismay and happiness.

I honored the heroes, people of all ages and ethnicities that sacrificed their lives for those of their companions.

I saw death. I saw it many times. My father's virtual one when he was only 16 and his real one at age 79. I saw that of his father, whom he never met, and that of his mother, whom he was able to find; that of my own mother, of my brother, of hundreds and thousands of sailors in the service of their Fatherland.

I saw my own death.

I entered Heaven. There I found my father, who had died ten years before me. He accompanied me on a spiritual journey filled with difficult choices, sometimes irreversible ones, and he guided me through the regenerating light of the Afterlife.

And, as the sentence "Game Over" scrolled mercilessly on the monitor in the Emergency Room, a miracle sent me back to my earth life. My heart, my heroes, my angels, they all allowed me another chance.

I was given the gift of an extra life.

Eight years ago, I died. And I was reborn.

This is my secret, and it's what makes me the luckiest man in the world.

I have the good fortune of being an adult, in fact, a senior adult, who looks at the world with the eyes of a child; one who is moved when looking at the petals of a flower, at a plane's contrails amid the clouds, at the smile of the woman I love and of people I don't even know.

I always have the good fortune to discover the extraordinary in ordinary things, and I invite everyone to do the same.

Eight years ago, I saw an incomparable light, a white, eternal, reassuring, and loving light, not a blinding one. Ever since that day, I have been seeking it, trying to describe it, reproduce it in my art, and convey it to others.

I have finally found the courage to tell you my great secret without timidity or censure. This book is not a biography, I would not wish to do that, nor would I have the audacity to bore even the kindest of readers with it.

These are events that really took place. I experienced those eight minutes through my father's eyes, his heart, and his guts. His life merged with mine, a fusion of blood and mind. When he cried, I suffered, too; when he smiled, I rejoiced, too.

During those eight minutes, I rediscovered the essence of our lives.

With all the energy I have, I can confidently say that life is beautiful, wonderful. It is a gift, and it must be lived to its fullest.

After this experience, I can guarantee that there are heroes and angels around us.

We cannot see them, but they are here. We, too, are angels, even if we don't know it.

CHAPTER ONE

DON SERGIO, MY FATHER

~

My father was an extraordinary man. He played poker with fate. And he never started with a lucky hand. He would just make it happen. He defied time, trends, and money. Always head-on. He was afraid but never retreated in the face of fear. He had courage, and he fed it on air. He was perfectly irresponsible yet had an enormous, unequaled sense of responsibility towards his family, never towards himself.

His eyes were deep and clear, you could swim inside them, as in crystal-clear waters, as if rocked by delicate waves, in a place where there was no danger, or where you could see danger from very far away, and you could always trust in his prompt defense. Through his gaze, you could see the approaching storm, and you understood that he knew how to confront it, that he had overcome it dozens and dozens of times. You clung to him, and you knew that he would never betray you. He loved the sea, even though the sea had taken his life. He loved it because it had also given his life back to him.

We played chess all the time; I let him win. He knew it, and yet, every time, he would play along and encourage me, giving me the feeling that I could have done more and beaten him. He loved me very deeply, and I often asked myself then, and I still do now that he is gone, whether he was able to measure the intensity of my love for him, as I did not show it openly, and, especially, as it was immeasurable.

My answer is always the same: he knew it. I was, and am, sure of it. I remember his eyes, I remember the tone of his voice, and I remember his warm and enveloping embrace, his intrusions into my thoughts. "What are you thinking?" "Nothing special, Babbo." He never pressed me. He knew what I was thinking, or perhaps he imagined that I was living some unique experience at that moment. Yet that was enough. We were on the same wavelength, even when we quarreled, and we fought a lot, sometimes fiercely. We loved each other.

We went to horse races together. When I was a young boy, barely older than thirteen, he took me with him as if I were a trophy, as if I were a guru that needed challenging. He preferred broken-down old nags with absurd odds against them.

"Look, look at number 7, the one with the jockey wearing the orange jacket. The jockey is having a hard time holding him back; he is so eager to sprint like a rocket. They listed it at 20-1 odds. That's our horse. Here, take 1,000 dollars, go and place it before others notice and lower the odds. We'll clean up!"

I obeyed because this was his bet, certainly not his intuition. He was an intelligent man, never a gullible simpleton. I was sure that he lied, knowing full well he was lying. I was sure he realized that the jockey was struggling just to keep that dappled bay standing while, in reality, the nag only longed to get back to his stable for a good rest.

The other horses overtook him during warm-up and seemed to be making fun of him as if he were the village idiot. His tack was second, or perhaps even third hand, and was too large for him. His noseband was worn and half twisted, and it hung over his mouth, having turned into a ball of leather and reddish cloth. His rivals would turn their heads towards him, and some would seem to show off their new golden blinders or the new red garters just above their hoofs while appearing to say, "Hello, clown, haven't you had enough of this?"

Not to mention the jockey. According to my notes, his races always ended the same way, with his nose behind the rumps of his adversaries, trying to avoid sprays of manure hurled by the other galloping horses, all faster than his. Depending on their final placing in the race, the other jockeys would reach the finish line with their goggles variously stained with grass, sand, or mud. Ours would cut the finish line all covered in mud but with great determination, having angrily spurred on the nag of the day.

Who would have thought of betting even one red cent on such a pair of losers? My father. This was not a strategy; it was a method he also applied to his life. He bet high because cautious steps do not pay, and they certainly don't provide adrenaline.

I would watch this show while trying to take in whatever positive aspect I might find, even though most seemed incomprehensible at the time. I saw betting offices filled with apparently decent, well-bred people who were ruining themselves, thugs who would offer spectacular deals under the table or a tip-off about an illegal arrangement between some stable owner and criminal elements.

They did not approach my father; they respected him. "Don Sergio, please allow me," they would step aside as he went by or stand to offer him a first-row seat. We were in Venezuela, in Caracas. The racetrack seemed to me like a science-fiction world, where anything could happen in just a few minutes, even being hit in the head by a lightning bolt. Worry was not among the feelings or emotions of those moments. He had none, so why should I? Just because I was a kid? Certainly not, I was with him!

My father smoked large Cuban cigars. He would have them sent directly from Havana, where we had lived a few years before, and had first been known as Don Sergio.

But what am I saying, "lived"!

In Cuba, my father had been like the boss of the island, of that whole country. Even Fidel Castro called him Don Sergio.

I think it was that bearded giant who had first adorned my father with that moniker.

I was four years old when the leader of the Cuban Revolution picked me up with his hands, much larger than my father's, so that his two thumbs rested against my sternum while his remaining eight fingers pressed into my spine. The dip between each hand's thumb and index finger acted as a perfect cradle for the space under my arms.

He lifted me over his head, up, up for me to touch the sky. I know you might think I am exaggerating, but do you remember when you were a little sparrow, and everything seemed out of reach? Siblings, friends, they were always bigger than you, even though they might have been only a couple of years older... yet they were better, greater in every way.

On May 31, 1956, I was born in Rapallo, a pretty little town on the Ligurian coast. On the sea. Every time my mother, Erika, became pregnant, my father would find a way to ensure that she would be in Italy to give birth. It was an essential rite of passage: their children had to be citizens of the same country so as not to run the risk of being pitted one against the other in a possible future world war. Claudio, the eldest, four years my senior, was born in Italy, so all the others had to be Italian.

I was conceived in Philadelphia, Pennsylvania, during yet another one of my parents' moves, one that took them from the United States to Mexico, thence to Cuba, which had seemed the right destination at the time, or, at least, a bit more stable than others. Then, too, my mother had taken a plane to Italy and had gone right back to my father after giving birth. I was American, Italian, and one could say that I was also entirely Cuban.

"Don Sergio," Fidel addressed him with the informal "you" as between old friends, but always with that "Don" in front of his name, "You cannot interfere with the destiny of a child of this land! He is Cuban. His nation is claiming him. I'm claiming him."

My mother, who always thought of me as a kitten in need of cuddles, conveyed his peremptory tone and theatrical gestures to me.

When my sweetest mother would repeat those words to me, my father, whom I adored, would start in with his own stories of long nights spent listening to Fidel and of how the atmosphere would soon change.

"He wanted to have near him people he valued, especially those outside of his family, whom he did not trust," my father explained, adding immediately, "and when I say value, I am referring to things that he knew he did not have, but that might someday be useful to him."

Don Sergio owned a paper mill and bookstores in the city. He was the only publisher of newspapers and magazines that were independent of Fulgencio Batista. That mill could have printed currency for Castro without having to rely on the Americans or the Europeans. Books and newspapers could be his personal bullhorns.

According to my mother's stories, Castro could talk from the early hours of the morning to the early hours of the next morning. He could go around the clock twice with his words. In Cuba, everyone would be glued to the radio, and every word of his carried weight in the hearts and people's hopes – hopes that were later to be largely dashed. Afterward, when his listeners were exhausted (not he), he would order a day of rest for all.

"The child you are showing me here is not a son of

Cuba; he is MY son!" That day, my father had no hesitation in standing up to Fidel Castro, who then set me down, perhaps without shaking me, but with an expression of rage.

"You must embrace the Revolution; you must put everything you've got into the Revolution. You owe it to your children. You owe it to Cuba!" said Fidel, underscoring his goal as if there was any need for it.

The beauty of my parents' stories, decades after those events, resided in their special inner strength, in their ability to always infuse trust, never hatred, however strongly they might have felt themselves about a man who later, brutally, would take from them a position that had been so fortunate and had lasted so long, and was unique. A position which my father had defended, without ever giving up, even in the days of Batista, who had also been eager to take over, yet had always been sent away empty-handed.

Don Sergio and Commander Fidel sparred while looking straight into each other's eyes, even though the Cuban had to tilt his head because he was over six feet tall and thus almost 8 inches taller than my father. One of them was bluffing, perhaps both. My father certainly was.

Neither would back down. Castro wanted the keys to the paper empire and control over the free-thinking that only Don Sergio's press could best highlight. But my father only answered to himself, not because of some political conviction or out of ethical considerations. That was just the way he was and how he had always been.

"I will not act as a bullhorn for your Revolution, and I will not be your puppet!" shot out my father.

Fidel held back from crushing that *gusano*, that Italian worm, right then and there. He would do it later, in another way, far more devastating and final.

When he reached this point in the story, my father

would appear triumphant, like a little David after defeating the giant Goliath with his sling. If you know that someone will break your bones, you might as well sell them at a high price! The most crushing defeat will have the scent of the most inebriating victory. That was how he saw things, and that was how he raised me.

Even my mother would smile. And this always showed me how much my parents loved each other, how their love was boundless.

No blood was shed that night. Castro would set down his cards the next day, getting his revenge without even having to show his royal flush.

The analogy with poker is not accidental. I cannot say that my father was a professional player because he never described himself as such to me. I only know that my Babbo always won large sums at poker and lost them almost as quickly as he had won them. As did the rest of us with him! And this is not a criticism; in fact, at this point, it is high praise.

Just after lifting me up and after that firm "Revolution? No thanks," from Don Sergio, Castro gave the green light to the nationalization of assets and enterprises belonging to all foreign residents, not just Americans.

That was in August 1960, and the bearded Commander had already decided to issue his first order as communist dictator but had first come to my father to offer him a chance to be a part of his rule. A position of power in exchange for his mill, and especially for what had been free thought and an independent press.

Once beholden to the corrupt dictator Batista, the military was to be, henceforth, under the command of Fidel and his standard-bearers. They entered houses in residential areas and offices in the center of Havana, looting and dragging away men whom they accused of plotting an anti-Castro campaign.

Many of our neighbors disappeared into thin air. My mother, over the years, tried to find some trace of them, tried to get in touch with them, but without any success, not even working through various embassies.

The events of those days in Cuba were particularly distressing for my mother, who had already lived through the horrors of a merciless dictatorship. Erika was Jewish, born in Berlin in 1927, and escaped Hitler's persecutions with part of her family. Many others had perished in the concentration camps.

The social contexts, ideological drivers, economic situations were diametrically opposed. But the brutal scenes of violence and abuse against individual liberties were identical in their lack of humanity. Young armed men entered homes, dragged people out with brute force, loaded them onto trucks. Here they wore a revolutionary beard; there, they had blond hair and blue eyes. The former were crazed communists; the latter were possessed nazis.

Together with my father, my mother would later encounter the cruelty of other perverse and totalitarian regimes, like Batista's, marked by the dissolution of values and by ever-lengthening banishment lists, whether of Jews, of anti-Castro activists, or *Desaparecidos*. All were equally rotten and ferocious regimes, solidified through terror and ignorance.

My father would never have left Cuba if he had not been forced to leave that country. He understood that Fidel was not bluffing. The seizure of assets had already been decreed; the pick-up trucks were already en route. He decided to hide his most valuable belongings, money, jewelry, property deeds, and documents of the paper mill and the bookstores.

He had an assistant, Alejandro Cuní, who had been living with us from the earliest days. He was Cuban, black as tar, a statuesque body. He was very close to my father, and my father was very attached to him. I don't know whether Cuní was his given name, his surname, or a nickname. A vast area of cultivated land surrounded our house. My father had given it to Alejandro and his family in a life-tenancy, for himself and his wife and their two children, our playmates.

My father and Cuní buried a small trunk containing our treasures in that land. Together, they dug a deep hole, and they built a tool shed with cement and straw just above that hiding place. We, the children, watched the scene from the windows. The moonlight shone on the only white surface, Cuní's white sleeveless t-shirt, floating in a ghostly way above the fruit orchards.

The plan was to return and retrieve the treasure as soon as the dictator/commander was deposed. Or, in case of his staying in power, to leave the house, the land, and the treasure to Cuní.

My father waited his whole life for that moment but died before it could happen. Nor were Cuní, his wife, or his children ever able to retrieve those documents and those jewels.

We left the island the next day, with only the clothes on our backs and little else.

CHAPTER TWO

DIAMONDS

IN A MATCHBOX TOY CAR

~

A t the airport of Havana, we could hardly breathe. Thousands of foreigners were trying to find flights to escape Cuba. In the terminal, sitting on the floor surrounded by the legs of my parents and other waiting passengers, I sat playing with the few Matchbox toy cars I had managed to hide in my pockets.

"They were full of jewels -- my mother would say --. Diamonds, emeralds, rubies. All we had left that was precious was hidden inside your little cars. Our money, on the other hand, had been confiscated as soon as we got to the airport."

"Vroom, vrooom, vrooooom," she would say, imitating the sounds and gestures that I did as a child.

"We would watch you play and pray in our hearts: please, don't let Fabio crash the cars into each other, as he usually does!" At this point, the story would assume the tone of both drama and comedy at the same time.

"Luckily, all went well, nobody was paying attention to your matchbox cars, and all that we had left of our worldly possessions was safe. But how frightening that was!" my mother always added, while a shadow would come over her face as she thought of Cuní.

Once our plane reached Panama, the destination my father had chosen because all flights to the United States or Europe were completely overbooked, we learned that our home had been ransacked, and our land burned, as had Cuní's house. The only news about him was that he had been taken away on a military pick-up truck and then tortured. He disappeared into thin air with all of his family.

The scene at the airport, surrounded by those long legs, as tall as venerable old trees, always brings back that feeling I mentioned earlier. When you are little, you see around you a world inhabited by giants.

I am talking about the kind of feeling that stays with you until the age of puberty, when, finally, everything seems to find its proper balance, and the world seems made to measure for you, too, not only for the heroes of your youth.

Sometimes this leveling turns out to be disappointing, so that you ask yourself, years later, "How could I have seen that person, that building, that car, as so large and important, so dominant?" Defects, excesses, and differences: all of these things can give you a jolt. I don't know about you, but cars give me a sense of relativity – no offense intended to Albert Einstein, who, in my view, is the absolute greatest, a scientist colleague of my maternal grandfather, someone I consider almost an ancestor. I don't own many books, but for the longest time, I treasured a book about Einstein. My father gave it to me when I was six years old, and it remained the only book to keep my enthusiastic interest for years to come.

At a certain point during my childhood, my father owned a Porsche 356 Carrera. It was fantastic. Or so I saw it then.

It was a coupe, metal grey, and it reached 200 kilometers an hour in the blink of an eye. We, the kids, sat in the back, two at a time. There were no actual back seats, just a narrow velvet-covered platform, but we fit there comfortably.

"Ready?" would grin my father, tapping his foot on the accelerator to rev up the engine. He would hold onto the steering wheel with his Porsche brand leather gloves. He had had them custom-made, he said. We never doubted it. And the engine's roar would become more and more exciting.

The Porsche would bolt forward like a rocket towards the moon, propelled by its enormous horsepower and knocking us back against the rear window. We laughed hysterically. Everything seemed huge: the Porsche and the trees alongside the driveway where my father amused himself with his flying half-mile.

I saw that same Porsche model quite a few times during my university years. And again recently. It is a collector's car, a classic car, as the old queens of the road are known today. I even saw one at an auto salon, alongside a new Carrera. I decided to buy it.

"Excuse me, may I test it?"

"Of course, it's the 911, just rolled off the production line of the German manufacturer, it can reach almost 300 kilometers an hour, and goes from 0 to 100 in less than 4 seconds…" the dealer was about to continue listing other details of the car.

"No, no. I meant the classic one. What year is it? 1960?"

"1961!"

They shone alongside each other. The new one, specs in hand, was 4 meters and 519 millimeters long. The '61 model was 4 meters and one millimeter long. Their width was practically the same – 1,666 meters versus 1,852 – except for the crowning over the wheels of the 911.

Impossible! They would have looked like a dwarf and a giant on wooden stilts if they had been compared side-by-side in a circus.

A mere half meter's difference, but almost sixty years. Has the world expanded to such a vast degree as I have grown up? How could it have seemed to me so large then, so spatial? I felt hampered in the driver's seat. I reluctantly left it behind.

As you might have guessed, I have always loved cars, their design, their curved lines and chrome plating, the progress of automotive technology from year to year. My father, especially after that scene at the airport in Havana, would buy me many more toy cars to stimulate my imagination (and his own), and I enjoyed souping them up. I would widen their wheels by using those of other cars in my mini-workshop, I would lengthen the exhaust pipes with drinking straws, I would apply stickers and adhesive stripes to prepare them for running in races I would later create for them.

I kept buying every new model, even as an adult, with the excuse that they were for my children. A laughable excuse, as I insisted on choosing them myself!

About horses? The same feeling. I would go with my father to the racetrack, and everything would seem unattainably high. The thoroughbred horses' legs were as tall as skyscrapers.

It may have been to level this perception that, as a head of the family who has always gone above and beyond, I bought a year-and-a-half-old racing filly; she was beautiful, very fast, a supernatural rocket. I told myself, and I shamelessly told my wife, that this was a gift for our daughter, who, since a very young age, had collected toy horses of every shape, breed, and size, made of rubber, hard plastic, or plush.

Betfair Lady, that was the name of our filly, won her first race paying out 16 to 1.

Nobody had bet a cent on that beginner from an unknown stable. Neither had I. Don Sergio was gone, otherwise, he would have cleaned up with my meteor pretending to be a nag.

I did not give in to betting because – very stupidly, you might say - I was not interested in the financial rewards of racing; rather, I was focused on the athletic and aesthetic aspects -- pure arrogance as an end unto itself. OK, I would tell myself, maybe next time I will bet on my filly. Of course, once she becomes a favorite. That first victory had brought with it a large prize, which allowed me to repay myself for her purchase and her training for at least another six months.

But a week before the second race, the trainer called me with a subdued and shaky voice,

"Betfair Lady...Betfair Lady..."

"Betfair Lady, what??" the tone of my voice rose on the phone, as I already feared some horrible disaster.

"She slipped, she fell from the van... she fractured her front left leg..."

Every once in a while, I watch the video of her first race, and my eyes still fill with tears at the deep emotion I felt at her victory. She had been last at 350 meters from the finish line. There were nine horses in front of her, all vying to cross the finish, with their mouths pushing forward, the jockeys stretched out over their backs, and the voice of the television sportscaster wild with excitement.

"Blue Wave launches a decisive attack on Gabardin, Holly Source and Belle Epoque are holding on by a neck. The outcome is absooooolutely unclear!"

"Blue Wave pulls ahead, Gabardin and Holly Source react, trying to push ahead. Blue Wave lunges forward... BUT HERE COMES FROM THE OUTSIDE, LIKE A TORPEDO, BETFAIR LADY! SHE DELIVERS THE WINNING THRUST!!! BET-FAIR-LADYYYYY!!!"

I keep that memory with joy and despair. The mafia, to eliminate a competitor, had lamed Betfair Lady. It was part of the dark world of illegal betting, which casts such a shadow on horseracing. I found out much later that perhaps, and I am only saying perhaps, the trainer had been paid to turn a blind eye while someone caused my filly to fall. Or, maybe, he was forced to take the money under duress.

In any case, matters would not have changed for me, my daughter or my super-filly, who had thus been forced to abandon racing and devote herself to giving birth to possible future champions. I decided to sell her to a good breeder, who would take care of her and of any future thoroughbreds she might foal. I never heard anything more about her, and I walked away from horse races forever.

I apologize for this emotional detour. As I was saying, the eyes of a boy see things very differently than how they appear through an adult lens.

"When you grow up, you will understand," at least once in our lives, we have all reacted poorly to that sentence, as pronounced by our parents, and yet we have later tried to feed the same to our children.

What, exactly, was I supposed to understand? That the things we experience as children are not important, that they don't have the same meaning, or, more generally, that they are pure fantasy?

When you grow up and look back on your early years, and you don't find those reference points that had seemed then so sure, so indisputable, at first you feel like an idiot. But then you turn that thought around, and your old idol becomes the idiot, not you. It was my nature not to choose one side or the other of a coin. At least not in an absolute and definitive way. Instead, I smiled at the thousands of facets of life, admiring it as I would a giant diamond.

The things that seemed to me extraordinary really were so. Even though time may have softened edges and re-drawn some shapes, this is how I always saw Claudio. I was a tiny ant, and he was strong, super cool. Unreachable. In any case, despite all his tall tales and, indeed, he told some very tall ones, he really was outstanding, a model to live by, always ready to prove himself the best in everything, but always pleasantly, without a trace of arrogance. A real expert in anything and everything, he could discuss any subject at all, enriching his stories with the most improbable anecdotes and experiences.

How I loved Claudio! He, too, like my father and my mother, is now a part of the immensity of Heaven.

Great fortunes and positive cycles characterized my youth. I had everything I wanted and my parents ruled over destiny, and nothing was out of their control.

Sometimes I have asked myself whether my memories of a happy past might not be a figment of my perception of the world, of the barrier I had built to keep out all problems and pain. It is possible.

I've always found good answers in examining the outcome of things. What did those events leave with me? Did I live them relying more on instinct or reason? Did I transform them into positive energy? So much the better. Excellent.

It does not much matter that when I've compared my memories of this idyllic childhood with those of my siblings - there were six of us - they rarely coincided. However, they only did with those of Claudio, who would remind me of this or that negative event that I had removed or rewritten. But he did it in such a funny way that my version of events was not affected and, in fact, only seemed to emerge stronger than before.

Of course, I am well aware, as I was even in my childhood, that our constant moving from one country to another, leaving behind everything we had built up to then, showed that not everything was well, that something had gone wrong, and that my family was not so much in control of the situation after all. I am aware of that, yet

I do not forsake any of my memories, even when they float back into my mind in rough, maybe even traumatic sequences.

A thousand times, my father became rich, very, very rich. A thousand times, he was left penniless. He started from behind in the race and always tried to catch up, while fate was mocking him. That's the way he was. I always admired his natural gift for reemerging from the depths and starting to swim anew, even better and more strongly than before.

However, I do not wish for him to appear to have been a spendthrift, someone born to spend money just for the fun of it, someone unable to accept the responsibility of providing a dignified life, not necessarily the life of a nabob, for himself and his family. Far from it!

Don Sergio was extremely generous but never for himself. He carried on his shoulders the whole burden of the wild swings between dark times and times of great wealth. My mother was his soul mate in every way. She supported him without complaining, his accomplice and architect of their existence.

His children, as well as the people who depended on him, sometimes entire families, all lived a life of ease, a life of prosperity.

My brothers and I understood this system as we grew up, and we adapted to it. We became willing participants in it.

My father believed in fate, and he knew very well that, however fast he may run, however much he may increase his speed, fate would be a bit faster than he was, and it would always leave him behind by a neck. He used to wager on seemingly hopeless nags for this reason: I think he identified with them, and he would project onto them his pluck and winning ways. He would raise them to the ranks of thoroughbreds, and he would spur them on with the strength of his thoughts so that they would give their best. He did the same with us.

A thoroughbred colt may indeed be extraordinarily spirited and yet be handicapped by the fact of never having suffered hunger. What I mean is that, as my father saw things, and as, inevitably, I came to see them myself, someone who has everything from birth, someone who has never had to worry about finding his daily bread, as well as providing for others, someone like that has no incentive to look outside his enclosure: there simply is no need for it. Such a person does not know sufferings, the kind that feeds subtle thinking, intuition, risk-taking, the kind that stimulates ingenuity, not deceit. He will not be inclined to share his riches, and even less any meager assets in times of famine, times that can act as a strong driver of altruism even in the hardest of hearts.

My father was a winner even when he lost. And the less he had in his pockets, the more he gave generously to others, to his family, to whoever might be in need.

His wealth did not come from gambling. It was the result of his ingenuity. Betting was a way to broaden his acquaintances, to get into places for which he did not have a membership card without having to join. His wagers were a source of personal pride, in a constant arm-wrestling match with destiny, with stakes that were often high.

I know very well that his time was not mine and that mine will not be that of my children. I don't think I have made the mistake of evaluating his life without taking into account the difference between the moment I was in and the one in which he was. One thing I am sure of, as I saw it myself and assimilated it as a rational adult, however much a dreamer and an idealist: his integrity was never in doubt. He never yielded to fraud, blackmail, or fear. And he paid a high price for that.

The paper mill, the bookstores, the Havana newspapers, all of these were not something he had won at a poker table. I never asked him: he would have told me himself, with a scornful smile.

On the other hand, he did tell me about another paper mill he came to own one night about ten years later, and this one indeed thanks to a bad card hand of a Venezuelan minister. And he told me how he had then lost it in another card game to a Polish man named Kowalsky. The latter, however, had cheated and did not deserve to collect his winnings.

Whenever possible, my father would take me to Cagua, two hours away from Caracas, in the Venezuelan hinterland, nothing more than four rickety shacks and his factory of *Pulpa, Papel y Carton*. The minister had given him ownership of a piece of land and an empty warehouse, which he had then proceeded to fill with machinery for manufacturing paper in all its forms, from banknotes to toilet paper. The equipment included the most advanced, cutting edge machinery, brought in from Italy and Germany (properly bought, on credit, in the certainty that he would be able to repay the debt, somehow).

This was another lesson I learned as a child. Never give up, whatever the difficulty. My father applied this rule with obstinacy, in fact almost obsessively. Castro had stolen his paper empire, and he was going to rebuild it piece by piece in Venezuela about ten years later.

Our house in Caracas was on a hill, the only one overlooking that metropolis full of skyscrapers and a warren of cardboard and asbestos lumber shacks. Those two worlds crossed paths on the horizon and were both very far away from us. The road leading to our large house wound up the hill and formed a curved path alongside the fence encircling our property. The entrance was just before the bend, with a driveway lined with trees and flowers that my mother lovingly tended. Behind the gate, there was a garage, which took up the entire first floor of the villa. The house was built with descending stories, following the shape of the hill. Three floors looked out towards the descending part of the road, on the side opposite to the curved driveway. The garage opened on that side of the road, as well.

My father often went to Cagua to supervise the installation of the machinery. At that time – and we could measure this on our mother's face – our life had a perfect routine, "tran-tran," as she called it. Home-school, school-home.

A phone call from my father suddenly disrupted that routine, like a thunderbolt out of a clear blue sky. "Load everything onto the trucks that are about to arrive at the house and leave. I will see you in Colombia."

Together with all of us, my mother rushed to pack everything in the trunks she kept in the garage. Those trunks were a necessary presence in her life. New country, new house. And my mother would empty the trunks again. Sheets, clothes, rugs, tablecloths, dishes, books, records, sculptures, paintings, silverware, photo albums. It would take at least a month to set up all our personal belongings, as they continued to grow in numbers. My father never got rid of anything, nor did my mother. I have learned to "travel light." I am guilty – but unrepentant – of having always left it up to my siblings to assist our mother with those trunks. There was nothing indispensable there for me, and I was able to make myself scarce quietly.

That time, however, I did help. It felt almost like a game until the doorbell rang. It was late afternoon, and we had finished loading everything onto a couple of large trucks with the help of the drivers. They had already been paid, and they knew the meeting place: there was no need for further instructions. My mother opened the door and was faced with a couple of unsavory-looking characters.

They were Kowalsky's men, and they were armed. They came in, pushing her back with the door.

"Where is your husband?" asked one of them while the other looked around.

There was nothing left in the house except for the kitchen appliances and the built-in bookcases. The large living room with the black and white checkered marble floor was also empty. We, the children, tried to make the scene appear normal, pretending to be playing a game of checkers and that we were the pieces.

"I don't know. I haven't heard from him all day...no, I don't know...," said my mother, with a pitiable expression, trying to keep the thug from becoming aggressive, while he, whether out of contempt or to underscore just how dangerous he was, pressed his shoe on the cigarette butt he had just dropped on the marble floor.

"Let's go!" he said to his crony, "Let's wait for him in the car, and if he does not appear within an hour, we will take one of the kids and..."

My mother wasted no time. As soon as the door closed behind those two, she gathered us around her like a mother duck with her ducklings, prodding us to exit through the rear door. The trucks were waiting behind the curve, with their engines running. Claudio and I climbed onto the second one; the others, including my mother, onto the first truck, and we set off, leaving the lights and an old television on to make the goons believe we were still in the house.

My mother left her car parked in front of the garage on the side of the main entrance. It was a bronze-colored Chevrolet station wagon, to which she had never been particularly attached. Cars were certainly not her favorite items, and, as she could not pack them up in a trunk, she considered them disposable. Under different circumstances, my father would have sold them or gifted them to someone. Not on this occasion, there was no time for that.

My mother did not like lecturing, even though she could speak and write in seven languages, and even though she had learned from very early childhood how to soften the blows of war and how to rebuild serenity for herself and begin anew. She was a practical woman, no-nonsense. She loved the truth and never bowed to the ephemeral. "What comes in with the 'fin-fi-rin-fi' goes out with the 'fin-fi-rin-fà'," was one of her favorite tongue twisters. I never asked her where she got it from; it was a mixture of Portuguese and Italianized Spanish, and it translated her thoughts on the matter: if something is not earned, it does not belong to you; it comes from nothing, so it goes back to nothing.

The match between Erika and Sergio was somewhat miraculous, especially when I look back at it through my memories. Two opposite souls, yet fitting perfectly with each other. He was a staunch fatalist; she was rational. He was impulsive; she was logical. She would try to set down roots; he would uproot her. I couldn't say who buttressed whom more strongly. Who was the dominating one: my father at a particular time, my mother in the long term. I cannot imagine anything more contrasting and yet more inalterable than their union. As, thanks to my luck, it is that between me and Alexa, my soul mate. But more about that later.

We traveled all night and all of the next day, without stopping nor switching the truck drivers, who showed no sign of fatigue, as if they had done this a million times. There was no highway for about a thousand kilometers, only roads with poor quality cement surfaces or full of potholes, and often long sections of nothing but dirt roads. No communication with my father. Although my mother was worried, she did not show it. The last stretch was uphill, in the direction of the Andes. Our destination was

Cucuta, a Colombian city at an altitude of over a thousand meters, with a population of two or three hundred thousand, where all the inhabitants, young and old, were used to sudden climate changes, and the comfort of coca leaves.

Chewing coca leaves, without ever swallowing them, is a tradition developed by Andean populations over centuries, apparently based on their original use by the Inca on festive occasions. This tradition has been handed down through the generations. Our drivers, too, stopped to resupply at a roadside stand. They started chewing it, forming boluses, which they shifted from one cheek to the other. The scene was rather disgusting, as they oozed saliva, and it dripped onto their shirts, already damp with sweat, and formed greyish lines on them. I was in the truck with Claudio, who was laughing and imitating our driver.

The man chewed slowly and, from time to time, added some *llijta*, a compound of vegetable ashes that he had bought at the stand together with his coca. He would dip it out with his fingers from a cloth pouch, and he would continue to knead it together, rolling it between his tongue and his teeth. That sort of homemade, mouth-made cocaine caused our driver to swing between euphoria and narcosis. We bet as to when he would bite his tongue, given all the potholes in the road. Suddenly, we heard a loud sound behind us, as if a large rock had fallen onto the road. Then another, and another, then a volley.

They were shooting at us!

My mother was in the truck in front of ours, with our other siblings, as theirs was a larger truck. Our man leaned out the window without slowing down as he went around the next uphill curve. He twisted and turned, pressing against the door with his left arm hanging outside the truck, in an attempt to calculate the distance between our pursuers and us. There was a line of at least four trucks behind us. He repeatedly yelled a series of *"coño"* and *"cabrones de mierda"* and other curse words that made us laugh hysterically and allowed us to hide our terrified trembling.

The barrier at the border between Venezuela and Colombia was just a few meters ahead: the Venezuelan border patrol was absent, they had switched places with their Colombian colleagues, a pair of undernourished twenty-year-old, who lifted the barrier without thinking twice, seeing that the first truck, the one with my mother, showed no sign of slowing down.

We crossed the border while shots were still ringing out. We could hear the sound of metal sheeting being hit. My father was in the truck behind ours, and he, too, crossed the border. Then another truck. Kowalsky's men hit the other two in their tires.

My father had lost half of his machinery, but he was smiling as he looked at the goons who were stuck on the Venezuelan side. When they turned around, Don Sergio disappeared for a good half hour into the tiny customs office. "I have to make a few phone calls," he said.

When he came back out, he paid the Venezuelan truck drivers with rolls of cash, then turned toward another group, the Colombian men he had hired in the mean-time. They climbed onto the remaining trucks, and we saw them disappear behind a couple of curves.

"My Erika, everything is in order. Home. School."

"Let's start up again!"

My mother kissed her hero, and he hugged us all.

"Let's go to the airport," my father told the taxi driver, who had come to pick us up with a van that was held together with tape and bungee cords.

Cucuta had a small airstrip with a single destination, Bogotá, the capital. A week later, my mother was absorbed in emptying the trunks, in a new house. We started attending a new school, an institution run by Dutch priests, the only school that would accept new students after the beginning of the school year.

Changing schools went hand in hand with our moving trunks. During the first 17 years of my life, I think I changed schools about twenty times. Because of the different curricula in the different countries, I had to repeat the first grade three times, in three different languages. The merry-go-round of schools began for me at the age of four, just before Fidel's holding me up with his iron grip and our escape from Havana.

I never understood why my father, for his entire life, loved to smoke those long and large cigars. Perhaps it was to maintain his deep connection with Cuba: no other reason would have made sense to me.

So, my dear Babbo, here is where I have found a point of disagreement between us: those cigars. I could never stand their smell, that smell that you considered an aroma, a pleasant scent, like freedom of thought. No, I never did like that acrid and horrid cigar stench; it stuck to me like a diving suit, and I tried not to breathe it.

You would blow smoke rings while we played chess. You would puff away like a chimney when we sat at the racetrack waiting for the horses to start. I would hold my breath while trying to make myself useful, to give you the right tip. I would memorize the ranking of the horses, the jockeys, the stables, and the tracks. I would remember the lowest, the average, and the highest speed of each race.

I knew who would win. But, alas, it was always that race's favorite. And, indeed, it did win every time. And my father, as he did when we played chess, trapped me in his smoke and smiled.

In his view, to bet on horses that paid just a few cents on the pari-mutuel register resembled begging for alms on church steps. Also, the Don Sergio I loved hated easy things. He always fell in love with the one most likely to lose. And he did lose. He lost money, but not his smile. His smile only grew.

I loved him because facts, sooner or later, proved him correct. Despite my calculations, and without any crooked tips, he succeeded more than once in making a killing. Whenever one of those "three-legged" horses crossed the finish line and won against all odds, that was for me a lesson in living. One of the many lessons my father taught me.

"Fabino." That's what he called me. Sometimes "Pallino," sometimes "Pocio-Pallino": words without meaning, but that sounded very tender, and they were.

"Fabino, money comes and goes." And by that, he did not mean, "Luck comes and goes." No, he meant money. He had an extraordinary relationship with money. He did not accumulate it. Never. Even when he could have put together and saved considerable riches. Yet this was not a type of irresponsible behavior towards his family. My mother, that extraordinary woman, never criticized him for not saving some money. True, my parents loved each other unconditionally. Their bond was and is an eternal one. Now they are together, now they fly happily in the wind, as happy as they were on this earth.

My father's relationship with money was straightforward. He spent it. Period.

"Surely there will be a Saint there for us," he would say when it ran out. And God only knows how many Saints my father must have encountered in his lifetime because he never allowed us to be lacking for anything. I can confirm that we had whatever our hearts desired.

I grew up with this philosophy, I tried to live it in my own way, sometimes trying to hold back from spending what I didn't have. Eventually, however, I realize that I behaved and still behave exactly like him. I am glad and proud of it but sometimes I'm fearful, as he did not appear to have any doubts while I do.

I am proud, and I derive strength from this because I consider myself a very fortunate person, just as he was, even though luck hasn't always been on my side, as it was not on his. Yet, it has always come to my aid at decisive moments, and it has always made all the difference.

As did the fact that I have always had angels at my side. Even when I died.

Especially when I died.

My dear Babbo, it was beautiful to meet you in Heaven! You were waiting for me, with that luminous energy of yours even more enveloping than before. Pure peace radiated from you.

In eight minutes, we experienced almost a hundred years: I saw angels pushing back devils, I saw purification heal injustice, I gained a greater understanding and a sense of time.

I felt as if my eyes were open, and I admired you with all the intensity I was capable of; I bathed in your gaze, the strength of your spiritual voice was holding me up.

I contemplated my life: it had stopped flowing, yet it proceeded with calm and order. My eyes were shut, yet I could see; I could feel my breathing, even though my heart had stopped.

I smiled at you. With my mind, without moving my eyes or my lips, without making my teeth shine. It was a powerful and reciprocal smile; it was probably your smile that filled up my soul. Circles of pure love rippled out in that infinite white light, as do the waves created by a stone thrown into the water.

I felt the warmth of eternal life.

I let myself transition into another dimension.

I did not feel any physical change, nor did I feel the passing of those minutes. No clock moved forward, not even an imaginary one.

It was as if we had never been separated. It did not seem strange to me to be there, nor did I find unsettling the idea that the distance between life and death had been canceled between the two of us. I simply did not see the difference.

Today I can happily recount what awaited me when I did overcome that distance.

After I retraced my steps and returned to life, I kept my secret so as not to be assailed by questions, the answers to which could generate disbelief, if not derision.

Why did it happen to you? Were you sick? Why were you sent back? Is there a destiny already carved in stone, already wired into our DNA, or can we rewrite it through our actions, which are often unconscious? Have you asked your father these questions?

No, I did not, and I did not have them within me to ask at that time.

Nor did I have the main one, the milestone of all questions:

What is there after life?

CHAPTER THREE

A BALLERINA
AT THE NAVAL ACADEMY

∼

I t was as if I was afraid to answer the most human of
curiosities.

How is the Afterwards?

What is there on the other side, in Heaven? What is
Heaven like?

They are facets of the same request for information or
reassurance, which is addressed to those who, like me,
have died and been reborn.

I was on the other side, and I was filled with knowledge and truth. The answers to those questions were already within me. The Afterward was already within me,
and I was a part of it.

And it is precisely the Afterwards that I want to talk to
you about. Revealing my secret has acquired a profound
meaning for me.

"It is a beautiful secret, and it is a message of love and
hope!" I said to myself, and I need to let people know.'

It's not a secret about life after death; it's the secret of
life!

Now I know what awaits us at the end of life. There is
no discontinuity between mortality and the spirit world.
And it's as if I've always known it. We all know it, even
if we don't realize it!

Suddenly, my fingers started twirling on the keyboard
like butterflies on a flower.

I live the miracle of still being here. I want to tell you, and absolutely I have to tell you, why life itself is a miracle. Because, when I died, I did not see an endless black hole, but only light, the radiant light of my spirit and the eternal light of my father, united as they always have been.

No physical transformation, no friction, no panic or despair, no thought about having left behind my beloved ones, my wife, my children. They, yes, in sorrow and tragedy. Instead, I was experiencing the fullness of joy.

I reconnected with my father. I was with him in the world beyond, a spirit world, as if I had always been there. He wasn't even born yet. Through him, I watched his first journey into life; I saw it as if it was happening before my eyes.

"Babbo, we are traveling through time".

"Yes, Fabino." His voice filled my mind. Its tone was warm and calm, just as I remembered it.

My father took me by the hand and guided me to the origins of his existence and to the point where mine joined with his. His soul and mine merged enough to allow me to understand the real beginning of my earthly life. To understand him in order to understand me.

And, especially, to understand why I was in the spirit world with him.

"Look at the beginnings of my life: here, you will be able to discover the love that created me and the love that will accompany you throughout your life." I listened and assented.

I remember that moment very clearly. He could have mentioned many other things about his beginnings, perhaps different states of mind. But he conveyed only love. I never had any doubts about this, neither while I was still alive nor at this time.

My father was born in Italy, in Florence, on March 6,

1926, under the sign of Pisces. He was conceived not far from there, in Livorno, under a distracted and mischievous moon on a late spring night. He was born of a furtive encounter, the First Act of his destiny, the score of a symphonic play.

***

Fascism had gathered up, as if they were rags, the hopes of a population worn out by the Great War. Hopes coming from despair and hunger, to which millions of people clung, as if to a lifeboat in the middle of the Ocean. Little did it matter that it was, in fact, only a wooden plank, barely floating itself. The first harbingers of the next devastating conflict already appeared on the horizon.

The Naval Academy in Livorno was not just a military academy; it represented the cult of the Fatherland. It was an integral and imposing part of the city, a seaport chosen by the fascist regime to dominate the trade routes in the Mediterranean and centralize the enrollment of the best young naval officers. Admission to the Academy was gained through merit, which meant belonging to the wealthiest and most aristocratic rungs of society.

Giorgio Porzio was a cadet, a young man who was raised within a wealthy bourgeois family, one with a tradition of service to King and country. He was an up-and-coming aspiring officer. Extremely handsome in his uniform, a statue to admire, a man to be relied upon to hold up the military successes of an entire country.

A man, a mission, no wavering allowed in his educational path, no failures in his choices for his life and career. Yet there was one, the first and only one, and it was fatal to him long, long before he could even begin to follow the path into those much too narrow preset confines.

Just like he did, so many other attractive and vigorous

young men from bourgeois families attended the Academy. They were ideal candidates for mothers in search of husbands for their daughters. Their family names were well respected, and they were destined for success. They were raised for order and discipline, to command and be respected.

Europe in those days witnessed the growing popularity of the Charleston, imported from America. A fast and spirited rhythm deriving from jazz, it was syncopated in four-fourths time. It was a lively, sparkling dance. Just a few years later, in Paris, a dancing star named Josephine Baker would drive the well-fed gentlemen in the front rows of the Folies Bergères to distraction, with her miniskirt of cloth bananas and seed-pearls.

Adele had studied ballet ever since she was a little girl. Her family was wealthy and aristocratic. Her parents owned land and homes in Tuscany, between Arezzo and Florence. For her eighteenth birthday, she had been given a signet ring with her family's crest. Inside a golden shield, there stood a castle in the background, and above it a knight-in-armor.

This ballerina was a young baroness. In those dark and unstable times for most families, she could have afforded the luxury of playing with her dolls until the age of marriage. At which time, under the old rules of nobility, her mother would have chosen a husband for her.

But Adele had chosen to dedicate herself seriously to classical ballet. She dreamt of becoming the prima ballerina at the Scala Theater in Milan. The world would come to applaud her. She worked without giving herself pause, and her feet hurt inside her dance slippers. They burned inside the satin as the entire weight of her body pressed on her toes. Ballet was everything to her. The effort was not only bearable, but it was necessary. It was her future.

As did other opera ballerinas, Adele refreshed her body

and spirit with the pure movement and energy of modern dance.

The Charleston was vibrant. It had spread quickly across the Atlantic from South Carolina to wash over Italian music halls. It went beyond European musical creations. Dancers kicked their legs back and sideways, with their knees together and their hands swinging from one hip to the other. These contortions and jumps suggested a new way of conceiving and experimenting with rhythm. A new percussion instrument was born, one we still call the Charleston. It joined the regular percussion section made up of snare drums, bass drums, and kettledrums. It was composed of two metal plates, superimposed and facing each other upside down. A pedal activated them, and they kissed each other insistently while marking the dancer's moves.

Crowds of young people were enthralled by it, as if by some popular rebellion. It was not opera, and it was not even jazz. It was something more glamorous. Adele, swinging and crossing her arms and legs in this frenzied dance, drove the Academy's cadets wild. The audience was composed of uniformed young men gathered in the auditorium for the gala celebration of the end of their academic year.

Many were petty officers. All dreamed of America. Adele's lightly pleated skirt flapped about on stage, and it perturbed the minds of those increasingly excited uniformed boys. The cadets whistled, they yelled dinner invitations at her (and after-dinner ones, too!). Giorgio had fallen madly in love with her. At first sight. Adele had pierced his heart with her blue eyes and acrobatics, which so enhanced the sensuality of her body. She stared at him and aimed the thrust of her hips at him. She, too, was instantly smitten.

Giorgio competed with the other cadets to stand out

in the crowd. They pushed at each other, and they pulled at each other's jackets. Such an evening made up for a year of forced marches, of hours and hours motionless on guard duty. Adele was that evening's star, despite the other girls gyrating alongside her, with their headbands and their black garters and their inebriating scents. Face powder, lipstick, perfume all trapped the breath of those future officers. All of them were fantasizing about the "free" part of their leave, the only one after that year of compulsory service. They were all looking forward to the night that would follow the show.

Giorgio had won her smile. Adele held him firmly with her eyes and with the lively movement of her hips. The Charleston cymbals drowned out the loud voices of the other cadets. Everything else disappeared.

Not far from the Academy, the men of the city would rendezvous at the "colored houses." There were four of them in town. Their real names were forgettable, and most people referred to them by the dominant color of the sofas and the curtains in the rooms. The Pink, the Blue, the Green, the White. These were all houses of prostitution, or "closed houses," "tolerance houses," "controlled brothels," or, as they were often called in Tuscany, "little villas."

The government appointed the management, and kept track of the madams, visitors, and troublemakers. The boys from the Academy frequented mainly the Pink House, the best of the four, the most expensive. Their parents were happy to bear the cost. They would never have allowed their sons to come to blows in another brothel, especially not an illegal one, like the ones called "bad death", thus described because of the higher risk of contracting venereal diseases or being robbed.

The White House was the most accessible, its name perhaps indicating the fact that some of the "girls" were over fifty, or maybe even sixty years old, and their hair, under layers of color, was, in fact, as white as salt. Fees were lower, and there was a very high chance of ending up in a room with an older woman rather than a thirty-something girl. There were no twenty-something girls in that house.

You paid for the time of the encounter: two hours, one hour, half an hour, depending on the desired service: with the hands, with the mouth, *Spanish style*, with the woman masturbating the male organ with her breasts, full intercourse, anal sex. You also paid according to the number of girls involved: a doublet, a triplet. The girls traveled from city to city and, at each stop, they would build up a devoted customer base. There was generally a changing of the guard every two weeks, the so-called *fortnight*.

In the brothels of the fascist era, it was customary to pay the fee in advance to the madam, based on the service, and receive a "marchetta," or token, to be handed to the girl in the room. The more tokens a girl was given, the more money she would be paid in exchange for her services.

Illegal brothels were a different matter. These were private apartments where girls who had had no health checks would have relations with men who were even less healthy. Severe laws regulated prostitution. The term "closed houses" derived from a strict requirement that shutters be kept closed, for privacy, certainly not because of any restriction in access to the houses, as they were open to anyone over the age of 18. Anyone could enter, even peeping toms, who would pleasure themselves while admiring the girls' lingerie, without spending a cent, until the madam kicked them out.

"If you are not here to buy, you must clear the premises!" and thus, the madam would get rid of idlers. Among her duties was the essential one of managing the flow of clients and women and to prevent the likelihood of dangerous emotional entanglements.

Some of the girls were sex artists; others were clumsy, lacking in charm and imagination. The manager of the moment would do her best to keep the most capable, gradually letting go of the others, as the house's reputation was on the line.

The Fascist Party had an agent in charge of controlling each house. He would verify the clients' age, sometimes turning a blind eye if a minor was accompanied by an adult, preferably his father, and he also made sure that the gynecologist took good care of the girls' health, as they were required to undergo regular exams.

There were posters in all of the rooms aimed at stimulating the client's imagination. The black and white photographs showed smiling girls, barely covered by gauzy veils, with bare breasts, long, lean legs, black high-heels, and prominently displayed buttocks. They were a real part of fascist propaganda, even though such regulated houses had been invented at least sixty years before Benito Mussolini's regime. These houses, however, were also a source of information for the political police.

The Pink House was not affordable by the less well-to-do. The fee included cigarettes and condoms, and the State imposed a higher tax rate on revenues. The value of the clients was judged based on the kind of token they could afford to pay, not by their muscles or their penis.

The young men from the Academy had planned to meet at the Pink House. One of them, more experienced than the others, had made arrangements with the madam -- no waiting room, with a parade of girls waiting to be chosen. A private entrance, then straight to the rooms. No one would have had any objection to their presence at the Pink, as even high-ranking officers were regular clients there. Perhaps they, too, had chosen the private route to avoid being teased back at the barracks.

"Giorgio! So, it's all set. You, too, are on KP duty!"

This was a peremptory term in the military, and it referred to an obligatory shift doing the least pleasant chores, such as cleaning the latrines or peeling potatoes. It also indicated "little villa" duty. That evening, in the Academy's grand salon, the young aspiring officers were creating a tremendous racket with their excited laughter. There was an atmosphere of absolute disobedience: it was a part of their evening's leave, the part that everyone had been waiting.

Giorgio's mind was elsewhere. "Yes, yes, I know. The last one to arrive pays for everyone!" The words came out of his mouth instinctively; his answers to his carousing companions were words to the wind.

He had just written a note, and he was turning it over nervously between his fingers. His handwriting had been a bit shaky and somewhat indecisive. He had drafted it once, twice, three times. Each time he had polished it and added something new. Too offensive, too mediocre. Not intelligent enough. In the end, bursting with courage, he had set it forth in simple and direct words:

"I want you!"

The errand boy in charge of the musical instruments of the show had received modest compensation for his evening work. Yet he was over the moon. That cadet, the one so neatly attired in his uniform, so perturbed inside, had handed him the note and stuffed into the pocket of his jacket so many banknotes he could hardly believe his luck. Over ten: he did not know how to count them without putting pen to paper. They were more than ten, quite a few more than ten. However many, they were for him an astonishing amount.

"Did you understand? Knock at the dressing-room door of the prima ballerina, and just stay there until she opens."

"Then I give her the note and leave?" asked the boy.

"You hand her the note, and you scram!"

The boy approached the dressing room. His legs were shaking, almost as if he were the one asking the girl for a date. He worried about the possibility of having to return that roll of banknotes if something had gone wrong. He knocked sharply. He knocked three times, quickly. It sounded like a code, but it wasn't. He did not dare to wait. He slipped the note under the door and ran away fast, holding on to his pocket with the money inside.

Adele had not changed yet. She was sitting in front of the mirror, thinking about that handsome young man in his uniform. The dreams of a ballerina were now intertwined with the heartache of a young woman struck by love at first sight.

She saw the card slip under the door, and her cheeks turned crimson. Her heart beat furiously. She did not stand up immediately. She had understood whose note it was and had guessed its contents.

The future rushed before her eyes, as fast and intense as a storm. Her legs felt weak, her fingers trembled.

"My darling child. When the time comes, you will feel a flutter deep inside," her mother would often tell her while brushing her hair.

Of course, that was in the days when she was being raised on books of fairy tales and princesses. At the same time, her mother also knew that her daughter's husband would be chosen not so much based on love and devotion, nor by his respect for her feelings, but instead based on family titles, whether a Count, a Baron, a Duke, and on the land and properties at the disposal of her new family.

Over time, the difference in the weight attributed to being (loved and respected) and having (titles and possessions) had tilted in favor of the material offerings of a possible future suitor. Adele would never have received her parents' permission to dance in front of an adult audience unless the latter was made up of high-ranking people, such as the officers and the cadets of the Naval Academy.

Her mother had been present at the performance and had left for home with her husband halfway through the evening. To take their daughter home, they had entrusted the family's assistant, a sort of factotum, gardener, blacksmith, and cook.

She was their only child. Her brother had died. He had left when very young for the Austrian front, during the Great War. A telegram from the Army had quelled any hope that his parents would ever embrace Vittorio again. He had fallen during military action in the Tyrol. His love for the mountains had led him to wear the grey-green uniform of the Alpine corps.

In addition to facing enemy attacks, the boys were confronted with the harshness of the elements: snow blizzards, avalanches, and natural ice traps. The advance in sudden spurts and retreats into the trenches, often dug into the rock, did not stop despite the prohibitive conditions. In an attempt to occupy high strategic positions and to create fortified and inaccessible combat lines, the soldiers carried provisions and equipment on their shoulders. They pulled along mules loaded down with artillery.

"In carrying out his duty, even to the supreme sacrifice, Alpine Second Lieutenant Vittorio Dal Boni gave his young life on the Austrian Front. With undying sorrow in our hearts, and in the certainty that his sacrifice will not have been for naught, we offer his family these expressions of our most heartfelt sympathy."

A few days after the Army's message, Adele began receiving the full attention of her parents, who had just lost their male heir, that critical lever for the increased recognition of a faithful subject of King and Fatherland.

Until then, she had received piano lessons, dance lessons, lessons in bon ton. Her mother almost entirely managed these efforts, sometimes her grandmother. Raising a good, marriageable girl was their primary goal, both for the young woman and for her family.

In the few years intervening between the Great War and the fascist dictatorship, there had hardened a cult of militarism, athletic strength, and virility. The male figure was a glorious one, guiding Italy and Rome toward a new imperial splendor. The handshake, which was seen as bourgeois, unhygienic, and a sign of lack of authority, was replaced with the compulsory Roman salute, with one's right arm raised and stretched out at eye level, with the palm turned down and fingers together.

There had to be simplicity and composure, rather than frivolity and disorder in one's deportment and dress and speech. The model young person was inspired by cleanliness, with no facial hair and a lean physique. No makeup or beauty products for women, as they were viewed as synonymous with vanity and lack of seriousness. Males and females followed different sets of rules, and there were no co-ed classes in the schools.

According to the fascist canons, the social role of a woman was that of motherhood, to provide more healthy and strong children for the new Italian Empire. Adele's mother, too, had been working for a long time, and with great care and attention, to find an acceptable candidate to marry her daughter. The plan for her was to have a formal meeting with a "desirable-young-man-from-a-good-family" soon.

The twenty-year-long fascist Era molded the new generations. Three and a half years had passed since that rainy October day in 1922, the day of that March on Rome with which Benito Mussolini, who wanted the position of new head of the Government, had persuaded King

Victor Emanuel not to declare a state of siege, as the other political coalitions had asked for.

The King had summoned Mussolini to formalize his appointment to form a new government. The Duce appeared in Parliament a few weeks later with a list of ministers, holding by now in his own hands the reins of the Ministry of the Interior, as well as taking on the role of Foreign Minister, thus assuming a position of power that would be clear inside and outside of the country.

His photograph was in tune with the message that would give rise to the twenty-year fascist rule. He wore a long coat, reaching below the knees, with a narrow waist and open over his black trousers and shoes with spats.

"I could have turned this deaf and grey chamber into a soldiers' encampment; I could have bolted the doors of Parliament, and established a Government made up exclusively of Fascists. I could have, but I did not wish to, at least not in these early days."[1]

Despite this rejection of fundamental institutions, his Government was elected with a vast majority.

In the years to come, organized fascist action squads and armed paramilitary groups aimed at the repression of local political adversaries and trampled upon the rule of law and social order. Looting and intimidation set homes and businesses, and churches afire. Mussolini initially tried to contain the most intransigent groups but later made indiscriminate use of them. In order to increase his authority and consensus, he traveled the length and breadth of Italy.

He was greeted by large cheering crowds, attracted by this man of the people who had risen to such power. The image relayed by the man in the street, by the radio, the press, the cinema showed him as "Duce," statesman, military commander. He was a pilot, a swimmer, a patron of the arts, a reclaimer of swamplands, a builder of new schools and sports centers, an urban planner, a founder of new cities. He promised triumphs, a new rebirth, work, and education. The masses idolized him.

In January of 1925, five months before the Academy ball, Mussolini had taken all power into his own hands, the Government had officially become totalitarian, a dictatorship. Adherence to the regime was extremely wide, sometimes even unanimous. The degree of enthusiasm varied, depending on age and social class. Young women and young men grew up with the idea of a country victorious in all fields.

From inside her dressing room, Adele thought she could hear the boy breathing outside the door; she imagined him still bewitched by her acrobatics. She went over her childhood dreams in her mind as she brushed her hair with long and delicate strokes, unconsciously repeating her mother's gestures. She looked at herself in the mirror, but her mind was elsewhere.

She knew she would cause her mother and father great sorrow. Much more than that. Her charmed life, the one aimed at creating the mother of an entire squadron of strong subjects for the Duce, the King, the Fatherland, this life was about to be swept away by a storm of hormones.

The girl picked up the note. It was folded over four times. She opened it anxiously, as she would have opened an invitation to an audition at the Scala Theater in Milan. She was hoping to read what she already had imagined in her heart. Her eyes filled with curiosity and desire.

She opened the door with a sudden move, even though at least ten minutes had gone by since the errand boy had knocked. She had racked her brain to figure out how she would manage the situation with her family's factotum, with her parents, with the script that had already been written for her future as a betrothed woman.

The possibility of an elopement alternated in her mind

with her dreams of a future as prima ballerina at the Scala. Fairies and gnomes swirled in her head, and they stung her like pinpricks.

The suffused light in her dressing room lit up Giorgio's face. He stood there, perfect in his military attire, as if ready to raise the Flag. Heels together, chest held out proudly, straight shoulders. His sight blinded Adele.

She saw the elegance of his uniform, his carefully combed hair, his chiseled features, the luminous eyes of this young man who had declared himself so explicitly.

He removed his cap and held it tightly against his belt.

"You are beautiful. What is your name?"

"Adele. Adele Dal Boni," she answered with a deep sigh, trying to control the blush she felt spreading over her cheeks through a mix of shyness and the warmth filling her inside.

It was one thing to stir the interest of this young man while dancing on stage, where she felt unreachable, although she would have been happy to be swept away even then. But it was a different thing altogether to have him right there, standing in front of her full of excitement, and to be without a chaperone or any other kind of protection.

"Dance some more, please. I want to look at you for hours on end."

Adele stood there. Her arms dropped to her sides, the note floating down to her feet.

"This time, I want you to dance for me only!"

He stretched out his open hand towards her, with his palm facing up.

"Come with me." His voice was inviting, both sensual and authoritative.

Adele instinctively picked up her shoes, and she threw a long shawl over her stage costume. She allowed the cadet to pull her along without even closing the dressing room door, hopping first on her left foot, then on her right, as she slipped on her shoes while also keeping up with her knight.

A chauffeur was awaiting the young man in front of the Academy. No one spoke. He opened the car door for her, taking care not to damage the silk veil as he closed it. During the short trip, they did not exchange a word: intimacy was already a part of them. They would occasionally exchange glances, holding on to the moment to make it even more exquisite.

The journey was short, intense, and memorable. He got out of the car and invited his lady by holding out his hand to help her. She leaned against her petty officer with an elegant twist, holding her knees together and her shawl around her waist with one arm. The shawl covered her shoulders and her body. Her legs remained bare, despite her efforts with the silk cloth.

They entered into an elegant old building. She asked no questions: she knew in her heart that he would not have brought her to a place that was unworthy of that moment. The doorman and the bellboys greeted him with an almost military salute, and she felt somewhat reassured and freed from her family's conditioning as she recognized the respect shown to her unknown seducer.

He knew nothing about her, but her surname had revealed her aristocratic roots, and he would never have dreamed of offending her. His soul was in harmony with Adele's purity, although his passion was not, and his blood was coursing wildly in his veins.

When the door to the room closed behind them, they stood still, staring into each other's eyes. He dropped his cap, which he had held tightly in front of his body out of habit and politeness. He touched her face lightly with one hand. They continued to study each other while still standing, memorizing every detail of each other's face.

They penetrated each other with their gazes.

Their first kiss was endless. His hands wrapped around her in a firm embrace. He lifted her dress while his lips and hers remained glued together. The sequined fringes hit his chest with a musical and sharp tinkling sound. That sound was the last subliminal attempt to wake the two out of their passion. But they did not hear it.

He kissed her neck, nibbled at her ears. She held on to him tightly, digging her nails into his back. Their bodies followed the music inside of them. His hands were everywhere. They moved with small steps toward the bedroom, just beyond the front room. There was not much of his uniform left on his body. Her little Charleston dress, her dance shoes, her underwear were all strewn on the mahogany floor and traced their rushed and wavy path toward the bed.

Adele's legs wrapped around Giorgio's waist. They were both prisoners of desire.

Their lives were about to change forever. They swore eternal love to each other; they embraced tightly and rocked within one another in an endless love dance.

The ballerina and the petty officer fell into a harmonious, tender, and complicit sleep, exhausted and gratified. They had not had the time to tell each other about their aspirations or ask each other why they were there, nor why they would have liked to stay there forever. They would do so tomorrow. And tomorrow came too soon. The morning light washed over their faces with urgency.

Fine golden dust filtered through the satin curtains in the suite in the Excelsior Hotel, which Giorgio's parents had booked year after year during his time at the Academy, to attend the promotion ceremonies. His father lived in Milan, in Lombardy, three hundred kilometers north of the Academy. His father's father had been an officer, as had also his great-grandfather. Going back in time, his family had lived with the pride of medals, the strict respect for authority, the honor of high military ranking.

Giorgio had just dishonored them.

Giorgio was married. His parents had chosen for him his career, his wife, and the mother of his future children. All had been carefully planned ever since his earliest childhood, and he had shattered all of it in one all-consuming night of love.

CHAPTER FOUR

A CAGED TIGER

≈

A dele drew closer to Giorgio through the crumpled sheets and delicately pressed her cheek on his chest. She started kissing him again. He held Adele tightly, with his arms around her shoulders. Their morning embrace confirmed the promises of the night before. She smiled and let herself go alongside Giorgio's body.

The night had not calmed their desire to play, far from it. The girl tickled his nose with her hair while he wrapped a leg around her body. Adele pressed Giorgio's wrists against the pillow to hold him still while she lay on his pelvis. The glimmer of dawn highlighted the supple naked body of the young ballerina. He was speechless at her beauty and breathless with his own emotions.

Adele started to nibble at his lower lip, feigning naughtiness, while her breasts pressed against his chest. Her feet drew lines along his legs. She was insistent and inviting. Giorgio did not react. To her, he looked like a lion about to pounce and possess her once more. She couldn't wait to become the prey of such a warm and enveloping body.

"I am married."

He freed himself of an anguishing burden with a faint voice, knowing full well that that massive weight would fall right back onto him and again nail him to his responsibilities.

Giorgio had been raised with military severity and had never tried to neglect the duties imposed by his parents and his studies. At home, both discipline and loyalty were words carved in stone. He was the only male of his generation in his family: his three older sisters would not be able to carry on the family name, nor would they have been able to present themselves in an officer's uniform on their graduation day.

He had played some pranks as a young boy, but nothing serious. Just jokes played on his classmates, not as a bully – that wouldn't have been like him – rather in a lighthearted spirit. But even on those occasions, he had not gotten away with it, as he had been taken to the office of the principal and scolded in front of his parents. His mother, Ginevra, would have forgiven anything of him, not out of favoritism towards the boy, but because she trusted his judgment and his ability to distinguish between good and evil, as he had been taught.

Even the thrill of his first kiss had been shared, willy-nilly, with his family, first of all with his sisters, who subjected him to a third-degree interrogation. Sofia was a classmate of his youngest sister, Sonia. What a pair they were, Sonia and Sofia, two little vipers in Giorgio's eyes! Sofia was just over fifteen years old, and he was just fourteen. They liked each other and flirted from a distance; they challenged each other with smiles. One winter afternoon, Sofia took advantage of her best friend's distraction, as she had left the room with innocent complicity and gone to join her mother in the kitchen.

Giorgio followed their movements with a lively imagination, leaning with one hip against the wall facing the door as he peeked through the crack left open by the girls when they knew the boy was there. It was part of their game of seduction, of their first experiments in conquest. The boy moved quickly from his position so as not to be seen by Sonia. When he moved back to the wall, he gave a start. The room was empty, and neither of them was there. How could he have been so distracted?

Sofia surprised him. Like a panther, she jumped out of the corner where she had been hiding and planted a kiss on his lips. He let her attack him a second and a third time before taking the offensive.

"Sofia, can you join me in the kitchen?" called Sonia loudly to give her friend the signal to retreat.

By evening the whole family knew. His mother had noticed the boy's dreamy expression but did not want to act cruelly towards him, adding to his sisters' needling.

His father, Captain Gian Guido, who had been informed as soon as he got home, just examined him from head to toe with a severe but pleased look. His child had just discovered his masculinity, and he was already looking forward to weaning him at the merry-go-round of the brothel girls. According to an unwritten law, it was up to the fathers, especially those from well-to-do families, with stars on their uniforms or a high rank in the party, to carry out this mission, and they were happy to do it. It was like a ribbon to pin on one's chest, a source of pride with friends and colleagues.

It was for the boys something resembling the debutante parties for the girls. At the appropriate time, Gian Guido had chosen the best for his son and heir. He had arranged with the madam for a private tour among some newcomers and some pleasure artists. His father chose for himself a blond girl, plump, with large breasts and buttocks. Giorgio chose a fresh-faced girl with short black curly hair, lovely pink nipples, and small breasts, soft pearl-colored skin. Her name was Wilma, or so she called herself for the world. That evening he brought in high earnings for her.

He had then gone again many times to the girls' carrousel, with his comrades-in-arms or on his own at the time of the bi-weekly changing of the guard.

He tried to understand where his life had taken such an unbearable turn. Why, how, and when had his parents decided that his career as a husband was to start, and that of a father, too, in short order.

His mind was now empty of memories: none of the faces of those girls emerged from the mist of the past, no names, not even a scent. Even less did the thought of Violetta, his wife. No. He had only Adele inside, over him, in his head, in his heart, in his belly. On top of his belly.

Adele had covered his eyes with her hands. She was astride his abdomen, just above his groin. She had been caressing it delicately, trying to arouse his desire, as it seemed slow to awake.

Giorgio's confession took her breath away.

She pulled away abruptly as if she had felt a spider crawling on her back.

"Oh my God!?!"

She rose suddenly, pulling back from that body that had suddenly become as painful as a fakir's nail-strewn carpet. She covered her mouth with her hands to keep from screaming, although she probably wouldn't have had the strength to do it. She wanted to scratch him, hit him, and hurt him. She burst into tears, holding her head between her knees. She curled up on the side of the bed, she wanted to run away, but she did not know where. She remained there, riveted.

"I don't love my wife. Forgive me. I swear. It was a marriage arranged between our two families, and we were betrothed to each other from the age of 15. Our parents did everything, and everything was decided: my military career, my private life, my position in society – everything."

"I swear. I beg you to believe me."

Giorgio shook Adele's body, which had now lost all its warmth and softness, and resembled a marble statue by Canova. A blade had pierced her heart and turned her into stone. She was unresponsive.

"I will find a solution: you are all I have ever dreamed of in my life," he promised.

In his distress, Giorgio continued to make promises he knew he could not keep but hoped would materialize, as if by magic. His head was quickly filling with a sequence of images: his father's ruthless look, the horrible feeling of his uniform being torn from him, and his being thrown into a lion's den. The wild merry-go-round of consequences was spinning ever faster, hinging on his legs.

"Adele, look at me. I love you! I want to live the rest of my life with you."

"Adele, I beg of you. We can be happy, believe me."

She did not move and continued to sob hopelessly. Her tears had dried up. She had used them all. Her skin seemed drier than the Abyssinian Desert. Giorgio caressed her. She didn't even try to push him away; she did not react to his attempts at drawing her back to him.

The young petty officer desperately wanted to obtain her forgiveness, to retrieve her love but he knew he was a caged tiger. His thoughts rushed from one side of the room to the other as the space was closing in around him. There was no escape. He knew it very well but did not want to contemplate that fact nor confess it. His life and that of Adele were in grave danger, and he knew it, as did she.

It was June 10, 1925. Women had no rights. Further, the separation between spouses was not permissible under any circumstances. Giorgio and Adele were guilty of adultery; they were criminals in a world that did not allow second thoughts. A world without forgiveness, full of honor and punishment.

Adultery was an extremely serious offense, not only a crime against one's family, but an inadmissible violation, an unforgivable sign of lack of loyalty to the Fatherland. To make matters worse, he was a member of the military. Not just a foot soldier, not just a boy willing to go on forced marches in exchange for a piece of bread and daily rations, not just a young man sent to face enemy cannons armed with nothing more than a simple gun with a bayonet.

Giorgio was an Academy cadet, part of the elite of high-ranking officers: a future captain, a commander, and an admiral. A white-gloved life to be lived in the service of the Italian tricolor flag. A path far distant from muddy trenches. Such an honor brought with it great responsibilities.

The military code called for doubling punishment up to the death penalty in cases of dishonor, treason, and desertion.

Adele did not have medals or ribbons on her radar, neither before nor after that night of love. Adultery, according to the fascist code, was first and foremost the woman's fault.

"The woman must obey [...] She is analytical, not synthetical. Has she ever been an architect over all these centuries? Ask her to build just a hut, not a temple! She couldn't do it! Architecture, the synthesis of all arts, is foreign to her, which is a sign of her destiny. Any opinion concerning her role in this State is in opposition to any form of feudalism. Naturally, she must not be a slave but were I to grant her voting rights I would be subject to ridicule. In our State she must not count."[2]

Benito Mussolini's dictate left no room for permissions or concessions for the fair sex. She was supposed to be a mother, a parent, and a producer of new men for the Fatherland.

Many fascists, the Duce first among them, led other lives outside of the family hearths: they kept lovers, not just the women in the brothels. He did not practice what he preached. He introduced severe penalties for blasphemy, but he was not a man inclined to put up with the

Church's dogmas. He severely punished infidelity within a family while being the first transgressor himself.

According to the fascist ideology, force resided in numbers. Women had a pivotal role in this, but as mothers, not as women.

"Some unintelligent people say: there are too many of us. Intelligent ones answer: we are too few. Numbers are the strength of a people who have sufficient land, and this hardly needs to be proven. But numbers also constitute the strength of people who do not have sufficient territory if they can stretch their minds and muscles to conquer it. Conquering it within the Fatherland, by making use of every free inch of land, by reclaiming and farming it in the best possible way, or by conquering land abroad, wherever there might be a superabundance or an empty space."[3]

Mussolini entrusted women with the task of nurturing the race and the power of his armies when he spoke of millions of bayonets ready to serve their country.

"[...] We must see whether the spirit of Fascist Italy is or isn't irreparably diseased with hedonism, bourgeois-ism, philistinism. The birth rate is not only an indication of the increasing power of our Fatherland [...], but it is also the thing that will distinguish the Fascist people from other European people, as it will be a sign of its vitality and of its will to transmit this vitality down through the centuries [...] Now, a Nation does not only exist as history or territory but rather, as a human mass that reproduces from generation to generation. Otherwise, it would be servitude or the end. [...] A Fascist Italy that has been reclaimed, cultivated, irrigated, disciplined, has room and food for another ten million people. Sixty million Italians will make their weight, and their history felt in the history of the world."[4]

Not even the daughters of proper, well-respected families were granted much. Demographic politics, which included taxes on unmarried citizens, led women, as wives and mothers, to be viewed as reproductive machines to create a great nation.

In one night, one single night, Giorgio had broken all honor codes and had dragged Adele into an abyss without return, a place where she would be expected to respond to the charge of casting an evil spell over a knight of the realm and of leading him to perdition.

She would have to suffer the punishment warranted for having loved a man with body and soul before binding herself to him in legitimate marriage.

As she sat on the side of the bed, she pitied herself for having followed her ardor rather than her conscience, for not having held on to her dreams of the Scala Theater, for having believed in the fable of a Prince Charming. That night's love had now become a nightmare, the scent of the new morning was now bitter, the perspiration on her skin seemed a harbinger of the anteroom of Hell.

She thought about her father Anselmo with dismay, imagining with fear and anguish their next meeting; she thought about her brother, Vittorio, whose undying smile she missed, of her mother, Agata, and of the dedication with which she had been preparing her for her great day, hoping to lead her daughter to happiness, although, more likely, she would become a disconsolate and luckless spouse. She and her mother had looked over the list of prospects, and they had rejected the ones that were too snobbish, the ones with a paunch, the rude ones. She wanted one with light-colored eyes, and her mother rejected all others. Someone who was a hard worker but a subtle thinker, someone well educated but not pedantic. Someone intelligent, of course, but not arrogant.

Agata would flesh out the list, then thin it out. Her main objective was to have Adele marry the best match, as secretly chosen by her daughter. That fleeting and transgressive love encounter would change everything. Adele knew it, and it crushed her.

Her family would react as any important family would have done then: very severely. They would not support her in anything that might be even just slightly outside of the rules. They would not tolerate the shame of having a daughter, who had been complicit in, if not the very instigator of, adultery, a daughter who was guilty of desecrating the institution of woman-as-mother.

Giorgio's parents would also react in the only conceivable way: this was dishonor, to be paid for dearly, even at the cost of sacrificing their son before a criminal court and a court-martial.

Both young people knew perfectly well what world and what times they were living in this fairy tale that had become a tragedy in a heartbeat.

She was pierced through by the shards of a shattered dream of love; he was overcome with remorse for having wounded her and was tormented by the idea that there was nothing he could do to distance himself somehow from his wife, his family, the Academy. To escape a trial for infamy and for crimes against his Fatherland.

The sun was already high in the sky, and the hotel suite was engulfed in the light of day. The large pendulum clock overhanging the wall mirror continued its inexorable marking of the passing hours. It was part of the room, part of a stage without an audience.

The unfolding drama put everything out of focus, as would a camera lens, capturing the two young people and accentuating their disintegration. Dazed, they were awaiting the fulfillment of their destiny.

Giorgio's fellow cadets had gotten drunk at the Pink House; they had had sex until their souls were stupefied. They had bragged about their performances, and they had challenged one another as to who could collect the most girls, like soldiers etching notches on their gun to tally the number of enemies killed.

The night spent at the Pink House had been gratifying. The cadets met in the parlor and talked politics, military tactics, women, and soccer between one girl and another. They would agree to meet hour by hour; they would exchange girls, praising their amorous conquests and boasting of their performances. They would later meet back in the sitting room, tease each other, and the merry-go-round would start up again.

The rear entrance to the brothel resembled a wharf, with a crew disembarking after a voyage of many weeks on a stormy sea. The boys staggered out onto the road in a stupor of smoke and alcohol, and sex. Their uniforms hung from their young athletic bodies, their jackets were open, and their belts were not tightened as they should have been. Some walked barefoot over the harbor side cobblestones carrying their shoes in their hands.

The stones of the pavement were still damp; the sun hadn't yet dried them completely. That group of petty officers gave off an acrid, unmistakable smell, a mixture of tobacco and a jumble of scents, a pungent cloud of vapor that would accompany them all the way to the Academy.

There would be just time enough to pull themselves together, comb some brilliantine into their hair, and show up for the flag-raising fully uniformed, with hat and gloves and their gun held up over their chest. Their commanding officer would look them over sternly, he would examine them with a fine-toothed comb, through a magnifying glass. The ill-treatment doled out with a scornful sneer by someone who had spent the evening in the same place as they had, but with greater experience and a favorite girl.

The evening of leave ended at six in the morning. Military rigor did not allow for detours, excuses, and failures. Even that evening, the evening ending the term at the Academy, did not allow for breaking off from the mandatory period of service, not even for temporary leave, except in cases of *force majeure*, such as the death of a parent.

Giorgio had not come back. The Captain noticed it immediately, at the first roll call, when the boy's names were called out in a decisive and loud tone, and they were supposed to answer without hesitation and with an equally ringing voice.

"Lanfranco Antonelli."

"Here, Sir."

"Carlo Bignami."

"Here, Sir."

It all lasted just a few minutes in rapid sequence like an exchange of saber strokes between the Commander and his troops.

At the letter P, confident of an immediate response, he snapped,

"Giorgio Porzio."

"Desertion!" he exclaimed, after exactly ten seconds, as he had counted them mentally with the "one Mississippi, two Mississippi, three Mississippi...ten Mississippi" method.

The Commander's aide-de-camp made a note about it. At the same time, his superior officer continued the roll call until the last sailor.

A year had gone by since the last unjustified absence by a cadet. That, too, had been a missed return after the evening's leave following the end of term. The serviceman was lucky in his bad luck, as he had fallen off a wet dock and hit his head against a stone before falling into the water. He had been completely drunk, stumbling forward as his body listed sideways with sudden swerves.

His friends, just as tipsy and over-excited after the night spent with the girls had formed a human chain and helped him out of the water with the aid of their belts, thus saving him from that scrape. But the cadet struggled to regain consciousness because of the alcohol and the injury sustained after slipping. His hair was soaked in blood. They had to call an ambulance and have him taken to the hospital.

In the end, he got away with a few stitches on the back of his head, a reprimand by his parents, and a charge of desertion that was commuted to expulsion from the Academy. Thanks to the help of a well-disposed fascist high official, his family avoided having him court- martialed.

The military criminal code in force in those days was that of peacetime. Absence from the unit to which one belonged, without authorization, called for various levels of judgment. Not returning to base at the end of a regular leave period was a serious offense, punishable by arrest. During wartime, it was considered an offense worthy of the death penalty. The Academy always chose the most severe path.

At the end of the assembly, a warrant was issued for Giorgio's arrest.

"We have a deserter! Bring him in immediately," added the Commander of the Academy in handing the police that warrant against Giorgio Porzio.

They informed his father, who moved heaven and earth to find him. He could not believe that his son could be guilty of such dishonor and behavior so disrespectful of the Flag. He had no idea of what had happened but answered the call of his peers:

"We will find him!"

That turned out to be easier than he might have expected. Captain Gian Guido Porzio called the Excelsior, "Prepare my suite. I will be there shortly."

The concierge overcame his embarrassment and told the father that the room was already taken.

"Your son, Sir..."

"Have you seen my son? Do you have any news of him?" added the officer with an apprehensive tone, looking for some hopeful news: perhaps an accident. Something minor but sufficient to save Giorgio from being court-martialed.

"Your son slept here last night."

"But where is he now?" His tone became austere, inquisitive.

Adele lay motionless, not a breath, no sign of emotion. Her world had stopped. Giorgio was staring at the ceiling, lost in a world that was breaking up and scattering in a thousand directions. They paid no attention to the pendulum clock. It showed ten o'clock in the morning. They didn't notice that someone was knocking.

The military police ordered the hotel concierge to open the door to the suite.

"Sir, you are under arrest!"

Giorgio did not offer resistance; he put on his military uniform and slipped into his shoes but didn't have the time to tie them. His mind was elsewhere. He took his cap and put it on his head without paying attention to form. They took him away in handcuffs.

The charges were serious and varied. In addition to desertion for not appearing before the Flag at assembly, there was adultery. A badge of infamy for the Royal Navy, for an Italian, for a fascist: a deserter and a traitor.

Adele was left where she was, with no comment. Without a glance or a word from the military police. They had not come for her.

When Giorgio's father reached the Academy, he was furious; he could have beaten him to a pulp. He was also heartbroken; he would have wanted to save his son. He was read the charges against Giorgio. He was to appear before the military court the next day. The civil case would proceed at a slower pace.

The boy seemed unaware of what was happening to him; he kept thinking about the night that had just ended, about Adele's smile, about her crystal-clear eyes, about feelings he had never experienced before. His mind was suddenly, almost magically, free of all worries, of all fears about the future. His wife? She did not exist. The military code? Neither did that.

They confined him to a cell as grey as lime, a place designed and built to crush prisoners and enemies, to lead them to madness. There was hardly room enough to turn around. By the Kingdom's prison regulations, a military man accused of desertion was required to be placed in solitary confinement, furnished only with a prison bunk and a blanket, and fed bread and water.

The small window overlooking the inner courtyard let in very little light. It had no glass panes to let the air in, and only two horizontal bars and two vertical ones joined at their intersections. Even if he had had the tools to saw the bars, the space was too small for him to escape.

It was an old jail that had last been used during the Great War, and no one had been imprisoned there since then. Giorgio sat with his feet on the bunk, his shoulders leaning against the wall, his uniform just thrown over his body. His jacket was on the ground, his belt was still undone over his trousers, and his shoes still untied.

That night at the Excelsior had been magical. Adele had loved him with all of her being. He had possessed her without restraint. The young couple had desired each other without second thoughts.

Neither Adele nor Giorgio had questioned the truth of their love. They could have a family, and have a child. Better still, one conceived during that beautiful night of love.

My father was already on his way!

***

Babbo, I remember this story! You described it to me hundreds of times, in its smallest details. And you always said, "See how lucky I was? I was conceived with Love." I could hear the capital "L" when he said the word "Love."

"Just as you were, with Love." Don Sergio's extraordinary ability to consider only the positive side of things, and ignore everything else, will always accompany me like an unhoped-for beacon in a stormy sea. "When you see nothing but problems around you, you must be the solution," he would say. And he was right.

***

Giorgio's father was tormented by shame and by a sense of guilt towards his co-in-laws and Violetta. He found the courage to tell them about the terrible event. He did not ask for their forgiveness, nor was he seeking it. Of course, he was hurt in his military pride, but even more was he shaken by his son's fate. Gian Guido was at the Excelsior Hotel, lying on the same bed where just a short time earlier there had taken place that most incredible story of love and damnation. He stared at the ceiling with his arms under his head, despairing for his son, while his boy spent the night in that miserable isolation cell, awaiting a sentence which he already knew would not be a merciful one.

In the silence of the night, guards marched along the hallway of that abandoned wing of the prestigious Naval Academy, with the military rhythm of their heels on the ground. Their footsteps made a frightening sound, presaging verdicts with no appeal.

The squad stopped in front of Giorgio's cell to take him before the military judges. The jingling of their keys replaced the sound of their boots but did not replace the atmosphere of foreboding.

"Captain! Captain!" the men called for their superior officer.

Giorgio was hanging from the bars of the window, with his belt wrapped around his neck.

His life had ended at the very moment when it had really begun.

It had been a night of intense, eternal love.

A night worth an entire lifetime.

A night from which a life is born. A new life.

Little Sergio, "Sergino", had just been conceived, and fate was already slapping him around.

***

Did I feel those slaps on my own skin?

NO.

I let myself be guided by my father's smile: I was able to absorb all of his positive energy and reciprocate it.

Perhaps this is the true dimension of the Afterworld: love and its positive energy.

CHAPTER FIVE

A RESTLESS BOY

~

A dele contracted the muscles of her legs. She was no longer on the dance floor. Her dancing shoes, her dreams, her love, all had been left behind in that suite at the Excelsior. Nine months earlier.

Her parents had sent her to Florence to stay with her uncle Aldo, a jurist and a man much respected by the Government.

Aldo was Anselmo's younger brother; he was intelligent, practical, a man of common sense, but very much loathe to engage in emotional entanglements. He had not married, and no dalliance had been able to convince him to make a serious commitment. Also because his weakness was the obsession with the family name. The name was a value to be preserved.

He secretly did not wish to be viewed as a firm follower of fascism. He knew in detail the supporting framework on which the Duce intended to build the new Italy.

"The nation is not simply the sum of living individuals, nor a tool of the parties for their own ends, but an organism which includes an endless succession of generations, of whom single individuals are the transient components; it is the supreme synthesis of all tangible and intangible values of the lineage [...] If a man cannot feel joy and pride in continuing as an individual, as a family, and as a people, laws will have no power, however draconian they may be, in fact, all the less so, the more draconian they are. Laws must spur behavior."[5]

On the one hand, he felt a political threat pressuring

him to form his own family as soon as possible. On the other, he was steering a course that allowed him to remain a confirmed old bachelor, by now in his fifties. The Dal Boni name had become a shield for him, both against women seeking a husband and to keep fascist party officials and spies at bay. He preferred to be made fun of as a "human" case.

He put up gracefully with snide remarks about his resistance to marriage, albeit not to women, as long as he could avoid attracting attention for not contributing to the procreation of the new Italian race.

He had carried out exhaustive research in heraldry. He had reconstructed the Dal Boni family tree to its first appearance in Tuscany, in the Casentino area, one of four valleys in the province of Arezzo, near Mount Falterona, the source of the Arno River. Casentino has its roots in the earliest prehistory. Aldo Dal Boni considered himself a direct descendant of the Etruscans, and he was a dedicated scholar of their history. The Arno, in his mind, possessed mystical energy.

He had had the family signet ring cast in precious metals: it contained symbols of courage, strength, work, and glory. Stylized armors, phoenix wings, laurel leaves. And a crown with seven pearls, the aristocratic symbol for a Barony.

The ring decorated with the family crest was not simply a piece of jewelry, nor was it a sign of snobbism. Aldo wanted to represent, as he felt was his absolute duty, the heritage handed down to him by the civilization of the Etruscans.

Wearing that ring clothed him with the mantle of tradition, with an identity, with loyalty to his lineage.

He would never have allowed an insult, however slight, to tarnish his family's name. This was the reason for his staying away from an official engagement, even though at a certain point in his life, it would have been desirable for him to improve his status through marriage to a woman of high rank, mainly for financial reasons.

At the end of the Great War, his law office, not far from Piazza della Signoria, had seen a considerable decrease in the number of its clients; many businessmen and wealthy upper-middle-class clients were almost bankrupt, others kept their assets hidden out of fear that they might be confiscated. The whole country and its cities were on the edge of starvation. Shopkeepers, leather merchants, booksellers were all silently eyeing each other, trying to measure their respective financial situations.

Giada Lombardi was the daughter of a jeweler who, in addition to a flourishing portfolio of customers between Venice and Rome, had been fortunate enough to marry a girl from an excellent family. Some said it was a deliberate conquest rather than a stroke of luck.

Giada and Aldo, who was then close to his forties, had gone beyond mere courting. She was eight years younger and the daughter of a Countess: her dowry was impressive. Aldo was in love with her, but, shortly before presenting himself to Count Lombardi to ask for his daughter's hand in marriage, he discovered that the Count had squandered his fortune through a lavish lifestyle and that, to cover his losses, he had also used up his wife's assets, which were now reduced to a pittance despite the sale of land and other property.

Aldo would have had to rely on his limited resources to support the family he was about to form, as well as to keep Giada's family afloat, taking on their foreclosures, debts, and mortgages. He would have done it gladly, out of love for the girl, had he not understood that he had been the prey in a preordained hunt by her father.

The disappointment had made the idea of being able to abandon himself to love vanish, while the drive to save his good name had had a regenerating effect, so much so that it was able to dominate again.

The value of his lineage became once again the main focus of his thoughts, while the search for a spouse was put on the back burner. Anselmo's request dramatically changed his prospects. He would never have expected to have to find a husband for his niece. And in concise order.

He knew he had to guide Adele's parents in choosing a husband with an appropriate name and social position. An important one, but not one to obscure that signet ring which would, someday, go to a new male in the family, someone with a different name. Even a foreigner, if necessary, in defiance of the regime, but not to the extent of diluting their Etruscan blood.

Aldo, whose profession dealt with other people's woes but without personal involvement, never expected to have to live through a personal tragedy himself and to be responsible for its outcome. As a literary genre, it was like a tragic play, rather than a cloak-and-dagger novel, something to read, perhaps, even something to write, but not something one would want to live through.

The year was 1926, March 6, to be precise. In Florence, publisher Roberto Bemporad published "Short Stories for a Year" by Luigi Pirandello. Aldo read them and loved them. He found them enthralling in their desperate superimposition of truth and authenticity, without any logical link or thread. He was fascinated by how the paradoxical situations created by the writer, where reality and fiction were indistinguishable, found echoes in real life.

He tried to take inspiration from a story in the collection called "All Three," in which the wife of a minor country squire, to resolve the issue of how to deal with the fruit of her husband's adulterous dalliances, located an affluent but physically unattractive notary public to marry off one of the adulterer's mistresses, who had had a child by him.

Aldo had dreamed of bright horizons for his niece, a radiant future, a noble and faithful husband, and children, especially male children.

That afternoon he was suspended between a theatrical stage and real life, between a Pirandello-like paradox and the frustration of seeing the failure of his plans for a new generation.

Letizia was a very experienced midwife. It was said of her, whether true or false, that she had assisted in the first childbirth of some members of the royal family and that the offspring of aristocrats and high military officials had been born with her in attendance. Fascism ascribed a primary role to women as mothers. It punished abortion with great severity, to the point of adding it to the criminal code a few years later. Consequently, even midwives were essential elements in the promotion of demographic growth.

Florence was at the intellectual center of the regime and thus a center for both information and disinformation. Alessandro Pavolini, a young representative of Florentine Fascism, a bloodthirsty member of a fascist action squad, who had risen to the position of Minister of Popular Culture, the so-called Minculpop, by the express desire of Mussolini, focused considerable attention on the work of midwives, which he called *"the art of childbirth."*

Letizia's hands possessed an almost sacred halo, an aura of mystery. She had swift, subtle hand movements, a lucid and calm mind, never a trace of anger, envy, or coyness. Her actions were like a sort of mystical surgery. In the fraction of a second, in a duel against time and physics, she would take the new life in her hands and ease it out gently, without forcing, so that it would slip out of the vagina without hindrance. Then Letizia would cut the umbilical cord, and help draw out the newborn's first breath, the first liberating cry.

She had performed these movements thousands of times, and she followed an almost superstitious routine. When she felt the breath of life, she would make the sign of the Cross, asking for help from the Virgin Mary. She would raise her hands and join them in front of her mouth while allowing the memory of her mother to well up inside her, the recollection of the woman who had been alone in giving birth to her while her father had gone to seek help. Her mother had died at that very moment. She would have been proud of her and would never have let her go without a smile, a smile that unfortunately she never saw.

She breathed in, gently laying her hands on Adele's head while asking her to push down one more time. Adele had been following the midwife's instructions for more than two hours, at increasingly shorter intervals, while unconsciously opposing resistance to them. She did not want to detach herself from the life she carried in her womb, and she was living childbirth as if a final goodbye to her love, to Giorgio.

Her uterine contractions had become more vigorous, and her eyes were crimson red. She had been crying ever since the beginning of labor. These were tears she had held in since that night of love, a raging river that she had held inside during months of hysterical apathy. Her mother had force-fed her: she was not alive, did not smile, and was absent. In her heart, she was clinging to life only to keep the child alive, at least until his birth.

Adele's lungs filled and emptied with increasing speed, but their movements were mechanical. She did not moan, and she did not scream. She did not cooperate. In the hospital room, one could only hear the voice of the midwife, who pressed her with increasing urgency, "Come on, come on. Come on. That's right!"

"Push, push."

"Come on! You're almost there. You're almost there. Come on!"

Aldo was not far from there. His house was a block from the hospital.

But his mind was very far from that hospital. His work was entirely different.

Ever since the early morning hours, he had been receiving young men, older men, noblemen, landowners, artists, fascist party officials, businessmen, notaries, and architects.

He had listened to references, asked for information about family lineages, and he had explained the situation, examined family trees, educational diplomas, ambitions, financial assets.

At least a dozen suitors did not seem too much below Aldo's dreams, as he glanced frequently and quietly at his signet ring, hoping that it would not be noticed. He was hoping for a sign that would resolve the matter.

While Adele was about to give birth, her uncle was examining the proposals he had collected for his niece, a girl who, although no longer a virgin, would be able to guarantee, in exchange, a very prominent social position.

The scandal for the Dal Boni family would be washed away by a wedding ring. A bitter pill, but one that would be made sweeter by wealth and by a step up in society for a husband willing to share his bed with a woman who had been loved by another man and who was about to give birth to his child.

The fascist regime doled out punishments and rankings and, at the same time, valued and recognized loyalty in its highest form, that to the Fatherland. Aldo had been working on this angle for many weeks.

It was clearly understood that there was no possibility for a spark of true love to be lit between the betrothed and

Adele. This was an irrelevant detail in the negotiations. The focus was instead on the financial and social rewards.

Adele did not ask for anything, nor was she consulted in the choice of her husband. Any request she might have put forth would have fallen on deaf ears.

The midwife did not let go. She was working on Adele's legs and her breathing.

Adele decided to push. That creature was all she had left; now she wanted it with all her strength. She could no longer hold it in. It was impossible to resist the call of life.

She pushed and pushed.

"There, yes. Yes. That's good. There we are!!"

A scream tore through that moment. It made the walls shake.

Adele experienced the moment of birth as if it had been resounding applause in the Scala Theater, with the audience in the front row on its feet, the ballet master jubilant, the audience in the gallery throwing enough flowers to cover her feet.

Her voice had not reached such peaks since that beautiful and terrible night. She drew out that sharp note with rage, letting go of herself. She screamed with all the breath she had within her. She gripped the armrests of the birthing chair, pressing her nails into them.

The midwife was in tears from exhaustion and emotion. She had, once again, been blessed by angels, and they all had her mother's features.

The nuns working in the hospital had told her about Adele's story. In helping her to give birth, Letizia suffered with her and for her. During almost thirty years of work and deliveries, she had always identified with the new mother, but never as much as she had this time.

"It's a boy. A boy!"

She emphasized the baby's sex forcefully, hoping that his future would be brighter than that generally expected for females.

"It's a little boy," her tone softened as if he were her child. She handed him over to his mother's embrace.

Adele's scream turned into sobbing. She cried from joy, and she kept weeping as the baby, wrapped in warm swaddling, lightly touched her face. "He's my son," she said to the midwife, mixing incredulity and protectiveness.

"Sergio, I will call you Sergio, my love. You are beautiful!"

When she was a little girl, Aldo would tell her fairy tales and fanciful stories of knights and valiant men. The bravest of all was Sergio. He was a character entirely created by her uncle, but he would keep her spellbound, and she would fall asleep thinking of her hero.

In story after story, Sergio had been a knight who saved princesses, or a seafarer landing on unexplored beaches, a violinist, a juggler, a general, a prince, and finally a king. An opera singer, a scientist, a man of letters, then, again, a prince. And an emperor.

Adele would not let go of her baby: she was waiting for Sergio to open his eyes. She wanted to be there for him, to convey her love to him. She wanted to cover him with hugs and kisses as soon as he opened his eyes. Her hero would recognize his mother, and the two of them would cross deserts, mountains, and rivers together.

She received no visitors at the hospital. She was not allowed. Not one relative. Not one friend. Not even her parents. None of the people she knew, nor any of the girls who had been her dancing companions, would ever have come to visit her. Having an unwed mother in the family was the most inappropriate thing that could happen in respectable society.

The midwife was the only person allowed in for medical check-ups. Some of the nuns were kind and attentive in changing her sheets and bringing her food. They prayed for her and her child. Others were more brusque. They saw her as a symbol of sin. They saw him as a fruit of sin.

Uncle Aldo thought of everything. That was the way it was supposed to be until he could find a husband for her; in the meantime, weeks went by.

She had Sergio, a beautiful child with two eyes as big as cherries and a smile that lit up the whole hospital room. Thin little legs, a skinny little boy constantly moving his hands and feet.

"An enterprising kid," noted the midwife, "he seems to want to get out of here as soon as possible."

"I have seen many babies. Yours is special, and he knows exactly what he wants. Just look at him!"

With her vast experience in the matter of newborns, Letizia recognized in this baby bold energy that struck her as indicating a daring character.

The girl's uncle walked down the hospital hallway at an unwavering pace. When he reached her door, he let out a sigh. It was the first time he had entered the room. The baby had been born a couple of months earlier. Aldo had been kept informed by the midwife and the nuns about the health of the mother and child.

He knocked at the door before entering. It was more for theatrical effect than out of respect or politeness.

"Ah, here is your boy. What is his name? We must register him."

"Sergio," answered Adele with emotion, gathering up her courage.

"Uncle, I gave him the name of the hero of your stories. Don't you find that he is just like the one you used to tell me about?"

Aldo's mind was overwhelmed with the exhausting negotiations, which had drained him and almost possessed him. He could think of nothing else, he had nightmares and kept thinking about Giada and her father. Pirandello's stories only increased his agitation.

The future of Adele's life and that of her child were in his hands, as were the family name and the crafting of a history that would not damage the good name of that family and could absorb ironic quips by colleagues and acquaintances, but without falling into the fascist police's surveillance list. His was a labor of embossing and chiseling, an art that the Etruscans called "Toreutics."

The practitioners of that art work the metal from more than one direction simultaneously: by embossing a relief in the negative on the back of the sheet while using a chisel to shape it in the positive on the front and to add in more details.

The tools used are complementary, and the object being crafted is perfected by taming the material without injuring it but by enhancing it. Aldo felt that he was something of a Toreutic artist. Just as when the elaboration of fine details in crafting a precious object out of metal leads the artist to reflect, reflection is helpful for research.

He would not have gone to see his niece without a contract in hand, one already perfected in its details, polished and unassailable.

Adele relaxed. She knew she could at least trust her beloved uncle.

"His name is Sergio."

"Sergio Dal Boni. It sounds good! Don't you think so, uncle?"

"Here…" Aldo froze her with his subdued voice.

The nun, who was in the room, quickly took away the dishes. She had been almost invisible until then, but she chose to disappear. She left and closed the door without taking a breath.

The room fell into silence so thick one could cut it with

a knife.

"My girl..."

"Well, that is not really how things are going to be. I have found you a husband."

Adele was stunned as she listened to him. She did not offer resistance, although she felt her stomach churning, and her head seemed about to burst.

Aldo ignored the chair that would have made it easier to manage his words. He loved Adele deeply as if she were his daughter rather than that of his brother.

"...You know...he is a good person. A responsible person."

Adele was no longer listening to him.

"...He is almost twice your age, he has never been engaged, and he comes from a family of notaries..."

Her uncle now spoke more slowly. The tone of his voice became more compassionate.

"...He is an excellent prospect."

"The wedding will take place here, in Florence, next month."

"Your parents will come, too."

"...Just after the ceremony, you will be able to go and live at his home..."

He kissed Adele on the forehead. The girl had slumped against the bed's headrest. His gesture was aimed at prompting her attention. He hadn't finished yet.

Something sinister hovered over mother and son, black and frightening vultures were about to swoop down on the two to feast on them. Her uncle was speaking in the singular ...

Adele pressed Sergino to her chest so much that his breathing coincided with hers.

"My dear Adele...this boy will be better off in a religious home for orphaned children," said her uncle, turning toward the door to avoid the imploring gaze of his niece and to avoid resting his eyes for too long on the child. It would not do to fall prey to second thoughts or regrets.

Fate was again mocking my father. But I believe it was making him stronger.

"Nooo, Noooo!" Adele stood up suddenly, holding onto Sergio as tightly as possible.

She kicked her legs out of bed, tearing off the sheets covering her. She spun around as she used to do when dancing the Charleston.

She dodged the hands of her uncle as he reached out to hold her back.

She ran barefoot down the corridor, dressed only in her petticoat until the nuns stopped her.

They pulled the child away from her arms by force.

Sergio had started his gamble for life. Alone, facing his most capricious stars.

Adele's life had again been put through a meat-grinder, with no future, no love, no meaning. She collapsed, exhausted and devastated. Uncle Aldo took her baby away, assisted by a nurse, without saying another word, and full of sadness and shame for that irreversible action that would fill him with guilt for the rest of his life. He lived out his days no longer as a confirmed old bachelor but as a bitter and lonely old man.

Sister Erminia, the Mother Superior who received my father into the orphanage, was used to this kind of task. She carried out her duties without any particular emotion, or so it appeared. She was born 65 years earlier, just when the Kingdom of Italy was being proclaimed, of noble parentage, with bishops, marquesses, and feudal lords on both sides of her family. She had been promised in marriage at birth to the son of a neighboring Duke. Through a series of bad choices – political, military, and territorial – her father had squandered the family's assets.

Erminia was the last asset to offer in a bid to rescue the fortunes of her family's coat of arms. She was used as a sacrificial lamb on the altar of promissory notes, with a very long repayment date, one lasting 18 years. In exchange, her father could get back lands and mines lost along the path of his endless failures.

Having come of age, at the time appointed for her to marry the eldest son of the Duke, a miserly and lazy and even physically unattractive young man, Erminia found the courage to refuse, thus embarrassing the two families as they gathered together for the great day. She escaped that preordained marriage by hiding in the family stables before they could drag her into the church. She had organized a rendezvous in the hay barn with the son of a blacksmith, an amusing twenty-year-old boy without any schooling, with a bold face but gallant and free-spirited -- a real scandal.

The two of them were discovered almost immediately. Their little escapade, whether driven by love or convenience, was enough to upset any marriage plans entirely, and to drive Erminia's father into a total rage, as he now found himself suddenly needing to pay back, with interest, what he owed according to the terms of a contract he was no longer able to fulfill. Thanks to a stroke of good fortune, as well as a capable accountant, he had succeeded in turning over the income flow from his agricultural production. He could have renegotiated his debt with his daughter's future father-in-law. He could have saved his daughter from that torture, but ultimately he didn't do it to keep his word.

Erminia had concocted the plan with that young man, who was in love with her and was willing to be burned at the stake for her. He said the plan could not go wrong. If the two were to be found in a compromising situation, she would certainly be discarded as a bride in an arranged marriage. Neither a Count nor a Marquis would now have accepted her between his sheets as she was thought no longer to be a virgin. But Erminia had not taken into account the consequences for herself, which would be even more unbearable.

As punishment, she was locked up in the attic of her family's mansion until a high prelate close to her family finally advised them to compel her to enter a convent. This would be a favor to the Church, as it was always seeking nuns and Catholic educators, and it would shine further luster on the father, and give him greater influence in the eyes of the Monarchy.

Erminia's life, spent praying the Rosary, doing penance, and in the company of holy images, became a stillicide of deprivations. She was not cut out for the religious life, a life sprinkled with renunciations and marked by the vow of chastity. She detested the cloistered existence imposed on her, one that was sending her youth up in smoke to expiate the sins of her penniless parent. Both frustrations and rancor had accompanied her during the first thirty years she spent in the convent. She took out her anger on the novices or the mothers of the children entrusted to her care year after year. Many of those children were, in fact, the offspring of unwed mothers who, unlike her, had experienced love. She didn't ask herself whether this had been out of force or out of tenderness, for money or because of a crush. That was none of her concern. She didn't care.

Sister Erminia was mean and irascible. She stayed that way until menopause; then, her life had brightened, although she certainly did not change into a meek little lamb. She started reading and studying philosophy; her temperament changed. Although Sister Erminia remained authoritarian, she was no longer stubbornly cruel. Even she, over time, had acquired a bit of that human kindness that one might expect from someone in the service of the Faith she professed, someone supposed to understand human frailty and provide solace to the soul.

The softness of her youthful features had disappeared under the weight of the rage that had consumed her all those years. Her traits were a blend of her father's Austrian ancestry and her mother's Mediterranean heritage. She had had wavy blond hair as a girl: now it was short and sprinkled with white, although the grey was well hidden under the linen band and the wimple covering her neck. But her eyebrows still showed some of her natural colors, a bit of ash blond, like the mustache of a chronic smoker. Her dark eyes, which may have looked hazel once, now only appeared grey. They resembled polished steel when she put on her reading glasses. A slight asymmetry of her cheekbones accentuated the shape of her nose, which was thin and sharp, and of her thin and pale pink lips. Her skin was fair, her height was average, closer to that of her short and plump mother than to her father's, who was about six feet tall. Her habit hid a slender body, although her thinness revealed itself through her hands and their long and pointy fingers.

Her reputation as an iron-fisted Mother Superior ensured that she would be the first to be chosen by someone needing an institution managed with order and discipline, a place to which one could confidently entrust a child still in need of breast milk, of nurturing, educating, and, especially, one needing to be kept away from his natural mother and the eyes of the world.

Sister Erminia was waiting for Aldo Dal Boni's car in the open area in front of the orphanage she managed and ruled over. Aldo had announced his intentions while he was still engaged in the negotiations.

The uncle and the nurse holding the baby got out of the car and exchanged formal greetings with the nun.

The Reverend Mother bent down to check the contents of the bassinet, a basket with woven straw handles, in which Sergio was sleeping wrapped in his little blanket, still fragrant with his mother's scent. The nurse had not allowed this out of concern for the baby, nor as a way to keep him from crying. In the excitement of the separation from Adele, the child had been transferred directly into the bassinet, just as he was.

Sister Erminia put her hands under Sergio's back, taking him out of his blanket and raising him in front of her to make eye contact.

He started to kick and move his hands as if to create a whirlpool capable of swallowing up that monster he could hardly discern, and that appeared like a black shadow surrounded by a sadistic glimmer.

It was as if he were already planning his first escape from this prison for abandoned children.

"What is his name?" the nun asked the uncle, moving the child away from her face as she had already sensed his obstinate character, that of someone difficult to mold.

"Sergio."

"Sergio and then..." the Abbess pressed on.

"Sergio N.N.," Aldo cut her short.

N.N. was an acronym given to children without a father's surname. It was not conceivable and not tolerated to give a child his mother's name. Those were children of N.N., children with an indeterminate father, nobody's children. To face the world with the brand "Nomen Nescio" [Latin for "Name Unknown"] was not the best of beginnings.

***

The images flowed in front of my eyes in slow motion. I felt I had known my father long before I was born. I had acquired a new level of awareness about my existence, one that I had never reached when I was with him in my earthly life.

"Babbo, you always joked about that N.N. Perhaps you were even proud of it."

My father always saw uncle Aldo as a positive figure. Not necessarily one to be emulated, but at least worthy of respect.

I extracted only one more smile of him, but it spoke volumes.

***

Sergino almost fell out of the nun's hands as he flailed about on hearing her nasty tone of voice. He was already trying to free himself from the witch's hands.

"We have a restless one here, don't we?" concluded the nun, turning her back to uncle Aldo, who got back into the car without another word.

As he was closing the car door, he heard Sister Erminia's prophecy.

"Look at how you are kicking about, my boy! When you grow up, you will travel around the world. But for now, you are going to stay right in here!" promised the Mother Superior with a scornful laugh.

CHAPTER SIX

HURRAH! WE ARE AT WAR AGAIN!

~

At that moment, I might have classified the separation I had just witnessed and felt like mine as an injustice and an intolerable act of cruelty. And it was!

Yet, my father's self-controlled reaction, one filled with unconditional love, did not allow me to stray away from the "Afterwards" trajectory.

In the world beyond, we find our doubts, our ambitions; we find our reference points, our Saints, whom we may not see, but who are always present, on earth too. There, we find our shortcomings, our merits, our moments of glory and ruinous falls; we see everything there, clear and accurate.

Yet, with an enormous, essential difference. The value of time. During these past years, while I tried to organize my thoughts to make sense of my near-death experience, and while I was writing down these lines, I gave much thought to the value of time.

By which I mean the value-of-time, not just time.

The value-of-time is the most inconstant of the variables of our life. If you have the patience to accompany me on this journey of discovery, we will often find ourselves dealing with this absolutely incalculable, unpredictable, uncontrollable variable.

The-value-of-time governs our happiness, our fears. Like the fear of dying. Or of living, in the broadest sense of the word.

Paradoxically, the fear of death takes on meaning only during life. It is because we try to measure the-value-of-time without fully understanding its equation. And we are not really able to do it. We fear death because we are responsible people: responsible for our actions, ourselves, and the ones we love. Dying is a terrible transition, a separation, perhaps just like the separation from our mother on our first day of life. Without being aware of it, except subconsciously, we carry that feeling, that fear, with us for the rest of our lives. Separation can last a second, an hour, or another fraction of time. But when we are dead, it stops tormenting us; it disappears as if we were returning into our mother's womb.

Just to be clear, I don't think I ever gave much thought to the end of my days while I lived my (first) life. I always lived as if I were a superman, believing myself to be immortal or acting as if I were so.

Given that I did die and came back to life, you might well ask whether I am afraid of death now. No, I am not scared of death as it enveloped and fitted me perfectly, just like a tailored suit.

But what I do have is a terrible, unconquerable fear of dying. I tremble just at the thought of that separation, now that I know how it happens, how it can devastate the feelings of those we leave behind, of how it can swallow everything up in an endless vortex. Luckily, we are helped by that value-of-time I have learned to understand better than I ever did before, not completely, of course, but better than before.

To try and be more precise, I'll go back to the paradox I mentioned above: if the fear of dying frightens me, but death does not scare me because it comes just an instant after life and has the power to stop everything, then the fear of dying, which is part of life, should not interfere with life itself. I must live life better, to its fullest; I must give it as much value as I find possible, and even impossible, and not only hope to live to a ripe age.

"Here, my son, you will find a part of that value."

My father knew everything about me; he guided me through my childhood, which reflected his own, however different his was from mine, in search for friendship, in its youthful passions, in the dreams and ideals of youth.

Together, we entered a large building.

***

The Catholic Institute for Orphaned Children was tenuous in its shades of color, austere in its forms, and was immersed in the Tuscan hills near Florence. It looked out onto cultivated fields and their variegated striations of green, from olive to clover, from pine to asparagus.

It had been built during the Middle Ages, and it had later suffered attacks by Vandals as well as wars and incursions until it was almost completely destroyed and rendered uninhabitable for centuries.

Towards the end of the 1700s, sufficient funds were found to rebuild it completely, thanks to the intervention of some noblemen close to the Court of Peter-Leopold Hapsburg-Lorraine, Grand Duke of Tuscany and second to last Emperor of the Holy Roman Empire. He was a reformer, especially for agriculture; he eliminated duties and tolls and reclaimed the marshes in the low-lying areas near Siena.

However, his relationship with the Church was nasty from the beginning. It was made worse by the abolition of the mortmain, a type of landed property which, among other things, sanctioned the tax exemption for farms and buildings left to religious institutions by the wills of dying and devout country squires.

Yet, this enlightened Duke, who did away with many codes that had become crystallized through time, such as that of lèse-majesté, the confiscation of assets, torture, and capital punishment, this ruler was not contrary to religion. In fact, he supported the autonomy of local religious institutions, even financially, and was instrumental in restoring churches, monasteries, and orphanages.

The orphanage was almost entirely hidden from view. A high iron gate blocked the entrance to passersby, as it also blocked the exit to all those within: the nuns, the children, who were all boys under the age of 14, and the Reverend Mother.

The building was ageless: it did not show any signs of the passage of time since its restoration. It was immobile, impenetrable, and unreachable. A gigantic wall of inlaid bricks defended the property from prying eyes. The cells, the common areas such as the visitors' room, the choir room, the refectory, the frescoed central nave, the early XVII century altar, all were immersed in a cold, dense, almost creamy smell, a mixture of the scent of blown-out candles, home-made soap, oils, and herbs. The religious sisters hand-washed drapes, sheets, and clothes with wood ashes. They scrubbed the floors with lye, which they obtained by boiling ashes in water after straining them to eliminate small pebbles and bits of coal.

The nuns' hands were smoothed by the ashes and whitened by the lye; everything everywhere was aseptic, immaculate. They walked very quickly in the hallways of the barracks-like orphanage, with tiny steps, moving almost like penguins on the ice. They were everywhere, at all times. An army of ants, busily working away, all terrified of their queen, Sister Erminia.

Seen from the other hills, some higher, some lower, the building looked like a sleeping snake, curled up onto itself with interminable cypress spires. Those trees were beautiful as they stood proudly, lean and elegant. They took care of themselves: nobody pruned their branches nor clipped them into shape. They had been that way for hundreds of years and would be that way for hundreds of years to come.

Sergino had a close relationship with those cypresses. He had studied them during his early childhood. Inside the barracks-like prison for trapped children, there were nuns and cypresses. Cypresses and nuns. Both stood in rows before him, and both prevented his escape. But while the former were well-disposed, the latter were inflexible, obedient to the orders of the Mother Superior.

The cypresses had been there long before the building. Much earlier, earlier than the Middle Ages, earlier than the Holy Roman Empire. They had been there ever since the time of the Etruscans, and this fact, somehow, unconsciously created a special bond between them and this exuberant child. Maybe it was because those trees were calm, able to adapt to the wind, unbreakable and unscalable.

They could not offer refuge in their height. Cypresses do not have the kind of branches you can scale, as they are short and intertwined. They don't have leaves behind which to hide because their leaves are, in fact, like small scales attached to those small branches and crowded against each other.

But their mystical presence provided for him the only refuge from the constant anguish of his confinement in that place. They provided fodder for his imagination. They were perennially present, like strong and understanding parents, silent yet able to convey energy and hope.

Nine long, very long years had gone by since when he

had been left at the orphanage by his great-uncle and had been taken in hand by the Abbess. He had no memory of that time. Nor any trace of his mother: not a photograph, a card, or even a visit. Never. Adele was forbidden from coming near him.

He had no idea of who his father might have been or of the reason why no parent ever came through the gate -- neither for him nor any of the other orphans. Michele, the oldest of the boys, had just turned 14. He had packed a large suitcase made of pressed cardboard and metal corners; and tied it with a string. A couple of books, an illustrated comic book, a small accordion, a couple of mended jerseys, one pair of trousers and a vest made of faux suede. His meager belongings were hardly sufficient to fill half of that suitcase, but that was all he had. The nuns had found him a job in a tannery near San Miniato, halfway between Florence and Livorno. He could have an honest life, a job. He could form a family of his own, have children.

The boy was utterly disoriented. He was happier than he had ever been, just at the idea of getting to the other side of the iron gate. He was also frightened, as he would be stepping into a completely unknown world. A world that had seemed not to exist up to that moment. The smile on his lips was bright, etched in a fire. He was going out into a new realm, but his guard was low. He would have done anything to escape that prison.

The school year had just ended, and Sergino had just finished third grade. Three years during which he had been rapped on his knuckles every single day. The nuns had little patience with his lack of discipline. He did not answer the teacher's questions in class and always ended up behind the blackboard as punishment. He did not study, did not do his homework, and did not hand in quizzes --just blank sheets.

He was not a model student, but he was not a rotten egg either. He loved reading: he had taught himself to read by listening to the older boys, sneaking books out of their classrooms. He was much more advanced than his peers. At age six, he already knew how to read, write, and do his math.

He had no interest in the curriculum set up by the nuns. It was all old stuff, already chewed up, an old and smelly mush. He preferred to be sent off, even as punishment, to a place where he could be alone with his thoughts. He would muse on Galileo's experiments or Leonardo da Vinci's inventions; he would build excellent mechanical devices to escape beyond those walls in his imagination.

He still thought back to when he had met Oreste, the boy on the other side of the wall. Just after lunch, when the sun was at its brightest in the sky, the boys were allowed to go outside and play: not outside the gate, just out in the garden. Recess was the most eagerly awaited half-hour in their grey days, between the morning lessons and the afternoon homework. The nuns had dug up somewhere an old soccer ball. The leather strips were unglued and worn, faded and somewhat moldy, but still contained some compressed air inside. The ball was deflated and heavy, like a bag of flour, but still, it was a soccer ball.

"I will be the goalie." Gianpiero would yell, a boy who dreamt of soccer as his path to the future and claimed for himself the role of Gianpiero Combi, the best player on the Italian national team, a legend between the goalposts. Young Gianpiero was clumsy, yet he did not hesitate to dive right and left to block shots by the opposing team, scraping his skin on the stony surface they used as a soccer field.

Sister Pia was the youngest in the congregation. The other nuns had gladly left the role of referee to her as the games always ended in a brawl. Gianpiero was always the first to dive onto the ball when she appeared with her whistle, leaving the others to form the teams. The two captains, Teo and Francesco, two of the older boys, did the choosing.

"I'll take Giacomo." Teo would say, pulling the chosen one to his side.

"I'll take Manfredo." The other would answer immediately.

This ritual went on until they reached the benchwarmers, the ones nobody wanted on their team. The game always started just then: Gianpiero would throw the ball into the heap, and the brawl would begin. Everybody would dive into the scrum, and nobody paid any more attention to team formation.

"Pass it, paaaass it!"

"Kick it, come on!"

"What the fuck are you doing??!!!"

"Jerk! Didn't you see that I was right beside you? You don't understand shit!"

"It's a foul, Sister Pia!!"

"No, it isn't, you blockhead. Go on, play!" she would reply in the same tone.

Everything was allowed during that half-hour, swear words and buckets of insults. They learned the words from the tradesmen who had access to the orphanage: truck drivers, bakers, and blacksmiths. The kids memorized them and handed them down to each other as if they were treasures. They laughed about them.

The boys released their anger while amusing themselves ferociously, sweating like fountains. They spit on the ground, hit each other, and swore. Sister Erminia, who had gathered a few pearls of wisdom from books she had read, applied the "bread and circus" method, as had done the ancient Romans, to keep her crowd of kids in check. There was not much bread to go around, so foul play was very much allowed.

To reach her goal, the Reverend Mother was generous in encouraging the game of soccer, which she considered rather a game of kicking each other. In fact, after recess and study time, the boys had free access to the library where, among the books on sports, there stood out prominently the Italian Soccer Yearbook, donated to her in its official edition by the Florentine director of the FIGC, the Italian Soccer Federation. That large volume contained names, stats, rules, calendars, and results of the games played by the national team. It was their favorite book, and in the evening, before going to the refectory for supper, they gathered in groups to read, listen, and comment freely.

In 1930 Italy won the International Cup, then it achieved a glorious double success in winning the World Cup in 1934 and 1938. The Yearbook was 430 pages long. Its cover was edged with the red, white, and green colors of the Italian flag, and contained the image of a group of men wearing long knit pants and a little cape embroidered with heraldic symbols.

This, too, was a printed work of propaganda, albeit brought about by circumstances. The regime used sports as a strong point and as a way to attract a following. The successes of the Italian team increased Duce's popularity. He appointed as head of the Federation a friend and early member of the Fascist Party, Leandro Arpinati, who reformed the single series championship, and was instrumental in the choice of Italy as host nation for the second edition of the World Cup, the one that saw it victorious in 1934.

The Yearbook narrated this course of events in its first pages. Still, the boys skipped those to go straight to the biographical cards of the "Azzurri," the Italian team, immersing themselves in the exploits of this or that champion:

[...] The member organizations were by now six hundred. The sports movement was growing very considerably: large playing fields were being built as the crowds were ever more numerous for national and international games; the techniques of the game were being perfected so that the Azzurri national team was able to brilliantly assert itself even over teams from countries more advanced in the game of soccer.

[...] The soccer institution was reformed in all of its aspects: its hierarchy, its sportsmanship, its finances; through this reorganization, the Federation had been entrusted to the Honorable Leandro Arpinati, who, in August 1926, established the office of its Federal Board of Directors, its new highest organ, in the city of Bologna. The Federation was filled with the sense of discipline and the spur to action that Fascism infused in the nation. Its new President, a man of high authority, vast ideas, and an indomitable will, instilled in everyone the call of duty and led Italian soccer on the path to today's greatness![6]

During one of those games, Teo kicked the heavy ball over the boundary wall with a crooked and clumsy shot.

"It was high!" yelled Gianpiero, jumping as high as he could, with his arms raised and fingers stretched out. His goal area had no crossbar, and two cypresses acted as goalposts. The boys relied on Sister Pia to decide whether the ball was in or out, whether it was a goal or not. But then, as the boys never agreed, they would fight among themselves and tug at the nun's habit to have her say that they were right.

Nobody protested on that occasion: the shot was definitely out. The ball was so high that it had gone over the orphanage's brick barrier.

Under the frightened gaze of Sister Pia, who feared a reprimand from the Mother Superior, the boys created a human tower to retrieve the ball. But just two of them were not enough. They asked Sergino, who was almost five years old at the time, and who had been sitting on the sidelines drawing with his pencil on a checkered notepad, to climb up.

"Come on! Quickly! Put your feet on my knee! Climb up!"

"Come on! Climb up!" The kids urged the little boy to hurry up, as they couldn't hold on much longer because Sister Erminia was already on her way.

Sergino quickly climbed on the first boy, then on the second, until he stood on the latter's head on his tiptoes and was able to grab onto the top of the wall.

"Can you see the ball?" asked the two boys with one voice.

"Can you see it?" asked the second one, pushing Sergio's legs up so he could lean on his stomach on the highest row of bricks.

Sergino saw a figure on the other side of the wall. It was the first time he had seen a child on the other side of that wall. Suddenly the world expanded before him beyond measure. Everything outside was full of color; there were no obstacles to the view. From his high perch, he could see things he couldn't even describe to himself: there were fields of sunflowers, expanses of olive trees, animals, and...that boy!

He seems a big boy but was a little boy, just like him.

Sergino slid down the wall and jumped without a second thought.

***

That's the way my father was. Opportunities were to be seized without wavering. He was no coward, not one of those who stop in their tracks after making great efforts and torment themselves with doubts and questions. "What if I get hurt?" "What if...?" "But...?" and then remain stuck with their questions, and give up, time after time.

A thin thread separates caution from adventure, fear from momentum, calculation from instinct. Some cut it, and some tie it around their waist. This subject is far too serious to take lightly when discussing such differences, especially when one is responsible for raising children, caring for parents, and managing employees. The variables that need to be taken into account are too many and all too important. You must project courage but also profess prudence. You call for reflection, yet you encourage others to make choices. You are quick and wise, strong and understanding. Some believe in fate, some don't.

We live an eternal contradiction between black and white. We often take refuge in compromise, in half-measures which may seem convenient precisely because they are not only this or only that; because they offer us possibilities, and possibilities give us a sense of infinity. But do they succeed in painting life in its unique way? Is doing things halfway, which is not always the easiest choice, enough to lead the soul to immensity? Or is it, instead, a rickety bridge built by someone who is at a loss, who doesn't have a steady hand, and for this reason sets limits that he doesn't have?

Whenever possible, my father, and I like him, has always chosen the strong contrast and never held back. He has always preferred to choose decisively, to follow a clearly defined path -- risk rather than deferment. In the end, balance is nothing more than a set of variables in opposition to each other. The variables of our existence are unpredictable and surprising. But all are not equally decisive. When my heart stopped, and I died, I understood that one of them must be considered above all others: time. As I was saying before, the value-of-time.

I am not speaking about the flow of time, the space

between one breath and another, the duration of a soccer game, or about the time it takes us to get home from work, which may vary depending on traffic, on one's car, on who is driving, and so on.

No.

One second is one second, an hour is an hour, period, no discussion there. But the element that varies from one person to the other is the perception of that second, of that hour; such a perception can change in the same person, depending on age, state of mind, expectations. How we want to use that time determines what we do next and what we do after that.

I am speaking precisely about the value we attribute to time, based on our own free will, on rules, on education, on this or that condition requiring our compliance. What value does your time have?

***

Sergino lost no time.

Sitting astride the wall, he turned around and took hold of the brambles creeping up on the outside. He let himself slide, one hand at a time, climbing down like an inexperienced bear cub. Halfway down, he lost his grip and fell onto a laurel bush, luckily quite tall, that softened his landing. He had only a few scratches on his hands and legs. He got up and ran towards the little boy. The two looked at each other, mirroring each other's smiles.

"What's your name?" asked the boy.

"Sergino. And yours?"

"Oreste."

They didn't need to know anything else. They started running toward the shed where Oreste spent his days while his parents worked in the vineyards they tended on a sharecropping agreement. The two boys began playing hide-and-seek, and Oreste was the first to guard the hiding place and spot Sergino and declare that he had caught him. Then they switched roles. During one of those role-plays, however, Sister Erminia saw Sergino and took him back to the orphanage, dragging him by the ear.

Sergino never saw Oreste again. He was punished and fed bread and water for days. Yet, it had been worth it. It had been his first exploration of the outside world, not a real escape, although he would start dreaming of the latter frequently in the following months.

Sergino was thin, very thin. His clothes were always too large, and they hung on his body. His belt was pulled very tightly around his waist. The orphanage dressed the boys in hand-me-downs, pants, and shirts once worn by the older kids. They relied on donations, especially on items received from nearby churches, where families would bring clothes and personal belongings that once belonged to boys who had not returned from the Great War, or had died of malnutrition or illness.

In addition to enforcing its rules with an iron fist, the orphanage played an important social role. Many of the boys would not have survived hunger and cold. The primary duty of the Abbess was to keep order, avoid anarchy, and prevent the forming of unruly little groups of kids. But it was impossible for her to fully stop alliances from forming among the boys, even with the help of an army of nuns.

Sergino was well-liked by the older boys. They had taken him as a mascot. They saw him as he read while hiding behind the bookshelves in the classroom or under the dining hall tables. He would sneak into their dormitories. He would stay up reading until the early morning hours and then run back to take refuge in his little cot.

The evening before he left, Michele couldn't stop talking and asking questions of the other boys. And they had answers to those questions, though most were the product of legend or their imagination.

Others would soon turn 14 and would then leave the orphanage. Fourteen was the age limit set by the house rules. Beyond that age, they were considered full-grown men. The nuns were very good at finding jobs for the boys to give them a new, dignified life. A life of hard work, but also one of dignity. The large tannery a few kilometers away provided an outlet for a constant stream of those boys.

They would have a middle school diploma in hand, obtained by some with flying colors and by others just by a hair. That piece of paper would act as a sort of safe-conduct pass that would allow the minors to go straight to work.

The owners of the factory did not do it out of compassion or generosity. They needed young workers, as they were paid very little and were not shielded by patronage or relatives in high positions in the Fascist Party.

On the one hand, the boys would be kept off the streets; they would be fed. On the other hand, they would be exposed to a very high risk of death.

Transforming the skins of butchered animals into hides and leather to make shoes, bags, or furnishings, all without the controls that should have been in place, presented extremely serious health threats. The natural tanning agents that were used to keep the hides from putrefying smelled terrible and caused infectious diseases. They penetrated the lungs of the workmen and devastated them, especially in the case of malnourished boys with insufficient clothing. Production proceeded without pause. So did the diseases.

"They told me I would be going to make leather wallets and ladies' handbags. Maybe one of them will take care of me, don't you think?"

Michele repeated to them precisely what he had heard from the Reverend Mother. He hadn't missed a word. He was about to leave, and he was giving the others expert advice. He was already proud of the new life that awaited him beyond the great gate.

"Now I even know my full name. I am Michele Dolci. Do you hear? Michele Dolci!"

The boys were incredibly excited: their older comrade was leaving the following day, and they were sharing in his happiness amidst gales of laughter.

Sergino's little head was all aflutter. He smiled as he listened to the older boys talk while browsing through the pages of a picture book about the solar system. He was enthralled by the planets and by the earth's rotation. Life was entirely contained in those pages and those drawings. What amazing discoveries he would make! He was daydreaming and listening to Michele.

"His last name is Dolci!"

He understood immediately. He had seen Sister Erminia's office many, many times. He could have drawn it inch by inch. Every time he was punished, the nun in charge at that time would take him to that room, where he would receive yet another reprimand, always beginning with these words,

"Oh, Sergino, Sergino. I understood from the very first time I held you that you would give me trouble. Why do you do this? Don't you understand that I see in you...," and there would follow words about the nun's childhood and adolescence, while the child's attention would turn away.

Behind the massive wooden chair, the Reverend Mother had a large bookcase. There were no books. There were only large ledgers. He had never seen one open, not even on her desk. But he had always understood that they had not been placed there in that order, with years marked on their spines, just for show. The Mother Superior blocked their view with her imposing figure. She was more than a physical protector of the institute's most precious treasure. In there, were the stories of the boys, of each of them.

"Dolci!" When he heard Michele's last name, he had confirmation about those large ledgers.

"Guys, you know what..." Michele surprised his schoolmates.

"I'm just happy to get out of here. I'm not going to the tannery..."

"Seriously? What will you do?" curiosity mixed with concern. They all held their breath.

Michele revealed his plan. He had been working on it quietly for days. Now he knew he could trust them; he was creating his little squad for the future.

"Guys, we will stay together, in the future as well... and we will cover ourselves in glory!"

They were all mesmerized, listening carefully to Michele. Sergino even more than the others.

A few days earlier, a new group of children had arrived at the orphanage. They were between three and six years old. The scene was heartbreaking, as it always was. The nuns had to pull them away forcefully as they clung to the legs of the drivers, whether relatives or strangers.

During the confusion, one of the adults had dropped some rolled-up sheets of paper, and Michele had quickly picked them up.

"Listen to this..." he read out with authority the front page of a newspaper. It was titled *Il Popolo d'Italia*, it was Benito Mussolini's paper.

Michele was holding up the page with both hands. It was almost larger that he was, and the other boys crowded around behind his shoulders. That page was titled *Il Balilla*.

The National Balilla Organization (ONB) was founded

just after the defeat of World War I. Between the time of its founding, on April 3, 1926, a month after Sergio's birth, and 1937, when it was absorbed into the Italian Youth of the Lictorian Fasces (GIL), it had gathered thousands and thousands of young people into its ranks.

The name Balilla came from the nickname of Giovanni Battista Perasso, a Genoese youth who, in 1746, had thrown stones against some Austrian soldiers, thus becoming the symbol of that city's rebellion against its oppressor.

The organization was set up for assistance and the physical and moral education of young people. Between the ages of 8 and 14, they were called "Balilla" and between the ages of 14 and 18, the boys entered the Young Vanguard. At the age of 21, they became full-fledged members of the Fascist Party.

The future couldn't have looked more radiant. More valiant. More epic.

"TO US!"

"TO US!"

"TO US!"

Michele repeated the headline above the large illustration, just to be sure they all understood. And to give even more substance to his now convinced dedication to the movement.

Above that inscription, "TO US!" printed in big red block letters, was an image of two boys wearing a uniform with a blue kerchief around their necks and a gun with a bayonet in their hands. The two athletic-looking boys were riding a torpedo.

Michele continued reading. By now, there was a chorus, as the boys who could see the paper over his shoulders were reading along with him. It was already becoming an anthem for them.

That manifesto prepared them for an unexpected future.

"Those you see pictured here are two of your young comrades, children like you. Look at them! They seem to jump out of the page with that overwhelming fervor that enraptures the souls of the braves when the time comes to attack..."

The boys puffed out their chests, breathing in as deeply as they could.

"We are ready for war, do you understand?" said Michele to the group.

"Long live Italy!" the others exclaimed.

Michele continued to read with an even more triumphant tone.

"How many of you haven't imagined yourselves, in your innermost dreams, as ready to jump up to the edge of a trench, ready to defend a difficult passage with your bayonets?"[7]

Sergino had by now already jumped out of the trench.

While Michele was reading those lines, immersed in his frenzy and that of his friends, Sergino had tied together about ten sheets and lowered himself from the window of the older boys' dormitory. Below it, there stood the balcony of the hallway leading to the office of the Reverend Mother.

Opening the inside doors of that barracks-like building was child's play for him. He had made for himself a passkey by rubbing a fork against some garden paving stones. He didn't dare to approach the great outer gate, but the doors to the rooms inside had no secrets for him.

He had stayed away from the Mother Superior's office until then, as he had no interest in her papers, certainly not out of fear of her reactions.

He easily opened the door and took out the volume for the year 1926. He sat cross-legged under the desk and browsed through the gigantic volume, almost panting from the weight of the book and the excitement of the moment.

Sergio. N.N. 3.6.1926

The inscription was clear. That was his folder.

Mother: Adele Dal Boni

Father: Not known.

Born of an adulterous relationship. The family opted to entrust him to this religious institution for orphans.

There followed some more notes by the Abbess concerning the child's character, but he didn't read those. He closed the ledger, put it back in its place, then ran back to join Michele and the others.

Michele was finishing his reading of the Balilla manifesto.

"Join us!"

"The future of Italy is at the tip of your bayonets!"

The boys now had plenty to dream.

"Michele, I am going away with you tomorrow!" said Sergino.

"My name is Sergio Dal Boni," he yelled at his schoolmates, raising himself onto the tips of his toes to try and multiply his nine years enough to make him seem as old as they were.

"Sergio Dal Boni," he repeated with authority.

CHAPTER SEVEN

THE SEA! FINALLY!

~

M y father lit up with an even more intense glow, his eyes full of warmth and love. I experienced his most intimate thoughts, his feelings, and emotions at that moment in the institute, and in so doing, I was able to rediscover my roots. He was proud of it, and so was I.

Today I fully understand why my mother never tired of making comparisons between her children and my father. When it was my turn, she seemed to have no doubts.

"You took everything from your Babbo, look!" She always had a photo of mine, when I was little, at the ready.

Her favorite portrayed me by the sea. I was just under a year old and was standing up with great determination.

"At seven months, you were already walking!" she would say to me proudly.

Under my feet, there were pebbles and sand. I must have come out of the water, and my cotton panties were so soaked and heavy that they seemed ready to be falling off me. You could see my ribs; I was so thin. But yes, I was a beautiful child and looked a lot like Sergino.

I was his copy. And so I grew up, even unintentionally imitating him in his bold attitudes towards life.

"Impossible? Not for me! " He would have said, and so would I.

***

Michele Dolci looked at Sergino, narrowing his eyes. He had caught the determination in his voice and the sense of rage and folly that were an integral part of his being. He took him seriously.

"And how do you think you are going to do that? Come on, tell me what you are thinking."

"I don't know yet," said the boy. He didn't want to say that he hadn't the faintest idea. He had dozens of scenarios in his head but hadn't decided which one to implement.

The other boys also took him seriously.

A military ardor now filled the dormitory.

Stories proliferated, blending wonder and imagination, and the boys could hardly contain their exhilaration.

"Do you remember Nicholas the Red?" He was a tall and ashen boy with a mop of carrot-colored hair. A couple of years before, he was slated to go to the tannery, too.

"He is in the Young Vanguard."

"What is the Young Vanguard?"

"He's a hero!"

"A general?"

"Red? For real?"

"He's already gone into battle!"

"In Africa!"

"What is Africa? Where is it?"

"His picture was in the paper."

The confusion had become collective delirium.

"He was standing on a tank, carrying his musket in his arms!"

"But he wasn't in the war!"

"Where was he, then?"

"At Camp Dux."

"In Rome, the capital."

Michele kept on reading triumphant quotations from the pages of *Balilla,* and the boys partly followed him, partly ran elsewhere with their voices and thoughts. They all had something to yell, projects to carry out, mountains of fear to overcome, myths to enlarge.

Sergino was making plans for the next day. He would make them and then set them aside.

He was going to escape with the help of some sheets twisted into a rope, something he had already done a few times to move from one floor to the other of the institution. He first planned to tie a brick to one end, then toss the sheet-rope over to the other side…

…No. The wall was too high to throw the brick over it. Nor would a brick have been heavy enough to anchor his climb, even if he had succeeded in that impossible throw.

He meant to wait for the nuns to open the gate to let in the tannery's van. Then he planned to run faster than the wind, avoiding the nuns, including the Reverend Mother. He would keep on running until he reached the sea.

The sea. Sergino was fascinated by the ocean, by the power of waves crashing onto the rocks, by the murmur of sand and shells on the shore, by the blue color and the depth of the sea, by navigation, both above and below the water surface. Rowboats, steamboats, submarines. How fantastic!

The scent of the sea did not reach up to those hills, but he sensed it, breathed it in books, and absorbed it from illustrations, drawings, and epic tales.

There. That's where he would escape to…To the sea. He would get on the van, somehow and that's what he would do.

Maybe it would be even better than the last time. Sergino was seven years old, and he was sick and tired of staying on this side of the wall after seeing the other side with Oreste. In the morning, he would observe the procession of delivery vans, the milkman, and the baker. He would study their schedules and their movements and write them down on checkered sheets of paper, the same ones he once drew abstract sketches.

The men carried in sacks of provisions and crates of fruit on their shoulders, and they never brought anything out. Clearly, he could not hide in a sack or a crate, as they were never brought out.

So, he slipped into the wheelbarrow of one of the gardeners, and he covered himself with a cloth that was often used to protect firewood from rain and dampness. He curled up tightly, trying not to be seen. The man did not notice the extra weight because his exit path was downhill. He had to try and slow down, pulling back with his arms and using his legs for leverage.

A wind gust lifted the cloth just enough to catch the attention of Sister Antonia, who was guarding the gate. She became suspicious and stopped the man and the little fugitive.

"Stop there!" yelled the nun at the gardener who instantly froze with fear, almost falling due to the inertia of the wheelbarrow, which he had trouble stopping because the wheel was spinning so fast.

"What do you think you are doing, huh?" the nun moved away from her post and came over to the wheelbarrow; she leaned over and took a corner of the greasy and grimy cloth, pulling it back quickly in a cloud of dirt and pebbles.

The nun succumbed for a moment to the sin of pride, recognizing in herself an exaggerated skill for that maneuver performed with such mastery that it would have made the best of illusionists gnaw with envy when they pull the tablecloth away from a table set with dishes, cutlery and glasses, without moving them by a single inch. She felt a thrill of unexpected vanity go through her.

But it lasted only a minute; the next froze her and brought her back to earth as if in a kind of sudden punishment. She was dumbfounded and jumped back, furious at seeing only dry twigs and leaves and a crumpled wool cap. She recognized it instantly.

"Quickly!"

"Sergino has run away again!"

The gardener did not understand what the whole fuss was.

"May I go, Sister?"

"No, NO!..." "Well, yes,...go. GO!" she answered, panicking as she had allowed herself to be tricked so blatantly by the little rascal.

Sister Erminia arrived quickly, at her brisk martinet pace.

"What do we have here, huh? Sister Antonia?"

"I don't know, Reverend Mother. I thought I saw Sergino's cap in the wheelbarrow, and I stopped the gardener and..."

"And what? What?"

"He wasn't there, just twigs and leaves..." answered Sister Antonia in a shaky voice, pointing at the gardener who was by now well beyond the gate and was waiting at the end of the path to be picked up by the van belonging to the workers who, once a year, came to do the cleanup and planting of the grounds around the orphanage. This service was provided by the owner of a neighboring farm, who contributed a cash compensation to the farmhands, as the nuns lived only on the charitable contributions received in exchange for their sewing work.

"And, if you please, where is the kid now?" asked the Abbess in an anxious tone, turning towards the other nuns who had gathered around because of the commotion.

"He's not here. No one has seen him."

"Well," insisted Sister Erminia, "who saw him last? Let's hear it!"

"Where can a seven-year-old rascal have disappeared to, huh?" she added, knowing full well that, where Sergino was concerned, anything was possible and remembering his leap over the wall two years earlier.

"I saw him," said Sister Pia.

"He was sitting at the foot of the cypress, as he always does, with his crumpled little notebook, while the others were playing soccer..."

"The others went back to class...Sergino didn't. Sister Franca checked," concluded the referee-nun.

Sister Franca felt the need to add something, as did Sister Rita, and Sister Agnese, and Sister Rosa, such as, "I can't understand how he could have...", and Sister Antonia, "He couldn't have gone outside the gate, I would have seen him," and Sister Teresa, who...

"ENOUGH! QUIET!" ordered the Mother Superior.

They were instantly quiet.

Sister Erminia's head moved like that of a hound pointing its prey. First, she looked back towards the classrooms, then, suddenly, she turned her head towards the gate. Then to the right, staring at the cypresses and the wall, then quickly to the left, at more cypresses, more wall. And, again, suddenly still, she looked at the gate.

Her eyes would have withered anyone. Her teeth squeaked as she clenched them and ground them together, while a raucous sound came from her mouth, like a rabid dog's snarl. She swung her habit as if to draw a sword from it and raised her right arm, thrusting it forward, pointing her index finger at the gardener and letting out a scream,

'THE WHEELBARROWWWWW!!!"

"He's still there. Catch him!"

The nuns swarmed towards the farmhand to block him.

I must confess that, among my father's stories, the ones I remember most vividly are those about his escapes from the orphanage. He performed like a great actor, as he echoed the sounds of his childhood; he imitated, one by one, the voices of the nuns, even their regional accents, whether Neapolitan or Roman, Sicilian or Tuscan, Lombard or Piedmontese. "Three times. I ran away three times. I drove them crazy, poor things."

He did not make fun of them, and it wasn't even a rather good way of playing things down. These were, in fact, good memories, and he was used to reading the cards of despair in this way as well. He felt affection for those nuns, and he knew he was truly loved by the Reverend Mother, who saw in him the young woman who had been torn from the love of her parents; yet, at least, she had known them, whereas he never had. He was proud to have "completed only the third grade" and to have done it at that institute.

Sister Pia, the youngest, was the first to reach the gardener, and she planted herself firmly in front of him as if to try and freeze him there while waiting for the other sisters.

He was a young man, only twenty-five years old, and had no parents, as he had lost them both during the Great War; his father had died on the Austrian front, and his mother of a broken heart. He had lived at the orphanage until 14 and then had fallen ill at the tannery. He now worked wherever he could. Sister Pia couldn't have recognized him; the other nuns could.

"Luigi!"

"Tell me you don't have a runaway in there!" scolded him the Mother Superior, who had been slow to arrive. She knew well who that gardener was, and she had had him among her pupils. He had been a gentle boy, always diligent and eager to learn so as to have a trade; never in a scuffle with the other boys, always attentive in answering the nuns, and respectful of schedules.

When the time had come to leave, he would have liked

to stay longer, but he accepted the job at the tannery with good grace. He worked there, tanning skins, for at least three years before becoming gravely ill. He almost died because of respiratory failure but was saved by a hair at the hospital in Pisa. Once he recovered his health, he tried to enroll in the infantry but was rejected as being unfit for long marches, so he stayed and worked as a stretcher-bearer at the hospital.

Sister Antonia rummaged around in the wheelbarrow, sweeping up great armfuls of the leaves that filled it to the brim.

"Peek-a-boo!"

"Here is our runaway boy," said Sister Antonia, hoping to be forgiven.

Sergino was sleeping soundly on a bed of leaves.

Again, the Abbess pulled him up by one ear and drew him so close to her face that the boy practically stared into her open mouth. The image resembled that of an ogre about to devour a bunny.

"Again?"

"You're having fun, aren't you?"

Sergino pretended to be like Sleeping Beauty, but the nun didn't buy that fairy tale.

"You want me to believe that you just fell asleep in there by mistake?"

"And what about you, Luigi? What do you have to say for yourself?"

However loudly she yelled, the nun could not break the apparent complicity between the two.

She let Luigi go and brought Sergino back inside the gate.

The escape had only been deferred. He had had a nice ride in the wheelbarrow and created an uproar at the school. He had had a wonderful time of it.

He was taken to the headmistress's office, and again

sentenced to bread and water. But his intention of leaving the place was not appeased; it was just set aside for another couple of years, enough time to come up with a nun-proof idea.

Sergino and Luigi had become friends the year before. They only saw each other once a year, when fieldhands from a neighboring farm gave the nun's grounds their yearly cleaning and planting.

"Hey, you. You don't play soccer?" Luigi had asked the first time he saw the little boy sitting with his shoulders against a cypress and drawing with his pencil.

"I prefer to watch."

"Lend me a sheet of paper. I'll teach you something," had added Luigi.

"So, we fold it here, then here, and here, in half. Then you turn the page over, and you fold it in two. Then you make the wings. Here, it's done!"

"Come on, make it fly!" He had handed him a paper airplane that looked like a bomber.

Sergino had learned from his elders a technique to help it take off successfully. He had first to blow on its tip, with his mouth wide open and with all the warm air he had in his lungs.

The paper plane had climbed sharply and had done a double loop-de-loop around the cypress before hitting a branch and diving to crash onto the ground at Luigi's feet. Not bad, for a first flight. They had exchanged broad smiles, quite pleased with themselves. A solid friendship had been born around those flying pirouettes.

"Can you take me for a ride on your wheelbarrow?" Sergino asked Luigi the second year he saw him.

"Why not? Get on board. Where do you want to go?"

"To the other side of the gate!" the little boy widened the scope of his bravado, involving now that clean-faced adult.

"Well, if you want to go beyond the gate, we have to do something clever, otherwise…do you see that nun standing there? She will stop us!" Luigi accepted the challenge, a small act of payback after so many years of showing respect and of *"Yes, Ma'am!"*

"Wait here, I'll be right back," he told Sergino, and he returned a short time later with a wheelbarrow full of leaves and dry twigs. He even took a cover cloth from the woodshed.

"Here, lie down on the bottom. Curl up like a worm, as flat as you can!" He emptied the contents of the wheelbarrow at the feet of the child to make room for him.

Sergino quickly climbed over the rim of that one-wheeled vehicle and curled up in it, with his face resting in its cavity.

"Cover me," he told Luigi, as he now understood his intentions.

The young farmhand arranged the straw, the dry twigs, and a blanket of leaves over him.

"Can you breathe?"

"Yes, very well," laughed the child.

Luigi placed the cloth over the layers of hay, leaves, and twigs covering the boy and picked up the cap that had fallen to the ground as he climbed into the wheelbarrow.

They both laughed. "Now we'll play a trick on the nun; you'll see how stunned she will be," added Luigi, putting the cap just below the cloth, partly hidden, partly visible, like a lure for a pike.

"Shall I go?"

"Go!"

Luigi started pushing the barrow, although it tended to pull away from him on the downhill path. As expected, he was stopped by Sister Antonia, who lifted the cloth but did not touch the layer of leaves and branches.

When the bewildered nun let him go, Luigi started moving again, with Sergino laughing his head off under the leaves.

"We made it! We made it!" they both laughed, the adult and the child who did not really want to run away. He just wanted to take a spin outside the institute. They stopped to see what might happen and were making bets on how long it would take for them to be discovered.

The older boy gave a play-by-play.

"They have a pow-wow; they are idling. Now they are looking for you behind the shrubs, in the pots, inside the building. Here comes the Mother Superior."

"Wow! What a sneer!" he laughed with tears in his eyes.

"Now we are in real trouble," he kept laughing.

"One of them is running like a rocket, and she is coming here. Pretend you are asleep!"

"3…2…1…We're off!"

The evening before Michele's departure, the boys he had gathered together were daydreaming about war, honor, and arms. They comprised his age group, the class born in 1921, who would soon join him. They agreed to meet in Florence.

Among the sheets of paper Michele had picked up from the floor, together with the *Balilla* newspaper, was a letter from a high fascist official to the religious sister, announcing the need for young and strong hands to construct the Home for Italian fascist youth. Florence was becoming a hub for recruiting boys to join the Balilla and the Young Vanguard.

The nuns let the boys vent all night, as it would have been useless to try and get them to go to bed. It was a ritual repeated every time one of the older boys left the orphanage.

Early the next day, although he hadn't slept at all because of all the excitement, Michele was already up for the morning roll call. He had prepared everything, said goodbye to his friends, and was just waiting for the Reverend Mother to call him in.

The boy was already practically a soldier. He was frail, like the others, but he stood there, ramrod-straight. At his side was the cardboard suitcase, with its metal corners, also standing straight. Michele showed no sign of weakness, even though the load he was about to take away with him was no longer made up of just a few rags and some newspapers.

Sergino had succeeded overnight in convincing him. Michele was only supposed to walk a few feet to the van and would undoubtedly be able to lift the suitcase without showing anyone its actual weight. Sergino, who was extremely skinny, was going to curl up like a contortionist inside the case.

Neither one would be risking too much, even if they were found out. Michele would have left anyway. Sergino would have been punished, again, but just another punishment certainly didn't frighten him.

"Michele Dolci!" thundered Sister Antonia. "The van is here. Come on. Quick!"

The boy left the suitcase on the floor before going into the Mother Superior's office, where she would hand him his new documents, and with them his fate among the skins to be tanned.

The Abbess had eyes and ears everywhere.

"Mister Dolci!" she exclaimed, raising her eyes from the papers she was signing to allow him to leave the institute.

Michele stood very straight, with his hands along his sides, in front of the nun's massive desk.

"Or should I keep calling you Little Michele?... Given that you don't seem grown-up enough to face the outside world..."

The boy stood silent, expecting something dreadful to happen. The nun jumped up. "What is this Balilla business?!!!"

She took some crumpled papers out of the drawer and started reading them with a severe tone.

Dear Mother, I am proud to inform you that we have decimated the enemy after a long battle in the trenches. I am well, and I expect to be home again soon! Your Ettore.

"Signed, Ettore Renzi," said the Reverend Mother.

"Do you know what happened to Ettore?"

She took another envelope. At the top left corner was the word "WIN!" Instead of a postage stamp, to the right was a military rubber stamp saying, "Area without stamps." It came from the front and was addressed to the Renzi family in Florence.

She opened it and started reading it with a sad tone.

Dear Renzi family,

We have learned with intense sorrow of the glorious sacrifice made by your family member, Ettore, who has fallen in the war for his Fatherland. While we offer you our most heartfelt condolences, we assure you that his name will be preserved forever among the glorious ones of the soldiers who have fallen for the greatness of their Fatherland.

"You will not go to war; you will not do what those other boys did when they ran away from an honest job and a future..."

"IS THAT CLEAR???!!!"

Sister Erminia was sizing him up from head to toe, knowing full well what had attracted all those older boys as they left the orphanage. She was sure that Michele, too, would follow them, driven by the impetus of the call to arms. The tannery owner had informed her of the many escapes by her boys to enlist among the Balilla.

"YOU MUST PROMISE ME. NOW!"

Michele detected a weakening in this last outburst by the Reverend Mother. He understood that her yelling was not caused by the transgressions of the night before in the older boys' dormitory.

"Yes, Mother!" was all he said.

As the boy had expected, the nun fell back into her chair and made a gesture with her hand.

"Go, and may God protect you."

Michele left the office of the Mother Superior and picked up his suitcase without attracting attention to it. It was a heavy suitcase, but wasn't he a soldier now? He walked with straight shoulders to the tannery's van.

The boys of the orphanage, even the new arrivals, usually slipped through the meshes of the nun's human net to go and watch the departure scene. That moment would mark their entire existence in there. It was the long-awaited farewell. An escape towards the unknown, as they knew nothing about their parents, nor would they know anything about them until the moment of their departure. And, in many cases, especially in those of children taken from unwed mothers, as Sergino was, they would never find out.

The excitement among the boys was hard to control, but the nuns were counting on the fact that none of them would dare go beyond the gate. That institute was an orphanage, but there were worse places to spend one's childhood. The boys were constantly reminded of this, about reform schools or starvation on the streets, about begging or being abused by the wrong families. That gate had always worked as a deterrent and would continue to do so in the future.

Michele started to climb into the van when the driver suddenly stopped him.

"The suitcase."

Michele froze, sure that he had been found out.

"Give it to me," added the driver, while the boy broke out in a cold sweat, mainly because of his stowaway.

"I'll put it up," said the driver.

The van was packed with tannery workers and had a little ladder at the back leading to the luggage rack on the roof.

"Don't worry; we'll tie it down carefully…"

"…BUT…BUT…"

"What the devil do you have in here? It's as heavy as a cow that needs milking!"

He took the suitcase with both hands to lift it, but it was so heavy he then had to rest it on his knees.

"STOP!" burst out angrily the Mother Superior, whose voice could be heard from the window of her office, where she had been watching the boy's departure.

In just a few moments, all hell broke loose. The driver let go of the suitcase, and it slipped off his knees. He then stood there, at attention, as if he were the guilty party. The suitcase fell heavily to the ground with a loud noise that sounded like breaking a large terracotta vase to those listening carefully. Michele stood still and proud, as if before a firing squad.

All the nuns formed a retinue behind the Abbess as she marched forward with her head lowered, like a rhinoceros. The older boys, who were watching from the windows of their dormitory, started yelling,

"Sergino, run, RUN!"

The general commotion grew as the workers who had been in the van got out to see what was happening, even though by then they had understood full well. They were in the presence of a fugitive.

"OPEN THAT SUITCASE, YOU RASCAL!"

The Mother Superior pierced Michele with her gaze.

"Come on! Open it!"

The boy bent down over the suitcase, which was now

warped because of its fall, and the pressed cardboard was now all bent.

Michele opened the suitcase, fully expecting consequences...

"But what's this?!! IS THIS A JOKE??"

Michele's bag, together with his few clothing items and the papers promising him a bright future, now contained a dozen large stone blocks.

Sister Erminia took Michele by the ear and lowered his head over the suitcase.

"Now, Mr. Dolci, explain this. NOW!"

The nun picked up one of the stones to show the boy her strength when she saw a handwritten note behind it.

Farewell.

S.

The Reverend Mother immediately understood what that "S" stood for.

"Bring me Sergino. I want that brat here. NOW!" she ordered firmly, turning towards the flock of penguins following her. Immediately they started running wildly, in all directions, along a dangerous grid of intersecting paths.

"And you! What are you looking at? Get back on the bus!" The workers were not under the nun's supervision, yet they did not linger.

"Sergino isn't here, Mother!" the chorus of nuns' voices reached the large gate where the Mother Superior held Michele riveted with her gaze while holding on to his arm with an iron grip.

"I think he ran away during the night," said Michele to the nun.

"And what about those blocks, then? Do you think I am so stupid?"

Michele wanted to say that his schoolmates had put them into the suitcase as a prank. But he would have had to notice the weight. That story wouldn't have worked:

the nun's fury would only have increased.

He would have liked to tell her that they were souvenirs of each of his years at that institution...

"Naah!..."

He chose not to add another word.

The sister had already signed the papers setting Michele on the path to his new life. The matter no longer concerned her institute.

"Be off with you!"

"And remember your promise. Work and build a good family for yourself. Don't make those who love you suffer."

Hearing those words, Michele, who had no living relatives, understood that, underneath it all, that nun loved him. However brusque and fierce, the Mother Superior saw those children as "her" boys.

"So? Where is Sergino?" she yelled at the nuns.

"Mother, we have looked everywhere. He isn't here."

"Look in the van, on its roof, inside the engine. That little sparrow must have hidden somewhere."

The search lasted all morning.

"Bring all the boys to the main hall!" ordered Sister Erminia. She meant to question them one by one, searching their pockets for any clue.

"On your feet, and nobody moves!" They all stood at attention.

The police came, too, summoned by the nuns. After three hours of searching and scouring the van inch by inch, the Abbess and the police gave the driver the green light. The workers all got back into the van, including the newly hired Michele, and they set off towards the tannery.

The road was flanked by a double row of tall and powerful-looking cypresses.

The police left with a statement from the Mother Superior to the effect that a child in her care was "missing".

They would communicate this to uncle Aldo, who had signed the papers entrusting the boy to the nun's custody.

Sergino, who wasn't even ten years old, was now officially "wanted."

"Your Reverence! Your Reverence!" Sister Nicoletta was running excitedly down the hall towards the orphanage door, where the nun was waving goodbye to the police.

"Look at what I found..."

"It's a book."

Twenty-thousand Leagues Under the Sea
By Jules Verne

"It was under your desk, way in the back. It's full of handwritten notes in the margin..."

The Mother Superior took the book from the nun's hands and walked back to her office with heavy steps. She let herself down into her chair and, leaning both elbows on the desk, clasped her hands as if to pray. But she wasn't praying. That position came naturally to her when she had to think.

Suddenly, she jolted back the chair, all the way back to the window. While still sitting, she strained her eyes to look as far as she could under the desk. It was huge, large, and long enough for a married couple to sleep under it, and the knee opening was also very deep, stretching the whole width of the desk. It was an antique desk, entirely built of solid wood, and its four feet were barely visible. It had been brought in many years before, with great effort, long before Sister Erminia's time, and no one had ever considered moving it from that spot.

"You rascal, you..."

She was talking aloud.

"You just stayed here reading while everyone was looking for you outside. You hid in the only place where no one would come looking for you."

The Reverend Mother picked up Jules Verne's book

and dwelt on Sergino's notes.

Many pages were bent back at the corner, and several pages had words underlined.

The sea is everything. There is a reason why it covers seven-tenths of the globe. Its air is pure and healthy; it is an immense desert where man is never alone because he can feel life quiver all around him. The sea is the vehicle for a supernatural and prodigious existence; it is movement and love. It is a living infinity.[8]

She remembered when she first saw that restless little boy.

"When you grow up, you will travel around the world. But, for now, you are going to stay right in here!" she had mocked him then. The nun thought back to that challenge she had issued him when he was much too young to accept it.

"I know your destination. It will be the sea, in the end."

CHAPTER EIGHT

THE FIRST PORT

~

For the first time in her life, the Reverend Mother inspected under her desk. She was sure she could find clues as to how and where to go to apprehend her runaway. She expected Aldo Dal Boni to be furious when informed of the news. The loss of Sergino represented a severe blow to the good name of her institution.

Despite her age and a few twinges of arthritis interfering with the ease of her movements, especially now that she needed to bend her knees, she held on to the chair and lowered herself to the ground. With her head covered by a black wimple so tight that it seemed sewn on, she slithered and twisted on the floor like a wounded snake and was able to reach the back of the desk. She did not call any of the other nuns to come and help – she didn't want their mockery, nor did she want to wait for their arrival.

She angrily performed that difficult maneuver. She couldn't resign herself to being deceived by that little boy who had dared to do the impossible: to escape from *her* orphanage, even leaving that "Farewell, S." note, as if on a dare. Sister Erminia understood that it was not addressed to the nuns or the orphanage or his schoolmates. No, it was addressed to her personally, to the Abbess who had torn him from his family nine years before.

Sergino knew nothing about his mother or father, uncle Aldo, or any other member of his family. And certainly, he knew nothing about his aristocratic and wealthy origins, all the more so as he was living clothed in rags and on rationed food, in a barracks-like place inhabited by nuns and boys abandoned to their fate.

But the religious sister was well aware, as she bowed and lay upside down under her desk, that Sergino, as she and the other nuns called him, more because he was frail and skinny than out of affection, had witnessed the dramatic moment over and over again in which the children crossed that iron gate. However young, they sensed that they wouldn't be able to leave for years and years. It was a scene that was repeated endlessly and on which the boys, all of them, built their desperation and, therefore, the will to escape as soon as possible.

"Let's see...," mumbled the nun to herself while trying to find her reading glasses, as they had fallen out of her pocket during her hasty descent under the desk. She stretched her right hand along her side with a twisted movement that surprised her.

"What's this?"

"L3..."

"G"

The nun thought about all the adventure books Sergino had devoured while not doing the required homework or writing a single line in the classroom. She followed the boys' progress, and she knew the good qualities and the bad, the ambitions and disappointments of each of them.

She knew very well that Sergino was the main user of the large library of that institution, which was full of books donated by the families of boys who had died in the war. This was one of the reasons why the nuns did not allow him to fail at the end of the school year. He was always promoted to the next grade, but his promotions were unusual, tailor-made for his character. The best pupils were promoted with special praise and ice cream. He, on the other hand, while being encouraged for three consecutive years, had at the same time been punished and given a day without food.

The nun focused her gaze and tried to make out the writing at the back of the desk, etched by the boy as he lay there looking up. Sergino had carved into the wood, with that same passkey he had fashioned out of a fork, a series of numbers set out in a column, together with words, symbols, and rings linked to the numbers. None of it made sense to the nun, and she could not understand the meaning of what Sergino had carved on that personal blackboard.

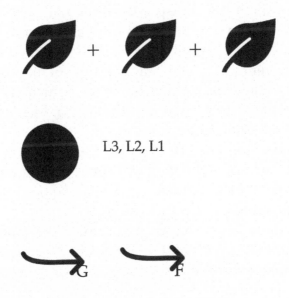

"Hmm, one leaf plus another leaf...three leaves?"

The nun was trying to understand by going over in her mind the nine years spent in that place by Sergino.

"Cypresses! Cypresses! Not leaves!" She remembered

clearly how long the boy lingered under the rows of trees when the children were allowed outside to play in the garden. They were like friends to him. Like older brothers who could mitigate his suffering, could listen silently to his flights of fancy, could whisper to him through the wind's breath new secrets about life beyond the gate. Many saw them as sad trees, trees that grow in cemeteries. Such people lacked the sensitivity of that little boy.

"But you couldn't have hidden in a cypress, even though it is true that you are skinny..."

She tried to imagine him climbing up one of those centuries-old trees, all the way up to reach its leaves and branches, but could not see how he might have succeeded.

She pulled herself up with difficulty, with another clumsy movement. Still, this time gratified at her discovery, even though its full meaning escaped her. She called Sister Franca, who was in charge of the older boys' dormitory, and Sister Nicoletta, of the elementary section. Many others came in to join them, too, like Sister Pia, Sister Robertina, and dozens more.

"I found this carved under my desk. It's by Sergino." She had memorized it well and could draw it on a sheet of paper for the two nuns.

"But...Mother, how did you do it?"

The nuns' astonishment was transparent. They knew she could do anything, but this inspection made them even more respectful and willing to obey. They certainly hadn't looked all the way under the desk when they had searched the orphanage looking for Sergino; this, however, they didn't acknowledge to the Reverend Mother.

Sister Robertina and Sister Elisabetta had gone through the Mother Superior's office with a fine-tooth comb. Still, they hadn't dared to violate what was almost a sanctuary, nor did they have the flexibility to bend down to check and see whether the boy might have hidden under there.

Sister Nicoletta, who was more scrupulous than the other two, had checked that office again and had found the book under the desk. The nuns exchanged a complicit look, and the Abbess understood what had happened.

"Let's forget about how he managed to hide and run away. The important thing now is to understand where he has gone. We must recapture him, or else there will be real trouble for this institute," cut short the Mother Superior.

The night before Michele's departure, while in the throes of excitement about military matters, there had taken place a long and intense exchange among the boys. Each of them had contributed effort and creativity in putting together an escape plan for their mascot, and they took the subject very seriously.

The idea of putting Sergino into the suitcase had come from Tommaso, who was now a month away from leaving the orphanage himself. An immediate chorus of approval had arisen from the others. Sergino had been helped as he bent double and into four, eight, and a thousand other shapes, to be able to fit into the suitcase without speaking, without breathing, without moving.

The rehearsals had lasted a long time; there was always something that needed fixing. A knee was sticking out too far, his head pressing against the cardboard side of the suitcase, toes that needed bending backward. The stratagem was a good one. After several attempts, they had closed the suitcase. Sergino fit perfectly.

Now for the weight test.

"Come on, Michele, lift it!"

"No, not like that. More casual…You should make people think it's empty…"

The other boys had helped Michele manage his movements, and act as if he were a relaxed traveler carrying few personal effects.

"There! Like that! Look at me!…" Michele had taken a

stroll amidst the cots, holding the suitcase at knee level, with his left arm hanging along his side and his right one slightly bent to show how easily he was moving. Sergino had held his breath and had not moved at all as if frozen. He was like a feather; his silent breathing made him feel as if he were floating.

"Yeah!"

"Hurrah!"io

"Tomorrow, you will be out of here, kid," had said one of the older boys, putting his mouth up to the suitcase, as a father might do when talking to his baby still in its mother's womb.

They had then reopened the suitcase, while their excitement had grown by leaps and bounds as they dreamt about their life in uniform, some as infantrymen, some as airmen, some as sailors.

Sergino had approached Michele and whispered in his ear, "We can't do it. They'll find us out. The walk down to the gate is too long."

"But it's a great idea," had answered Michele. "We can do it. You just worry about holding your breath, and I'll worry about the rest."

"I have a plan. I saw it in one of the nuns' books," had insisted Sergino.

"We will rely on the element of surprise. Don't tell anyone; let's just pretend that I am in the suitcase!"

"I like that. Go on!" Michele had joined in plotting the escape as if the two of them were already planning an attack inside enemy lines, as if they were already in uniform, in the name of their Fatherland. For each other, as friends for life, as brothers.

Sergino and Michele had snuck into the larder without making a sound, also protected by the other boys' loud voices and laughter - a din that the nuns tolerated. They had crept like lizards along the walls, opening one door after another without making the slightest noise. On the pantry shelves, alongside the often dried-out pasta, rice, and bread, were also stored garden tools, rusted implements, and stone blocks. The nuns used the latter to border the flowerbeds during the growing season.

The small pantry was at the far end of the refectory, the dining hall where the boys gathered in the morning for prayers before going to class. During the summer, when school was over, the nuns used it to assemble the boys for roll call. Just in case someone might have had the bad courage of running away during the night.

Michele and Sergino had brought along the suitcase and filled it with stone blocks. They had left it in the dining hall, under the chair where Michele usually sat. They had then run back to their dormitories to await the morning. The only sure and unshakable thing in their escape plans was the systematic and rigid observation of the activities, the rhythms, and the habits that the Mother Superior had imposed on the sisterhood. Their rules were utterly predictable.

At the end of the roll call, Michele had picked up his suitcase without drawing attention to himself and had walked with light steps towards the office of the Mother Superior. Sergino had gone back to his dormitory and had been looking out of the window into the courtyard.

When he had seen the nun pounce like a fury on the driver of the bus, who could not extricate himself with a heavy suitcase, he understood that the time had come. Nobody would have been paying attention to him. He had lowered himself into Sister Erminia's office and had hidden under her desk, as he had done many times before. The nuns would undoubtedly search the entire premises inch by inch. Still, they would not have had the agility, or the desire, to stick their noses under that massive wooden structure, the symbol of the Headmistress's absolute power.

The police always came in pairs to bring government documents to the Abbess or bring some dramatic announcement concerning a relative of some child in the custody of the institute. When they had arrived that day, the scurrying around the convent in search of the boy had quieted down.

The Headmistress had met the police and spoken with them in the main hall.

"Reverend Mother, we have finished. If you can sign this report, we will start our investigation as soon as we reach Headquarters," had said one of them, while the nun had signed the police report with irritation. Then they had left.

The driver of the van, on the other hand, had waited for a signal from the nun before assuming that he could go. He hadn't dared to leave the premises without her permission.

Having ascertained that Sergino had indeed disappeared, the flock of nuns had gathered again in the main hall: they, too, had awaited instructions from the Mother Superior.

The gate was still open and now unguarded!

Sergino had slipped away from the desk and pounced like an invisible cat towards the row of cypresses to the left of the great gate. Between the massive orphanage building and that iron barrier, there were two rows of cypresses in a semi-circle – three on the left to demarcate that side of the large garden, and three on the right to define the area used as a parking lot, where the van and the police cars had been parked at that time. The trees were tall, handsome, generous, and faithful. And the double row of those Etruscan trees marched in parallel ranks beyond the gate and down the entire hill.

He had stopped and stood straight and still behind

his cypress friend, on the left, the one Sergino had described as **L3** in his plan. He had pressed himself against the trunk, puffing out his chest with a deep breath.

Sergino had then sprung to **L2**, then to **L1**. Now had come the most challenging part. He had had to gather the strength of all his hopes, summon all the luck that had eluded him so far, seek in the depths of his heart all the energy he had absorbed from the tales of his heroes and the firmness he had borrowed from the cypresses.

As expected, **G** was still open! And still unguarded!

He had glanced over at Michele, who had winked at him and smiled to signify, "Go!"

It was like a pat on the shoulder, a gesture of sincere encouragement. In that facial expression was hidden the sign of a friendship born of the strange tricks of fate. Michele had in his hands the papers needed for his departure. They were like a good hand at poker. Sergino had only low cards; in fact, he had no cards at all. But he did have an ally for the first time in his young life. Someone willing to take a risk for him, with him. They would never see each other again. They both knew it. The bond between the two was enormous. Extremely brief, extremely strong, deep enough to give meaning to their lives.

Sergino had smiled at Michele and dashed away with one final sprint, away beyond the nuns, beyond the tannery, beyond the great, eternal, iron **G**. The Mother Superior would find his farewell note (**F**). He would by then have left for the unknown. With a smile on his lips, in his eyes, in his belly, and in his feet.

He had run as fast as he could, using the cypresses as cover. He had caressed them with his back as he hid behind them and with his hands as he thanked his evergreen friends. He had tumbled down the hill running in a zigzag.

He had remembered Luigi and his wheelbarrow. The

young man had given him some directions, and Sergino had kept them in his head as a travel guide.

"I, too, used to live here," he had told him the first time they had met when he had made the paper airplane for him.

"Really? And you never tried to run away?" Sergino had asked him, as he was always seeking information about life outside the orphanage. He had started asking questions after meeting Oreste and discovering the existence of another planet outside the gate. He sought answers in books, questioned the tradesmen who came in, and probed everywhere for clues, sounds, and smells different from those of the institute.

"No, I never had any idea of what was on the outside before I stepped out..." answered Luigi.

"...but I must tell you, I wouldn't mind coming back inside here."

"Why?" Sergino asked him back, listening carefully to the boy's words.

"Because I felt safe..."

"...and because things didn't go exactly how they had told me they would go, nor how I might have expected..."

Sergino had not interrupted him; Luigi was mainly talking to himself.

The tanning industry had developed in the Grand Duchy of Tuscany, between Florence, Pisa, Arezzo, Santa Croce sull'Arno, and was one of the most flourishing activities of these areas. Hundreds of thousands of items were manufactured every year, from processing cowhides to making soles and uppers for shoes, goats and sheepskins to making gloves, corsets, and other clothing accessories. The Arno River provided the means for moving livestock and merchandise by land and by water. And the presence of large wooded areas was very useful for producing the vegetable tannins that were used to treat the skins to prevent their putrefaction.

At the end of the Nineteenth Century, there had been an anthrax epidemic in the hills between Santa Croce and San Miniato. That infectious disease is caused by the anthrax bacterium and is spread by contact with the skins of recently butchered animals during bating. To make the hides waterproof and ready for processing, many steps have to be taken, from soaking to hair removal, from fleshing to splitting, from deliming to bating. Then, depending on the type of leather or skin product needed, the tanning takes place, using various substances and acids, all of which are harmful to health.

The leather manufacturing area was particularly active at the time of the Great War in the production of footwear for the military. Its importance was now growing again in the expectation of a new war. Boots for the soldiers were made of leather, with cowhide soles; gun holsters were leather, as were other items of military equipment; the driving belts for the tanks were also made of leather. All this made tannins and tanneries crucial to the military effort.

"…The nuns had promised me a future with work and a family, but I got sick at the tannery…I did not believe the boys I met on my first day…"

"…They had warned me… but they, too, ended up in the hospital, one after the other, day after day…I, too, ended up in Pisa, almost dead. I couldn't breathe…"

"Hey, boy, don't go to the tannery!" Luigi had said abruptly, lest Sergino became distracted.

"But the nuns did help me. Here, at Mr. Bruno's farm, things aren't so bad…"

Sergino and Luigi would meet only once a year, and each time they picked up where they had left off.

"And you, what do you want to do when you grow up?" had asked Luigi.

"I want to travel by sea!" had answered Sergino, immediately adding all the questions he had been saving since the year before.

"How is the sea? Have you ever been there?"

"Yes, I was there quite a few times. When I was in the hospital, they would take me down to the waterfront to watch the ships, down at the mouth of the Arno. The nurses told me that I needed to detoxicate. "Breathe hard, fill your lungs with air," they would say to me."

"And what does the sea smell like?" had asked Sergino while the older boy continued his story.

"When you look at the sea, you feel your eyes widening to take in the whole horizon. Near you, it is light blue, green, clear. Far away, it is blue, dark blue. But the line where it touches the sky is made of light. If you squint, you feel as if you could touch it with the tips of your fingers…"

Without realizing it, Luigi had made Sergino's dream even more vivid.

"…The smell of just-caught fish tickles your nose; it mixes with the salty taste that clings to your face…"

"… and there is always wind! Sometimes it caresses your eyebrows as if magic fairies were kissing you, sometimes it ruffles your hair, it forces you to close your eyes, you can't resist. But really, you don't even want to. It is nice."

"…and it pushes the sailboats as they glide on the water, with their retinue of little songbirds looking for food…"

"…There…Nothing is as vast as the sea. The ships are enormous, with cannons, with nets…," Luigi had blended together images of warships with those of fishing vessels.

"I went to one port where there were warships, but it wasn't Pisa; you should see it. You would be dazzled!"

Sergino had listened to him with excitement.

"Which port?"

"La Spezia! There, everyone is in uniform, some blue, some white, some covered in grease, some perfectly clean. They move carts, they load crates, and they march in single file…"

"… I would have loved to be part of it, but they wouldn't take me because I was in poor health…"

Luigi's tone had become melancholy. Sergino listened to him without speaking as if trying to take mental notes.

"…I presented myself at the office of the military command in Florence, and they sent me to the infirmary for a physical…I wanted to enroll…"

"…Instead, they handed me a paper saying "Unfit." At that moment, I thought it would be better to go back to the nuns…"

"…The Reverend Mother found me a job at Mr. Bruno's farm…so I am now near the institute where I grew up…a bit like being home with my family…"

Luigi had described to Sergio the hills and the road from the orphanage to the village, with its food shops, public school, church, and rail station.

"How can I get to La Spezia?" Sergino had asked.

Luigi had expected that question. The kid was very determined. He wasn't just looking for the sea. He was looking for a port. Not just any port; he wanted one with warships. The young man had spoken of La Spezia, not of Livorno, the largest of the two, simply because he had been there personally, otherwise he would certainly have chosen the more important of the two.

"The best thing…in fact, the only one…to do is to take a train…," Luigi had realized that the boy was too young and that, although he might have seen pictures of a train in some books, he would certainly not have been able to follow his directions. So, he had tried to simplify things a bit.

"I mean, you need to go to a place where you see rails, and when you see an enormous thing coming along huffing and puffing steam, there, that is..."

"A dragon!" had exclaimed Sergino before the other could finish his sentence. Seeing Luigi's stunned reaction, the boy had burst out laughing in a convulsed manner.

"Hey, I am seven years old. I am little, not stupid!" Sergino had said as he continued laughing, and Luigi had joined him in his giggle fit.

Then, still laughing, he had continued to draw for him a mental treasure map. "OK, so you get to the train, and you jump on. Not on the one made for people, that one stops at the station. No. You must take the one that slows down but doesn't stop because it is already loaded with the merchandise it takes to the port. That's the train you want."

He had not told him that many different trains were going to ports. Indeed, some went to La Spezia and then on to Genoa; others went to Livorno and then on to the south. He hadn't told him because he would reach a port in any case.

"And what do you want to do when you reach the port?" had asked Luigi. "Do you have a plan?"

"I am only seven years old. Maybe in a couple of years, I really will leave. Not now."

"OK. Come on. How about a spin in my wheelbarrow? Eh?" had suggested Luigi.

"Yes, sure. Let's go. The half-hour of soccer is almost finished," had answered Sergino, asking Luigi to cover him with branches and leaves while he curled up at the bottom of the barrow.

Chatting with that nice boy, always full as he was of good intentions, had clarified many of the thoughts fluttering in his head: about the nuns, about racing towards the sea, about touching the horizon with his fingers. That horizon was his destiny, and he had acquired a certainty: it doesn't matter if only the darkest part of a medal is shown to you. The other part exists, always. And it is not necessarily the same as the first. It is not written in the stars.

Luigi was the other side of the medal: an unexpected friend, someone with a smile able to break through sadness, despite his many disappointments.

Oreste, Luigi, Michele – my father felt less alone. Someone, through that light between sea and heaven, was sending standard bearers to cover his back.

The fugitive kept on running and reached the train station. He had nothing else with him but himself and a piece of dry bread he had taken from the pantry the night before. He was free to discover the world, to run towards the sea.

He jumped onto a freight train that was moving very slowly. The wagon he chanced on was for livestock, the best traveling companions he could have wished. No questions, no abuse, no judgment. Every once in a while, he would hear some reassuring bleating. He found refuge in the corner of the car and fell fast asleep.

When he climbed onto that train, he had no idea of its direction or where it might stop along the way. He woke up when the wagon made a sudden jolt. He rolled on the straw that had been his mattress and ended up against the legs of a sheep. She turned towards him and looked at him in a tender, maternal way.

"You have arrived, little one," that lady with mustachioed lips and a fluffy woolen coat seemed to say.

Sergino poked his head out of the wagon as the "La Spezia" sign passed before his eyes.

A scent that lifted his spirits enveloped him. He recognized it even though he had never breathed it before. Amidst a mixture of fumes from fuel exhaust, rusted iron, rotten fish, wet ropes, very sweaty dock workers, he unconsciously recognized the salty smell of the sea, as it washed over his face like a wave of happiness.

"The port!"

He jumped down!

CHAPTER NINE

THE NAUTILUS

~

The maritime military Arsenal of La Spezia was the jewel in the crown of the Royal Italian Navy. It is said that Napoleon Bonaparte was the first person to realize the strategic position of that bay for the control of the Mediterranean. Its development was strongly promoted by the Prime Minister of the Kingdom of Italy, Camillo Benso, Count of Cavour, who gave the green light to its construction in 1869.

As Sergino looked across the rails, he saw a warship, and at the same time, he heard a loud clamor from a crowd of men dressed in uniform. They were all sailors saluting the flag before boarding the ship.

He ran to the Arsenal building, a large structure embellished with Tuscan grey stone. The archway over the entrance was flanked by a double row of columns and looked out onto a circular open plaza. At its center stood a statue of General Domenico Chiodo, the officer of the Corps of Naval Engineers who had designed the Arsenals of La Spezia, in the north, and Taranto, in the south of Italy.

The boy reached the base of the statue. That solemn and majestic place slowed his steps, which became both fluid and still at the same time.

***

No, I am not talking nonsense. Have you ever felt a sense of ethereal movement? Perhaps while sleeping or daydreaming.

Mine was not a dream.

With my spiritual eyes, I saw that I was hovering with Sergino in front of that monument. I was in total sync with him. That movement was like a spiritual vibration.

You feel totally free, free to move wherever you want, with your eyes, with your hands. Your glow expands, you can soar to where you can view the world from above. You can explore without being seen. You can sing without awakening the consciousness of others with your song. You can spin around, turn upside down, see through yourself, and move through anything. Your body is air; your senses are weightless yet invincible. You are as strong as a horse, as imposing as a dragon, as sensitive as a leaf in the wind. Your mind can process impossible data, shape logic, and even draw the depths of the soul.

It is the power of imagination. Everybody has imagination. And the stronger we feel, the more we can rise to a state of purity that lets us feel like heroes or angels and behave as such. That same strength should come to our aid when we feel so weak that we are not able to perceive the angels and heroes around us. I am using the conditional because all too often, we take refuge behind a barrier of fixed rules, stratified bonds and invariable variables while rejecting imagination and eccentric thoughts as a waste of time, if not a guilty spawn of the absurd.

***

Sergino felt grown up, like an adult, a young man ready for a new life full of adventures and glory at sea. He looked up, with his nose raised towards the proud gaze of General Chiodo, who appeared to him sincere and protective. A hand as cold and hard as marble grabbed his arm.

"He responds to the description. He's the one!"

The nuns had asked the military police to keep all ports on the Tyrrhenian Sea under surveillance, from Livorno to Genoa, and had provided a description of the runaway. In any case, the only children allowed to wander in the vicinity of the barracks were wearing Balilla uniforms, with an open-collared black shirt, a light blue kerchief with a clasp in the shape of a shield decorated with a portrait of the Duce, grey-green short pants, knee-socks of the same color, a black belt and sash, a black fez. Chin out, straight shoulders, straight legs.

Malnourished, poorly dressed, dirty, and smelly, without a cap or the Balilla posture, Sergino stood out like a sore thumb and was immediately recognizable. The only river stone sitting right in the middle of the stream, a small and isolated obstacle, but one standing out just enough to deviate the flow from its natural course, bending straight lines into curved ones, causing the water surface to ripple with bubbles and sprays. He was like a bothersome insect.

The policeman's grip was such that Sergino could not get away. He writhed and kicked and screamed to no avail. A second policeman added a further grip, and they held him up by his arms. The boy was spinning around like a propeller but was unable to take flight. He looked at General Chiodo again, begging for help.

"STOP!"

A figure in uniform emerged from the Arsenal door, with rows of ribbons on his chest. A couple of young petty officers escorted him. He approached the policemen, who saluted the high-ranking officer with their free hands. Judging from the weight of his medals, his rank must have been at least that of a Navy Lieutenant. From their point of view, he might as well have been a Colonel.

"Good morning, Sirs. Tell me, what has this young man done wrong?"

"He escaped from the Catholic Institute for Orphaned Children in Florence, Sir."

The Captain, with measured and authoritative steps, walked around the police officers and the boy, who was still spinning his legs in the air, in an attempt to free himself.

One of the policemen took a page folded into four out of his pocket and handed it to one of the petty officers escorting the Captain. It was the telegram describing the boy and containing orders to take him back to the orphanage. The officer opened up the paper to better read it, but his superior froze him with a sneer.

"What's your name?" The Captain put his hands on his hips and bent over to get a clear picture of the fugitive's face as the latter stopped moving madly and tried to gain some composure, not so much out of respect for that figure, nor out of fear of worse consequences, but simply to be able to answer for his actions in a proud way.

"Sergio Dal Boni."

"Sergio Dal Boni, Sir," the Captain corrected him with a severe tone, already treating him as a recruit.

"Sergio Dal Boni, Sir," the boy replied immediately, in a ringing voice.

The Captain had long experience in reading into his men as he chose them for different missions. It took him no time to understand that kid, who was able to convert the sadness of his early years without parents into a burst of pure joy at the sight of the sea and of those ships. Sergino was the personification of the desire for a bright future; he exuded positive energy from his greasy curls and dirty nails.

"Courage, vehemence. Good. We will make a glorious sailor out of him! Italy needs boys like this. The King is asking for them, and the Duce is calling for them!" exclaimed the Captain.

"This young man belongs to the Royal Navy!"

Hearing these words and that tone of authority, the police officers let go of their hold. The child was entrusted to the two petty officers, who then withdrew after the customary salute to their Captain. Sergino disappeared from the view of the policemen, leaving behind General Chiodo and the thought of having to escape once more from the nuns or being taken to some reform school.

He was handed over to the local branch of the Fascist Party, where he was bathed, fed, and clothed from head to toe. A few weeks later, he was ready to take his oath, which he read aloud:

In the name of God and Italy, I swear to follow the orders of the DUCE, and serve the cause of the Fascist Revolution with all my strength and, if necessary, with my own blood.

He was then handed the ten commandments of the young member of the militia:

1. *Know that a Fascist, and particularly a member of the militia, must not believe in perennial peace.*
2. *Prison time is always deserved.*
3. *Service to the Fatherland can be rendered even by just guarding an oil drum.*
4. *A comrade must be a brother: 1) because he lives with you; 2) because he sees things the way you do.*
5. *Your musket, your cartridge case, etc. have been entrusted to you not to be wasted in idleness but to be saved for wartime.*
6. *Never say, "Anyhow, it's paid for by the Government," because you are the one paying, and you chose the Government, and it is the one whose uniform you are wearing.*
7. *Discipline is an army's sunshine: without it, there are no soldiers, only confusion and defeat.*
8. *Mussolini is always right!*
9. *A volunteer has no extenuating circumstances when he disobeys.*

10. *One thing must matter over all others to you: the life of the DUCE.*[9]

He thanked them for the clothes and food, which seemed real to him for the first time. His life had changed at that very moment. His smile was one of awareness, not of surrender.

"If I don't like it here, I'll run away from here, as well."

He found himself in the company of hundreds of boys, all dressed in the same way. The regime's organizations set the children born in Italy on the path of the cult of the Duce, of adulation aimed at the man who personified the Fatherland and sought victories and the birth of a new Empire. The Mediterranean had been the theatre of African colonialism by the Kingdom of Italy and other powers, such as France, the United Kingdom, and Germany, even before fascism. Italy ruled over Libya and, further south, along the Red Sea, over Eritrea and Somalia.

In October 1935, the Duce launched a new campaign in Africa aimed at conquering Ethiopia. Boys were easily drawn to the military call to action. The new campaign in Abyssinia felt like revenge taken against the Empire of Menelik II, who, at the end of the XIX century, had halted the advance of the soldiers from the Kingdom of Italy and driven them back.

After armed clashes lasting seven months, the Italian army entered Addis Ababa in triumph. Mussolini appeared at the balcony of Palazzo Venezia in Rome and announced the end of the war in Abyssinia and the formation of an Empire now called Italian East Africa.

The Duce's popularity reached its highest peak. The Balillas were proud and eager to participate in the new military missions. The spark of those colonial successes gave meaning to their shirts, their muskets, and their bayonets. Newborns in this new Empire were called "Children of the She-Wolf," echoing the legend of the twins Romulus and Remus and the founding of ancient Rome.

Alongside military exercises and fascist discipline, boys were trained in sports, from fencing to rowing, cycling to swimming, and track and field. Teachers, in turn, had to have some knowledge of physical therapy, foreign languages, psychology, military strategy, techniques of warfare, hygiene, anatomy, singing, and art. The military branches of the Balilla and the Young Vanguard covered many different areas of the territory in defense of the Fatherland and against enemy aggression. They were cyclists, skiers, airmen, and submariners.

Sergio became an excellent sailor: he was well-loved by everyone because he was lively, cheerful, intelligent, helpful, and never subservient. He was responsible, amusing; he played along when adults made fun of how he looked, of his ideas.

"We can see your bones!"

Despite the food being decent, he was skinny by nature, as he had been when he left the orphanage.

"Rest your brain, kid!" They valued him for his witty remarks, for his helpful ideas, for his creative genius.

Boys grew up and embraced weapons; they learned how to shoot, fight, and survive. The Royal Navy represented excellence, without exception. The training and commitment of its men were of the highest caliber. The boys would push themselves with tenacity and spirit, above and beyond the quantity and quality of the equipment at their disposal.

The pace of the production of tanks, cannons, aircraft, explosives, and naval vessels did not equal popular enthusiasm. The nation was ready to go to war, its armaments decidedly less so.

Between 1939 and 1943, Italian factories produced eleven thousand warplanes, less than half of the twenty-five thousand of the Germans or the twenty-six thousand of the British. The armored vehicles for land operations were just over three thousand seven hundred, compared to twenty thousand German panzers and twenty-four thousand Russian tanks. Those numbers were even less reassuring compared to the American aircraft and tanks built in 1943 alone, which numbered eighty-six thousand and thirty thousand, respectively.

On paper, in laws and proclamations, Italy was well prepared for a new world war. Every sector was studied and regulated. On October 13, 1938, the King decreed the new classification of Navy vessels.

VICTOR EMMANUEL III
BY THE GRACE OF GOD AND WILL
OF THE NATION
KING OF ITALY
EMPEROR OF ETHIOPIA

In accordance with Law n. 1178 of July 8, 1926, concerning the rules governing the Royal Navy, together with later modifications thereto, [...] the vessels of the Royal Navy are classified according to the following categories, with a warning that the displacements herein referred to are the ones indicated in the basic designs:

– *Battleships – Battleships suitable for use on the high seas, commissioned with principal armaments of over 203mm caliber;*
– *Cruisers – High-speed vessels with principal armaments of a caliber equal to, or less than, 203mm, with displacement equal to, or greater than, 3,000 tons;*
– *Torpedo-boat destroyers – Surface torpedo vessel with displacement between 3,000 and 1,000 tons;*

- *Torpedo-boats — Vessels able to navigate with displacement between 1000 and 100 tons;*
- *Submarines — Vessels able to navigate in total immersion to deploy underwater weaponry. They are divided into the following subcategories, based on their range, armaments, and nautical capabilities:*
  - *Ocean-going submarines;*
  - *Coastal navigation submarines.*
- *Gunboats — vessels with speed lower than 20 knots, and displacement lower than 8,000 tons, not for auxiliary or logistical duties, and armed with at least one cannon, of any caliber;*
- *MAS [Motor torpedo boats] — Units with a displacement lower than 100 tons, equipped with internal combustion engines and capable of hunting for submarines or carrying out torpedo operations;*
- *Auxiliary vessels — Ships assigned to auxiliary and logistical services. They are divided into subcategories, based on the particular purpose for which they are used.*
- *Local use vessels — Smaller auxiliary vessels intended for local service in fortified harbors.*[10]

The La Spezia Arsenal was an essential component of this strategy. Many of the categories described in Royal Decree n. 1483 were stationed and trained in that very same Ligurian bay. In particular, the first MAS flotilla, made up of Armed Torpedo Motorboats, was its pride and joy.

At the outbreak of World War II, that special unit would change its name to Tenth MAS. Its first attack missions would turn out to be less than encouraging, in fact, fairly disastrous, with the loss of very large numbers of men and equipment in battle.

The second strategic basin, the Southern one, in Puglia,

encountered difficulties even just in entering the war.

During a nighttime raid, on the so-called Taranto Night, between November 11 and 12 of 1940, the British Royal Navy planes inflicted serious damage to the Taranto Arsenal. The Naval Command found itself needing to send fresh troops to the South of Italy.

Sergio had turned 14 just a few months earlier and was old enough to be sent to the front lines. He was assigned to the Taranto submarine unit.

On the military transport train carrying him and the other boys to that base in southern Italy, the loudspeakers continuously broadcast the songs of their units and war.

They skim the black waters
In the darkest of the dark
And from the proud turrets
Their lookouts scan the seas.
Silent and invisible
The submarines depart,
With hearts and engines
Ready to fight Immensity.
They sail the vast expanse,
They taunt Lady Death,
They laugh at destiny.
They aim to strike and bury
All enemies they meet.
This life the sailors live
In deep and roaring seas.
No fear of enemies
Nor of adversity,
For victory, they know,
Will come to crown their day.
Down below grey waters
In the misty light of dawn,
A turret with the tint of lead

Now spies its passing prey.
And from the quiet sub
A live torpedo springs:
It has unfailing speed,
It knows its given path,
It's sure and straight
And merciless, it crashes
Through the target hull
And churns the frothing sea.
And now in the blue waters,
In the light of a new day,
Now all those engines murmur
A new triumphant song.
And then the underwater boats
Return to hidden bays,
And every flag that's waving
A victory does say.[11]

In the train's bathrooms, on the outside walls of houses, everywhere the boys would look on their way to the base, they would be prepared for war, for being bombed, for defending themselves against spies.

Don't speak with anyone. The enemy is listening!

This poster by the regime was categorical, without appeal.

The air raid against Taranto was viewed for a long time as the work of traitors or enemy moles conveying information about guard duties, service units, the best times to launch an attack. Many swore that they had seen ground flares used to indicate target locations to incoming aircraft.

At midnight of June 10, 1940, Italy entered the war with four battleships, nine cruisers, 59 destroyers, 69 torpedo boats, 117 submarines – belonging to 24 different categories depending on their armaments – as well as two subcategories for operations in the Atlantic and in the

Mediterranean.

The vessels built for ocean-going operations were larger than the others. Some submarines were armed only with torpedoes, others with one or two cannons for a surface attack, others were outfitted for laying mines.

The Italian defense industry was struggling to keep up with the German and British ones, also from a technical point of view. The Italian fleet of submarines entered World War II as one of the largest in the world but others were faster, could dive more quickly, and stay submerged in deep waters for longer periods. Yet the heroism and abnegation of Italian sailors were without parallel.

The submarines were little more than sardine cans. Men and torpedoes shared spaces that were reduced to the bare minimum.

Missions were mainly of two kinds: the destruction of enemy merchant ships and the oil tankers that could refuel military craft, both by sea and air, and the destruction of military vessels to decimate the enemy and protect the allied ships engaged in the war.

Ever since the night of the devastating British attack, the Taranto base had been placed under curfew. At sunset, the town would fall into a kind of catatonic trance, in total darkness. The sound of sirens added to the dramatic tension while awaiting orders from the High Command.

"Sergio!" exclaimed the petty officer on patrol, "Inform the Captain that another torpedo-bomber raid is about to happen!"

Running had always been one of his best talents. The Commander of the Arsenal was standing in the radio room. The alarm signal had now reached his hands. "Thank you, young man. You may return to your squad. Very good."

The boy would have liked to be able to give some news to the petty officer on duty. Still, his rank was not high enough to ask the Commander, nor were questions allowed in any case. You obeyed, and you carried out orders.

Planes flew over the base, both that night and the following one. They were spotters. Cannons fired repeated rounds towards the sky, but no enemy was hit. No other bombs were dropped.

High spirits returned among the ranks at the Arsenal. New vessels were en route, including two submarines: one, of the Atlantic type, and the other for deployment in the Mediterranean. The boys made bets on which one they would be assigned.

"Hey, listen to this."

Even when not necessarily all that funny, jokes lessened the tension and lightened the dark shadow of the (very real) possibility of death at sea.

The Axis between Italy, Germany, and Japan had already been in place for a couple of years, and the war was just beginning.

In the barracks of those three nations, Propaganda was busily at work. In sleeping quarters and in mess halls, postcards from "Good Friends in Three Countries" were handed all around. Cheerful-looking children carrying flags from the land of the Rising Sun, or ones decorated with nazi swastikas, or tri-color Italian flags with their crusader shields, or with portraits of Hitler, Konoe, or Mussolini, all celebrated belonging to the German-Japanese-Italian Axis. Servicemen used these cards to write to their relatives, to their wives and girlfriends, and this was one of the ways in which the message was spread to their families.

"So…there is a Japanese guy, a German one, and an Italian. The three challenge each other before embarking on their submarines. The Japanese says, "Our submarine is so long that we need bicycles to get from stem to stern."

The sailors nudged each other, laughing. Some tried to portray Japanese features by stretching their eyes with their fingers. Some stuck out their tongues. One mimed a sort of dwarf monster trying to push his mini bicycle forward.

"The German says, "Our U-boats are even longer. We need motorcycles to get from stem to stern!"

Another burst of laughter and cheer, and here, too, that same mime went to work in the part of a stiff-looking German, ramrod-straight, awkwardly pushing a motorcycle with wheels in the shape of swastikas.

"At this point, the Italian snorts, "Our submarines are so long that someone standing to the fore knows that there is a war, while someone aft doesn't even realize it!"

A long double whistle from the two battleships announced at that very moment a different fate for the Taranto Arsenal and for those young men who were ready for anything.

Suddenly the boys jumped up, helping each other: they looked like a long millipede.

An interminable roll call started blaring out of the loudspeakers. Sailors and petty officers immediately fell into rank to carry out the orders that kept coming through those croaking, iron voices.

Together with their names were announced, in order, the numbers and acronyms of their combat units, and the names of their vessels and captains. At the end of that long list stood the names of two cities: Naples and Messina.

"What is happening?" The buzz grew more intense, and it was hard to understand, while two lines of men climbed the gangplanks to board the two vessels.

"They are closing the Arsenal."

"What does that mean?"

"That they are going to transfer us. We are going to war, but not from here. The base has been compromised,"

Sergio explained to his comrades.

He was not just guessing. He had been present a short time earlier at the reading of a telegram from Rome. The Commander of the Arsenal was briefing his officers.

"The Naval Command has decided to transfer the rest of the fleet from Taranto to Messina and Naples. Divide the men into two groups: surnames beginning with odd letters go to Messina, even letters to Naples. We cast off at dawn."

Sergio was assigned to Naples. His vessel did not suffer any attacks during its navigation along the coast, nor was it spotted by enemy cruisers or submarines.

Long before he disembarked in Naples, he was handed his orders for the mission. His first submarine was ready to sail, and its Captain was awaiting part of the crew and supplies arriving on the ship from Taranto.

Sergio had daydreamed, even as a little boy, fantasizing about adventures aboard the *Nautilus*. He knew it inch by inch; he was in the good graces of its creator, Captain Nemo, and Sergio imagined himself as his first mate. Not surprisingly, his favorite book was *Twenty-thousand Leagues Under the Sea*.

The *Nautilus* had been designed for long sea voyages. Thanks to its two hulls, one inner and one outer, separated by watertight compartments, it could travel the sea depths at a speed of 50 knots. It was shaped like a cigar or a tapered seashell and was 70 meters long. It attacked enemy ships and ripped open their hulls with a kind of rostrum. Thus, the few survivors of such attacks would rave that a metal-eating marine monster had attacked them.

In the illustrations of Verne's book, which Sergio had memorized as he hid under the Mother Superior's desk, the Captain's grand salon walls on the *Nautilus* were decorated with tapestries and paintings. The floors were covered with Oriental rugs, and an enormous organ added a note of drama and mysticism to life under the seas. At the center of the Captain's quarters, Nemo had placed a large command table surmounted by a fountain in the shape of an oyster.

Most importantly, there was Nemo's great library, containing thousands of naval texts, epic tales, and stories from around the world. There were pendulum clocks and other wall clocks all around, arranged in ticking and chiming order.

Sergio descended the ladder into the Atlantic-type submarine. Other young men, lined up ahead of him and behind him, stopped to salute their Captain and went to take up their positions, clinging to each other like mussels onto harbor pylons. They had to bend their heads to avoid injuring themselves against the boat's instruments or its air inlet vents. Sergio's only book was the one he had slipped into his backpack before embarking. It was an illustrated section from Robert Louis Stevenson's *Treasure Island*.

Sergio was entering the world he had always dreamed of, and he was smiling. He smiled as he looked around, taking mental notes of everything. It was not the *Nautilus*, but it was a submarine, a real one.

No organ, no carpets, no gushing fountain here. The most important order was written everywhere, "Save Water!" This certainly was not the *Nautilus*. Yet, it was a sea monster without a doubt. And Sergio was on board; he was now hermetically sealed inside its belly.

CHAPTER TEN

THE LEMON

~

I must say that many of the things our parents tell us are then scattered to the wind. Or, as my sweetest mother used to say, "They go in one ear and out the other" -- an excellent way to say that you have nothing between your ears.

In a repetitive cycle, ever-revolving on itself, the "luck" of being listened to passes down from one person to another, from one generation to the next.

I will admit that the stories about the war and submarines were not among my favorites, if for no other reason than the fact that they always elicited sadness in me. However, most likely, my parents tried to keep those memories alive to make us understand that we should avoid weapons and wars at all costs. As I mentioned initially, my father hoped to ward off the chance that his children might find themselves pitted against each other in the armies of different countries.

When I experienced his youth alongside him, I, too, entered into that submarine. It seemed natural to me, and I felt I already knew what he was about to show me.

"Babbo, you are right. I have not forgotten: fascism, the war..."

His smile was able to bring daylight into the bowels of that small sea monster.

"Look again; there's much more."

He was referring to the men, to friendship, to the sea.

***

The Royal Navy was the most orderly and efficient example of what the Kingdom of Italy had to offer. It was the pride and joy of the fascist government. Embarkation procedures were planned in their most minute details: cleaning the loading wharves, unloading the freight trains, gathering joyful-looking mothers to wave off their sons as they boarded their ships, flags fluttering in the wind.

Everything was carefully studied to project the Duce's charismatic image. Such scenes were filmed and shown in cinemas triumphantly by the Istituto Luce, Mussolini's primary propaganda source. The wealthy bourgeoisie was fed the much-extolled military successes of the regime. Families, especially those less well-to-do, could rise with the tide of pride lifting their sons so well prepared for war. They were prepared to die for their Fatherland.

With the introduction of sound in the early 1930s, movies and cinema theaters became a primary means for the regime to spread its messages. To promote enthusiasm and generate consensus, over 500 films were produced in the space of 10 years. At least one in five contained direct proclamations, while others referred indirectly to the fascist machine.

Censorship was institutionalized, the Venice Film Festival was inaugurated, and Cinecittà was built in Rome, with the motto *"Cinema is the strongest weapon."*

Likeableness, creativity, and heroism were the talents required in movie characters for the release of a film to be granted. Control over foreign productions became obsessive.

Gangster movies came over from America and were very successful at the box office. To ban them altogether, the regime decided to use them for its purposes by changing the dialogues between the characters through expert dubbing or by editing out some scenes.

One such Hollywood film was "Scarface," by Howard Hawks, which told the story of Mafia boss Tony Camonte, inspired by the figure of Al Capone.

Italian importers decided not to purchase the film, as they were sure it would not clear censorship. Luigi Freddi, General Director of Cinematography during the fascist era, and Mussolini's censor explained the reasons for this many years later, after the fall of fascism.

"One film that the Italian audience was not allowed to see at the time because of me – and I still assume full responsibility for that – is the one about Scarface. [...] I had seen it in London, at a private screening room on Wardour Street; it was the progenitor and masterpiece of all gangster movies, a frenzied film in which the number of gunshots and people killed was greater than the number of frames! It was a film that didn't allow you to catch your breath, written with such diabolic skill as to keep the viewer on the edge of his seat for two hours. But, quite apart from the film itself, which is a real school for crime, we cannot forget that all the criminals holding up the framework of that terrifying subject, although living and moving in an American context, were carefully and deliberately classified as Italian." [12]

People old and young, housewives and athletes, even in the most remote towns and villages, all had access to the cinema, as it was the regime's most encouraged form of entertainment. Adults were allowed to smoke, even though that bad habit was seen as inappropriate for a fascist man. Spectators would sit either in rows of velvet seats or on wobbly wooden chairs. Before the film, there would be a showing of the latest newsreels created by Istituto Luce.

Those newsreels could never be followed by a gangster movie, as it might impress in the minds of the spectators the idea that an Italian could be a ruthless killer. The music that accompanied the reading of the news was unwavering, as were the images. The voice-over was firm while at the same time singing respectful praises of the highest authorities. Together with the expressions on people's faces, the words conveyed honor, dedication, sacrifice, and affirmation.

The audience watched the newsreels in silence, with focus and admiration. The black and white images scrolled over the screen, leaving in their wake pride and participation.

[...] Solemn celebrations of Italian military glory at the Altar of the Fatherland, on the twenty-first anniversary of its victory. The torn flags and the glorious banners of the regiments of the Roman garrisons are being raised together with the emblems of the National Fascist Party, greeted by the population which fills the Imperial Forum with very loud ovations. [...] Thousands of Italians were present in Taranto at the joyous launching of the submarine "Alpino Bagnolini" a new unit in a submarine fleet without rival!"[13]

The enormous propeller of the *Bagnolini* was its most eloquent show of strength. It was like a giant octopus, rotating its blades without the slightest chance of enemy resistance. The slipway frame was gigantic; the people in charge of the launching looked like ants working for their queen. The Bishop was imparting his blessing; a fluttering of little flags accompanied the smiles of the mothers behind the barriers set up to protect the launching site.

Sergio and his crewmates were among those greeted by the fanfare. Neither he nor any of his companions turned to greet the mothers, who were dressed in their best attire for the occasion, with fresh hairdos and cheerful smiles.

It didn't even cross their minds that they might be offending their parents or the military or religious authorities. It was simply that their mothers were not there. In most cases, they were orphans, or, as in Sergio's case, they had been taken away from their mother's breast just after leaving the womb.

Entering the narrow hull, completely black on the outside and with just enough light to prevent the young patriots from bumping their heads against one another, would have taken the breath away from even the most heroic amongst them. But not from these. They entered smiling as if they were resurrected to a new life.

For many of them, subconsciously, entering the submarine was like returning to their mother's womb, to those nine months spent inside her. To navigate the sea depths was like being rocked in amniotic fluid. Protected from the outside world, fed through an umbilical cord. Loved without ifs, ands, or buts.

It was like a blood relationship. The Navy warmed the boys' hearts, and they reciprocated with ardor and loyalty, grateful for being chosen. The submariners were the Navy's most dearly beloved members. They were its pride and joy, its standard-bearers. When they died, they all died together, without exception. Their gaze would shine forever inside that hull resting on the bottom of the sea.

They were young heroes, a hero production line calling on other heroes to enroll. In 1936, the Navy proudly announced a revolutionary solution devised to keep those heroes alive as long as possible.

The safety of submarine crews is guaranteed by a new device, entirely designed and built in Italy. It is the most important ever put to the test by any navy in any country in recent times. This device consists of a hermetically sealed turret, which can hold one man at a time. It is launched from the submarine and very quickly reaches the water surface, where the man can free himself from that temporary prison.

Once the rescue is accomplished, the submarine retrieves the turret so that another man may take a place in it. Its descent can also serve to introduce into the submarine men and materiel needed for repairs or recovery.

Thus, finally, can be foiled the effects of one of the awful sea disasters, that of submarines forced by mechanical failures to lie on the sea bottom, becoming thus metal graves before any rescue can reach them.[14]

The Royal Navy was in Sergio's DNA. The boy felt a strong bond with the sea and was naturally drawn to warships.

He was unaware that his father, Giorgio, had been dedicated to the Naval Academy long before he was born, as had been his grandfather, Gian Guido.

Sergio hadn't the faintest idea of who his father had been. Nor could he ever have imagined that Officer Giorgio Porzio could have been the Commander of his submarine – a man who, even before his first sea voyage, had lived out his destiny in one inexhaustible night of love, when, without knowing it, he had given life to Sergino.

Sergio had impressed in his mind those few lines read in the Mother Superior's file just before escaping the orphanage.

In his mind, his mother was a princess, a scientist, and a woman of great intellect, perhaps a writer. He dreamed of giving her a gift of glory and pride. One day he would go looking for her; he would present himself to her in his white uniform, holding his cap at his waist.

Without knowing it, he would be dressed like his father at his first meeting with Adele.

Without knowing it, he, too, would be loved at first sight. With a purer love, that of a mother for her child, yet one no less overwhelming.

"Mamma, I know that you exist, that you are thinking of me," he would often repeat as he drifted to sleep. He would dedicate his last thought of the night to her. In the morning, his mind would immediately focus on the day's seafaring operations.

Submariners were given a short, concise training

course, mainly consisting of lessons in living together in very close quarters, with food and water carefully rationed. The petty officer conveyed to the boys a few fundamental rules and, especially, made them proud of serving their Fatherland.

The *Bagnolini* set sail after its "joyous launching" in Taranto and immediately made a name for itself thanks to widely reported successful operations. On June 12, 1940, just two days after the beginning of the war, that vessel – an Atlantic *Liuzzi* class submarine – under Lieutenant Commander Tosoni-Pittoni sank the British cruiser *Calypso*. It was a brilliant opening for the naval warfare in the Mediterranean. The sailors' caps were tossed high, the submariners anthem filled the air in the mess hall, where loudspeakers broadcast words of military triumph.

The successes of the *Bagnolini* raised high the troops' morale. They helped convince the General Command that they could quickly turn the conflict in their favor thanks to their dominance on the seas. This conviction was transmitted directly to Mussolini. It was, however, a short-lived illusion.

By the end of June, at least ten submarines had not returned to base. Hundreds of brave men lay at the bottom of the sea, cradled and sheltered in a metallic womb.

The war was a desperate tallying of equipment and men sent off to die, disdaining danger for the greatness of their nation. But only a few high party officials were aware of that at the time. By the end of the war, the tally of submarines would climb to three out of four sunk, destroyed, and lost.

The *Bagnolini* was the first to triumph on the high seas. It continued its proud service to the Fatherland in closed seas and open oceans, off the African and American coast, always bringing its crew back to base, safe and sound.

It would later be attacked several times by British aircraft, which dominated on land and sea with their raids. It always distinguished itself even after it was forced to change its Flag after the Armistice of 1943.

The *Bagnolini* would then be transferred under German command and converted into Unit UIT22, assigned to transport troops and goods to the Far East. In March 1944, American aircraft attacked it. After being hit by machine-gun fire and depth charges, it never reemerged. Together with its German crew and officers, 12 Italians died; most of them were twenty-year-olds, who had been sent on board in the name of non-existent cooperation.

By the summer of 1942, Sergio had already changed crews a few times. He had boarded half a dozen vessels and experienced war at the bottom of the sea, a few rare moments on shore, then, again, immersion. He had managed to grow up but not to put on weight. He was so skinny that, with a bit of imagination, one could almost see his bones, lungs, and heart.

He was too young to climb the rungs of the military hierarchy; he was still just a ship's boy. Everybody loved him, from the ship's engineer to the Captain. It was thanks to his gift of the gab, to the charm of someone who is in this world to live life, not to suffer it. He always had a ready answer, bright and friendly eyes, and an open and pure mind.

The older boys, and they all were older than Sergio, felt that it was their duty to give him advice on his future, to talk to him about sex and business, to give him suggestions on how to find his mother, and on what to expect at the end of the war.

As soon as Sergio had embarked, he was taken under the wing of the cook, Giuseppe Russo, who had just turned forty years old and was a submariner with considerable experience. He had survived aerial attacks and the sinking of his first vessel after a nighttime shipwreck on a rocky reef just off the Greek coastline. He had served meals to at least half a dozen captains and five hundred sailors.

The submarine was his home. He had no other. His beautiful house in Messina, in the elegant "Mille" neighborhood, had crumbled like a breadstick during the terrifying earthquake of 1908. And with it, he had lost his entire family, too. He was the fifth and youngest child of a tavern keeper who was very famous for his "arancini" in his town. People came from far and wide to taste those rice croquettes that look like pear-shaped oranges and are based on a recipe handed down in Messina from the days of the Saracens.

His eatery, which occupied the entire ground floor of an Arab-style building he owned, was called "*l'Arancinu di Giuseppe*," in honor of his grandfather. His father, Gaetano, and his mother, Olivia, did the cooking; his four sisters, Pina, Mirella, Marinella, and Beatrice, served tables. He had been too young to work in the kitchen, even though he spent his days there. He was the official taster. His father adored him. While stirring a sauce or cutting meat, he would describe the dishes he was cooking, preparing his son for the day when he, too, would wear an apron embroidered by his grandmother Regina with their specialty, which was to be eaten while standing and with one's hands.

Four days before the New Year, preparations were at a high pitch for the season's festivities. It was that time of year when Sicilians have the most incredible appetite! Just before dawn, a loud and booming sound woke up Giuseppe. In an instant, he was covered in glass and plaster fragments while wood splinters shot into him, wounding him. As the house pillars collapsed, the entire second floor, where the family lived, fell through. The ceiling fell onto him. The earth continued to shake with the same vigor as his mother used to shake the tablecloths to get rid of the last crumb. That movement was brusque, decisive, and repeated with sudden and strong snaps violent enough to kill an elephant.

The Ximenian Observatory in Florence recorded something unheard-of:

This morning, at 5:21, the instruments of this Observatory began recording striking, extraordinary data. The amplitude of the graphs was such that they could not fit onto the cylinders: they were over 40 centimeters wide. Something very serious is happening somewhere.[15]

Giuseppe looked at his bleeding hands and at his legs, also covered in red stains. He was full of cuts, luckily only superficial. He felt no physical pain, but his mind was clouded. A large wooden beam had fallen over a doorframe just above him, and that strange defensive refuge created by fate had saved his life. He was covered in rubble, and his eyes were grey with dust and plaster flakes. He heard a voice calling for help from under a mound of debris.

"Help, I am here. I am here."

It was his sister Beatrice, who was a year older than he. He tried to reach her, digging with his hands and pushing away fragments of shattered furniture with his legs. He saw his sister's face as she lay crying and curled up in a panic. He succeeded in pulling her out by the sheer strength of desperation. They held each other in a long embrace.

"FATHER?"

"MOTHER?"

"MIRELLA...PINA...MARINELLA?"

They both yelled endlessly, at the top of their lungs, in the hope of finding their family by sounding through the rubble.

In 37 seconds, the earthquake had destroyed half the

city. Death and destruction were everywhere. Nobody answered. As they tried to get out of what was left of their building, their prison, they found the trapped and lifeless bodies of their three sisters and their beloved father. Their souls had flown to another realm. Holding each other's hands, they were finally able to find a way out amidst clouds of dust, without turning back, with tears frozen on their cheeks.

"Mamma, MAMMA!"

The siblings found the strength to run towards Olivia, who was sitting with her head bent over her knees and her hands covering her face.

"Giuseppe, Beatrice…"

The three of them embraced under the dark sky that hung over the desperate cries of their neighbors and the sinister creaking of buildings still standing unsteadily. The old street was a river of devastation, and in front of them stood the broken sign of their restaurant.

Aranci…

…iuseppe

The survivors of that massacre started running towards the sea, out of an instinct for survival and of a desire to get as far away as possible from any new building collapsing. Their flight was accompanied by explosions and fires caused by gas escaping from broken pipes. The road was strewn with sinkholes. Olivia, Giuseppe, and Beatrice joined the long human snake seeking safety at the harbor. But that black morning was not over yet: it was as if the devil had taken total control and was amusing himself in spreading death and destruction.

The picture appeared even more terrifying once in view of the sea: they saw the sea pull back, leaving its bed exposed to the air. The line of people understood that they were trapped and screamed with one voice,

"A TIDAL WAVE. A TIDAL WAVE!!!!"

After pulling back to form a wall about 10-12 meters high, the water turned into a giant octopus, writhing with fierce brutality. In a fraction of a second, with a demoniacal howl, it unleashed itself in the direction of the city, sweeping away and crushing everything it encountered along its path. That marine monster pulled back and regrouped at least two more times again, swallowing up trees, houses, trains, and people.

As sharp as a saber stroke, a slash of water hit Giuseppe's hands with violence and made him lose his hold. In an instant, his mother disappeared to his left, his sister to the right, and he was lifted up high, then slammed down in a nose-dive, like a seagull onto its underwater prey. A vortex threw him against the ruins of a church, and he lost consciousness. The water kept on pushing him until he remained entangled on a cross that stuck out amidst the wreckage. Yet again, a structure formed by fate had saved him from death.

Exhausted and aching all over, he regained consciousness at the very moment when a generous soul was fumbling around to pull him down from the cross and lay him down on the rubble. He didn't even have the time to thank him or to ask for any more help: his rescuer had already disappeared inside the ruins of a small house in search of other survivors.

The child, crawling amidst piles of rubble and pools of water left by the fury of land and sea, made his way back to what had once been his house. He sat on the side of the wreckage of a boat that now took the place of that building's façade. He waited for his mother and his sister to reappear. He hoped and prayed. He waited, he hoped, he prayed, for hours and hours.

It became late night.

"Hey, kid."

"Kid!"

A sailor was shaking him by the arm to make sure he was still alive. Giuseppe stood up with difficulty; he was weak and confused.

"What's your name?"

"Giuseppe Russo," he said with great effort.

The sailor wrote down his name on a crumpled piece of paper he had in his breast pocket. He bent over and lifted that human bundle, laying him over his shoulder like a sack of potatoes. He carried him to a torpedo boat that had been outfitted as a hospital ship. Giuseppe never left the Royal Navy after that. As time went by, he was adopted by it, and, as his contribution, he brought the art he had learned from his father.

"The time has come for me to start a family," Giuseppe would tell himself every time he returned from a sea voyage.

He had already gone on a couple of missions with Sergio. He saw him as the son he would have liked to have, the one he would not have wanted to be away from, ever, for any reason. And the one he would certainly never have allowed to board a submarine. Every time he stumbled across him, he would have liked to give him a gentle smack on the bottom.

"Still in the Navy, little sparrow?"

Then he would hug him, lifting him off the ground.

Giuseppe was the largest man on board. He carried a few extra kilos of weight around his waist, not more than five or six, but more than he needed.

After days and days at sea, they had all grown beards, some thick, some more stubble. Water was too precious a commodity to waste on shaving. The cook's beard was soft and golden.

"Sergio, listen to what I have to say."

It was the same story he had heard every day, no new details. The only thing that changed was the tone if the boy wasn't paying enough attention.

"When you first came on board, I gave you a lemon. You still have it, don't you?" The cook's words were more of a threat than just a question.

Sergio's thoughts were elsewhere, focused on the stern voice blaring out of the internal loudspeakers. The Captain had just ordered a rapid dive to a depth of 30 meters, then 45 meters. The submarine was on a transport mission northwest of the island of Crete, in the Aegean Sea. Shortly before dawn, the officer on duty had caught sight through the periscope of a destroyer traveling at high speed just above them. They were too close to launch torpedoes, too near not to be subject to enemy attack. A squadron of reconnaissance aircraft escorted the British vessel.

The cook put his hand on Sergio's chest, shoving him abruptly against the bulkhead. That hand was like a giant ox plowing through his bones; the boy could almost feel them being crushed without resistance. The hand now went up to his throat, and those fingers were like roots tangling with the boy's breathing. He was suffocating; he couldn't answer that screaming voice.

"Do you have that lemon??? Where is it? Show it to me! I told you always to keep it in your pocket."

Sergio wasn't able to open his mouth and, even if he had, most likely, he would have had to swallow the enraged cook's saliva, as the man's face was by now right up to his own.

Giuseppe felt a great deal of affection for him. He adored that little sparrow.

"I'm doing it for you!" he said.

"You are just a little boy; how did they allow you on board? You don't even weigh 50 kilos, and you are all skin and bones."

On the other hand, as Sergio could judge from his position at that moment and the creaking of his ribs, the cook must have weighed at least double that: he was a giant, tall, and wide. A bear. Sergio had seen bears in an illustrated book. He tried for the first time to free himself from the grip of that hairy creature.

How had they allowed him on board? He took up at least the place of three men in a space just big enough for forty sardines. His cooking kept the men cheerful, and his stories lulled them to sleep.

He loved all those kids, and he also scared them to death.

"It's to keep you awake; danger doesn't wait for you to open your eyes," he would say. No one dared question his words. He had authority.

"So, show me that lemon. Do you have it?"

Sergio kept it in a cloth pouch in his trousers.

"Here it is. Here it is, Sir."

He had received it on the day when orders had been handed out on board. Sergio, however, did not have any particular duties; he was the boat's aide-de-camp. His sailor's cassock was perfect, in the sense that in the evening it also served as his blanket. Yes, Sergio was definitely small and thin. He fit in it twice, but it was the smallest one available.

"It's too large for him," they said, as they were handing him his kit when he first came on board.

"No. It makes me look older," thought Sergio.

"You can sleep here. You will be my helper," the cook had ordered.

"How old are you?" asked the big bear in a huff, as he already knew the boy's age. However well-disposed, he would rather not have taken such a flea on board "his" submarine.

Even before he could answer, he started calling him "little sparrow."

"So, little sparrow, do you have a tongue? Or don't you know when your mother made you?"

"Sixteen, Sir." His voice struggled to come out, while his hand was guided to his trouser pocket by an involuntary protective gesture, one as irreducible as maternal instinct.

"What do you have there? Show me."

"Your mother?" He read the notes that Sergio kept with him, not so much out of fear of forgetting, but to have a sort of identity card in case of heroic death.

A grin briefly twisted the cook's jaw. His teeth showed, and his lip curled up towards his enormous nose. "You are a foundling!"

Sergio did not know this word, even though it definitely didn't sound very elegant. Giuseppe had said it while turning towards the counter he called his galley. He grabbed a knife that was as big as his forearm and larger than the boy's entire arm. He waved it in front of him as if it were a fan.

He then started rummaging in the larder. He had done this before with other newbies, with other boys. Never, however, with such a little sparrow. He got out another lemon, one that was as hard as a rock, judging from the sharp sound it made when he put it down on the cutting board. It was no real cutting board as the counter wasn't any wider than his hand.

Giuseppe did all his work on it, and with great passion: the grub he made for the sailors was sacred. And once he had put away his cooking utensils, the kitchen would become his bunk, the bear's den.

TZAK! A sharp and clean movement of his forearm split that poor lemon in two.

Sergio was seized with uncontrollable laughter. Tears filled his eyes.

"There!"

Giuseppe slammed half of that lemon into the palm of his hand, squeezing it from his wrist to his fingertips.

He expected a question like, "What should I do with it, Sir?" But Sergio said nothing and continued to laugh, trying to control his emotions at the theatricality of that gesture. What if his head had ended up on that counter?

He laughed and laughed, harder than he had ever before. He brought his free hand up to cover his face and try to hide his grimaces. He tried to hold his eyebrows still and separate.

"LITTLE SPARROW!"

That harsh pronouncement almost lopped off the boy's head.

"Just watch out if I ever find you without that lemon."

Sergio said nothing. Not a single word.

CHAPTER ELEVEN

BOMBS!

~

G iuseppe did not wait for Sergio to ask him why his words were so tart, why they had an edge more pungent than the juice of that citrus fruit.

"Show me your lemon!" he said one other day.

He took the boy's hand, and, together with his own, he stuck it into the boy's pocket, where one could see a hard round shape.

Sergio was afraid of what the cook would order him to do with that dried-out old fruit, but he could not imagine how crude the subject discussed would be. He was just a young boy, and many of the words uttered by the bear were to make a rude entrance into his fantasies. Or, even worse, into his nightmares.

"I have seen too many gnats ruin themselves for a cunt!!" The bear was raging and yet, in his way, protective. Sergio twisted his mouth and his nose simultaneously while also squinting his eyes. He barely took in the meaning of that sentence, while a shiver went through him at hearing the word "cunt," a word that was still, for him, just "hearsay."

He had heard it in the jokes told by the older boys, in the stories they would tell about sex when they would always describe things in the most detailed way. The shape, texture, smell, and feel were all constructed inside his head by the simple power of deduction. He had not browsed through illustrated books on the subject in the nuns' library, nor had he looked for any. Nor would he have found any there.

"The lemon is your only defense!" yelled the bear, determined to hammer his advice into the boy's head.

"When we get to shore, to port, everyone runs to the nearest cunt they can find. Without a lemon, they would all be stuck through by an enemy bayonet!" He spoke using military jargon, even though female genitalia had nothing to do with maritime warfare.

"Syphilis, the clap. They cause more victims than the war. Do you understand, little sparrow?"

No, he didn't understand. Giuseppe persisted.

"It's terrible. You have no idea of how much damage can come from a cunt, and a dirty cunt."

The cook was not a misogynist, nor was he homosexual. He had not suffered abuse as a child, nor had his mother treated him like a scoundrel, far from it. During mission after mission, he had seen boys howling with pain, rolling on the floor with piercing cries.

As soon as the young men set foot ashore, they would run to the first available bordello near the harbor. They often did not wait to find a decent house, one of those subject to government control. They would often assault or be accosted by prostitutes who frequented the alleyways around the docks. These were often malnourished girls looking for food or older women seeking only meager pay.

In many cases, they had had sexual relations with many different unknown men during the same day. One after the other, with no protection. They had received their sperm, and the infections those men might have contracted from other women or from the lack of hygiene onboard their vessels. This engendered a never-ending chain of diseases. The lemon was not an antidote or a remedy. It was a preventive weapon.

"Do you know what they will do to you in the hospital before they send you right back on board ship?!"

Sergio was silent. He was spellbound by the bear.

"They will give you a shot of penicillin right there, at the tip of your penis," he bounced forward towards the boy's pubic area, causing him to clamp his legs together like a hedgehog recoiling in horror.

"The burning, the vomiting, the immediate high fever. You would be rolling on the ground as if a cobra had bitten you on the glans and injected its poison into you. You would scream like an innocent man sentenced to death."

He went on, adding rudimentary medical details and painting a dreadful, hellish outcome for the boy.

"Sometimes the infection is so serious that the only thing the doctor can do is to stick something up your penis, into the urinary canal, a device that looks like a miniature version of one of our torpedoes. As soon as the whole thing is in place inside your penis, he pulls it back with all his strength…"

Sergio thought he would faint…He raised his hand to his mouth to try and stop the uncontrollable wave of nausea that had come over him, and he repeatedly coughed to try and get rid of that sensation.

"The device opens up with four blades. Your penis would be opened up into wedges, like an orange. No anesthesia. You'd be wide-awake. You wouldn't even understand when your pain would ever end, as the doctor would be scraping your penis to get rid of the disease. Then he would sew you up with the gentleness of a fisherman repairing his net…"

Giuseppe shook the boy by his shoulders; he took his hand, still wrapped around the lemon. He yelled at him.

"Before you go with a woman, dip your fingers into the lemon, then touch her. Touch her cunt!"

The boy was overwhelmed with disgust. At that moment, he would have chosen never to touch a woman.

The bear then made a statement the boy would not

have wanted to hear.

"If the woman screams when you touch her with your hands full of lemon juice, RUN!"

"Run as fast as you can. She has lesions; she is infected!!!"

"Now, do you understand what the lemon is for?

***

I listened with bated breath to the story about the lemon. I cannot say that it did not make an impression, as I had heard it time and again during my adolescence, yet it did not immediately come to mind when I approached a girl.

"I know that you wanted to warn me, and I also know that you were never offended, even as you realized that I would completely ignore that bit of advice..." I said to my father, who was holding me in his luminous embrace.

I eventually realized, many years later, that by insisting on that lemon story, my father was only giving me further proof of his love and of his wish to protect me during my boyhood.

I had only focused on that lemon and the consequences of sexually transmitted diseases.

How far I was from the truth!

"Babbo, I don't know how I didn't understand it earlier!"

"Fabino, you understood it perfectly well, deep inside. Your heart is full of love."

The images from the past began to change again, and I became aware that something terrible was about to happen.

***

Suddenly the bear became tame, and he hugged the boy, who seemed to be getting thinner by the second. He had been swallowed up by his jersey, which seemed to have grown even larger on him.

Giuseppe lifted him. He placed his large hand on his head and held him even more tightly. He loved him like a son, and he had adopted him.

Sergio felt a deep affection for him. He felt like crying, but he held back.

***

I, on the other hand, cannot hold back. As I write these lines, my eyes are full of tears because I know how much I have received from you, my dear Babbo!

***

TWEEEEE-TWEEEEE-TWEEEEE-TWEEEEE...

They almost didn't realize that the signal had been screeching for about ten seconds, despite its piercing, constant sound, its high and low, fast and sharp tones. They had heard about it, but none of them had ever experienced that hammering announcement, not even the cook, despite his dozens of missions.

Sergio felt that Giuseppe was holding him even more tightly both to lighten the fear he had injected in him with the story about the lemon and because he understood the meaning behind that pulsating sound.

That bear hug had become very protective, more so than at other times.

The sighting of an enemy vessel was part of everyday life on board, as was the consequent rapid dive of the sub.

The firm and strong voice of the Captain seemed mixed with some labored breathing. It was an emergency, not just a maneuver to avoid the attack.

"Bombs."

"Bombs! Bombs!!"

"BOMBS!!!" The sailors were transmitting information to their coxswain, who would convey it to the compartment heads, and the Captain.

The boys were all at their posts. All of them. Sergio, too. They knew what to do. Each one of them had a task. Lights, sounds, engines. The small cabin became suddenly completely quiet. Not a breath from the lungs of these boys. They were prepared for anything. Even to become heroes, if necessary.

KABOOOOOOMMMM!!!

KERPLASH-SPLASH-SHHHH-SCRATCHZZ

AHHHH, AARGGG, AHHH, OOUU, OOUU!

The tremendous noise sent part of the crew flying against the bulkhead. Sparks flew, the sirens went wild, and water started spraying in from all directions while the keel began to shake.

"We've been hit!"

"Hit aft, Sir!"

KABOOOUUUMMM!!

KABOOOUUUMMM!!

The depth charges left no chance to escape. Three consecutive detonations shook the submarine, and it started spinning around like a wild top. The hull was rolling from stem to stern. The crew was being tossed from side to side; the sailors were thrown one against the other as they were being injured by the ship's equipment now torn apart by the explosions. There was blood mixed with water everywhere. Screams of pain blended with the Captain's orders as they were repeated along the chain of command, from the officers to the enlisted men.

"Minus 45, Sir."

"We are at minus 45 meters."

"The engines are not responding. The propeller is gone!"

The hearts of the submariners, especially the more experienced ones, were troubled at the thought of methyl chloride, otherwise known as chloromethane. Chemists called it CH3C1 as if to exorcise its lethal effects. It was the refrigerant used in subs' air conditioning systems.

The sailors communicated via radio. Sea legends were born during such exchanges between one vessel and another. The radio also conveyed orders from the Supernavy, as the Naval Command of the Royal Navy had been renamed. The radio broadcast war bulletins and bulletins about the missions of other vessels. No secrets were more widely known among the crews than military ones.

The *Archimede* was a Brin class vessel launched in Taranto. On June 19, 1940, it sailed from the port of Massawa, in Eritrea, on its first mission, but it had to turn back because of a methyl chloride leak. The men had been seized with coughing fits shortly after departure. Four had died almost immediately, two more just after landing. Eight crewmembers had gone mad, and another 24 had been badly intoxicated. A kind of curse seemed to have struck that submarine, as it was destroyed, while surfaced, by bombs dropped by the American seaplane *PBY Catalina* in the spring of '43, during its seventh mission.

Forty-two men had gone down with the *Archimede*, and of the 25 others scattered among the waves by those bombs, only one was rescued by a fishing vessel.

The boys knew of the methyl chloride on board the *Archimede* and about the *Macallè*, which had run aground, together with its intoxicated and crazed crew, on a reef off the Bar Moussa Kebir in the waters off Sudan.

They had all heard of the efforts made on board the *Perla* to fight back the effects of that terrible gas. The Captain had ordered the quick shut down of the air conditioning system. Still, the temperature inside the boat had reached peaks of 64 degrees centigrade in the torpedo launching room, which was unbearable. On June 21, 1940, the gas leak had first affected five men and then gradually poisoned almost the entire crew.

The *Perla* had succeeded in getting back to port in desperate straits. The second in command had gone mad, and many other sailors had shown signs of delirium and madness and had to be tied down to be prevented from injuring each other. Before they could stop him, one of them ultimately succeeded in opening the valves of his compartment, thus flooding it and sinking the vessel.

The Supernavy, after many incidents and a growing number of poisoned sailors, had tried to alleviate a situation, which it had earlier considered impossible, also because of the demagoguery of the time. The Italian fleet was invincible, and depth pressure could never be allowed to cause the collapse of the air conditioning systems of submarines. So, they decided to replace chloromethane with freon in the refrigeration systems as soon as a vessel reached port.

Yet, not all the submarines at sea had been approved for such a replacement. The conflict required all available means to be deployed.

The crews out on combat missions gave their all for the Royal Navy and their Fatherland. They adapted to the hardships of the long sea deployments with a spirit of sacrifice. Submarines designed at the time had difficulties with surface navigation in rough seas or with cross-waves, so they tended to travel in immersion for as long as the charge of their electric batteries allowed. The temperature was higher, and the stabilization of the vessel was not easy, even at a depth of 20-30 meters. Any slight imperfection was amplified. An enormous effort was required of those men, who were being asked to be ever stronger and braver.

Missions could last from a minimum of four to a maximum of six to eight weeks. For this reason, at the time of embarkation, the galley was filled to the rafters with food, as much of it as possible canned or such that it could be preserved for long periods. The limited space available forced the crews to seek improvised galley and food storage areas in the engine room and in torpedo launching tubes. The high temperatures and the dampness, which reached 100 percent levels in the case of engine breakdowns or discharged batteries, created an environment favorable to the spread of mice, cockroaches, flies, and other insects.

The cook defended his assets with all means at his disposal, fighting against those natural enemies of his food supplies. His tiny galley was where he would prepare the sailors' meals, as well as those for the officers and for the Captain, the only man on board to have a kind of private life, with a semblance of a private cabin, separated from the rest of the boat by a sliding curtain. There were some airtight compartments between one bulkhead and another, creating separate spaces within the hull in case of problems.

The officers' wardroom was located astern, in a space formed by a bench on three sides, a table for four people, and some shelves. After each meal, the tables and the benches were folded back, and the hallway was cleared. The men's creativity found ways whenever a space-saving solution hadn't been devised in the original design.

Amidst cables, pipes, and levers, duffel bags, tin plates, and supplies of various kinds were placed.

Submarines were minimalist living spaces; everything was stripped down to the bare essentials. Crew members on board always outnumbered the available bunks. The latter were stacked and folded back against the bulkhead to free the passage during maneuvers or set up for meals.

The torpedo compartment and the engine room took up the largest space aboard the submarines; the rest was shared, from the bunks to the toilet. A particularly well-equipped vessel might even have two toilets along the corridor but so small that there would hardly be room enough to crouch to defecate. The sailors worked 24 hours a day, which allowed them to take turns sleeping on the bunks, in six to eight-hour rotations, depending on the type of mission, which was called the *hot bunk*.

The clothes worn on embarkation day were the same worn when returning to port: greasy, soaked in sweat, wet, salty, filthy. A few men were able to change their underwear during the crossings. When the coast was clear of enemies, the Captain would order surfacing, to recharge the batteries, allow some fresh air to circulate inside the submarine and provide a bit of relief to the crew's eyes, after all the time spent in the dim and shaky artificial light of weak light bulbs.

The sailors would take advantage of those times to wash their clothes in seawater, but with poor results, as their garments would remain stained and smelly.

The air inside the hull would become unbreathable as soon as they cast off. It was a blend of sweat, rancid motor oil, diesel fuel, kitchen fumes, and smells, not to mention the crew's farts and the acrid odor of unwashed family jewels. Giuseppe avoided cooking with garlic and onions to avoid worsening the stench, nor did he prepare spicy foods that might have led to the use of excessive amounts of the tightly rationed drinking water.

Smoking was strictly forbidden, although the Captain did allow the sharing of a few cigarettes among small groups when the boat was in the open air. But never at night, because of the danger of being sighted by the enemy from a distance. There was no real doctor on board, so they tried to avoid the risk of even minor illnesses inside the pressurized capsule. But diarrhea, colic, and backaches were part of daily life.

Scurvy was one of the greatest bugbears of life at sea, even since the days of the large sailing vessels in the sixteenth century. Giuseppe would load up crates of citrus fruit among the food supplies, especially lemons, and not just to torment the young enlisted men. Lack of vitamin C was a real scourge at sea, causing gum bleeding, muscle weakness, and joint problems.

Life at sea had its own rules, some of which were not listed in any regulation manual nor taught at the Academy, but were even more stringent. They did not follow a single set of guidelines, nor could they be divided into subgroups. Everyone knew them, and anyone who did not follow them would be expelled, taken by his arms and legs, and tossed overboard to be at least decontaminated, or else shunned as if plague-stricken. They were rules of superstition. Numbers, colors, words, situations, it was like crossing a minefield. Particular gestures or signals were unequivocal in indicating whether a mission would fail or whether they would return home alive.

Whenever someone had been unlucky, even just once, he would be known for that forever after without forgiveness. On the other hand, if someone seemed to bring good luck, then everyone wanted him near. It was like an insurance policy on board. All sailors used some kind of amulet against bad luck, and each one kept his own good luck charm in his pocket.

During his life, my father went through many of them, sometimes because they had lost their esoteric efficacy, sometimes because he had fallen in love with a different one, one that appeared to be more powerful: minerals, coral horns, gold items, photographs, number combinations. Divination was always a part of his mindset. Still, there was only one figure to which he attributed healing, redemptive, transcendent powers: Our Lady of Grace of Montenero. There is a shrine dedicated to her on a cliff overhanging Livorno called Stella Maris. Above the altar is a statue of the Virgin Mary and a stained-glass window depicting a ship in stormy seas, lit up by a large star in the sky, the lone star protecting sailors.

"We are taking on more water, Sir."

Sergio and the other sailors tried to plug up the areas where the water was leaking with anything they could find. Their jerseys, blankets, rags, socks. It was like trying to stop the wind with your hands, like trying to stop a flooding river with a small pail.

COUGH, COUGH, COUGH, KATCHOOOUU.

The men in the control room were beginning to choke. The Captain fell to the ground, on his knees. He pulled himself up, holding on to the periscope, but fell again.

Kaboouuummm!

Kaboouuuum!

Other bombs were heard in the distance. The hull had been hit in its belly and was slowly sinking, rocking downwards. The bulkheads were creaking with a metallic sound.

EEEEEE!!!!!!!AAAAOOOOOUUUUU...

The alarm sound hadn't stopped providing the beat for that dance of farewell to life.

TWEEEEE-TWEEEEE-TWEEEEE...

The noise would not abate -- all kinds of noises, like the premonition of imminent and premature death. The hull creaked, letting out strange howls, as the bow listed towards the sea bottom. Pieces of instruments and provisions were flying everywhere; anything that wasn't tied down was knocking about left and right, hitting both sailors and equipment.

The seawater leaking through had knocked out the

batteries, and the countdown had started towards the crew's death by suffocation.

The submarine was sinking slowly, rocking as if on a swing. The boys nursed their wounds and curled up against each other. They clung tight, nobody spoke, and many coughed. The air was unbreathable; the water was already above the knees of anyone trying to remain standing.

Their faces were marked with resignation; their cheeks were stained with blood and tears. Their hands were blackened and cut by their struggle against the collapsing walls.

The camaraderie existing inside a submarine was the strongest possible among a group of people, not because of sharing a bunk or living in such a limited space. Each man was bound to all of his crewmates by a tight thread, a very tight one. They would open up to each other; they would share secrets, likes and dislikes, aspirations. They went to war knowing that they could count on the others. They would have given their lives for a comrade, as he would for them.

They were more than brothers! These were boys dedicated to sacrifice for the honor of their Fatherland, a supreme value, one that went far beyond any other aspiration. They were heroes for each other.

"No!"

"You will not die here, little sparrow!" exclaimed Giuseppe.

Papa Bear picked up Sergio by his suspenders, but they came off in his hands. The boy no longer had on his jersey or his pants. He had used them to try and plug the holes in the boat's hull.

The cook was a wounded giant. His face was soaked in blood; he had a gash splitting his left cheek in two from a tin plate that had flown into him when the first bomb hit the aft compartment.

He stretched out with a great effort to pick up Sergio and throw him over his shoulder. Just as the sailor from the hospital torpedo boat had done when saving his life after the Messina disaster.

Strength and determination kept Giuseppe going, even as he staggered almost out of breath. His knees bent down, one after the other. He stood up again.

He reached the hermetically sealed turret intended as a means to rescue the crew. He wanted to slip that small human bundle into the capsule and to operate its mechanism with his last breath. He would then leave it to fate to decide how to shape the end of that boy. Once on the surface, he would be able to free himself and wait to be rescued. Or he might be taken prisoner by the British Navy. In any event, he would not die at the bottom of the sea.

The mechanism to open the turret was stuck, and the handle had been torn apart by the explosions. The cook didn't give up. With one hand, he held onto the archway above the bulkhead in the torpedo room. Giuseppe wanted to try another idea before letting death take him by the hand and lead him to join his family.

To reach the torpedo-launching room, he had to climb a slanted steel ladder. Just four steps, but under those circumstances, they seemed like a mountain to climb barefoot, as he was at that moment, in fact, after being tossed about so roughly.

The sailors in the engine room and the torpedo chamber were at the end of their strength. A couple of them were lying facedown in the water, waiting to be listed in the annals of war heroes. They hadn't even had the time to realize what was happening. They were sleeping an eternal sleep, and they were floating in peace.

The other awaited their time. Their dismay didn't dis-

courage their pride. They helped Giuseppe without asking any questions; they didn't have the energy to waste
in useless explanations. They understood.

They nodded with an eloquent expression. "Come on!"

The bear took the speechless little sparrow and put
him inside an empty torpedo tube. The surprise attack by
the British planes hadn't allowed the time to arm it, but
luckily hadn't damaged its launching system.

"Farewell, my boy. We are going to accompany our
boat to the bottom of the sea. Your angels will decide if
you have another chance to see the light."

Papa Bear tried to give him instructions while he fum-
bled around the torpedo-launching device and the boy's
suspenders, which he had thrown over his shoulders together with his godson.

"Hold your breath…"

"…Blow all the air you have inside against your ears,
and swim up as fast as you can."

He tied to Sergio's arms two small buoys he had kept
as a memento of his first mission on board a destroyer,
and he covered his face with a Davis mask he had taken
from his bunk. This was an artificial respirator invented
by the British Royal Navy and also used on Italian submarines to rescue men in case of underwater abandonment
of the hull.

These were among his treasures and good luck charms,
together with an inlaid oak cutting board gifted him by a
nobleman after a dinner prepared for about twenty fascist
high officials. He also owned a rare collection of Sardin-
ian, Spanish, and Corsican knives. And he always kept
with him his father's apron, the one with "Arancinu di
Giuseppe" embroidered on it by his grandmother, something he had found while digging through the rubble
some days after the tragedy. He kept it folded carefully,
and he had never worn it. He didn't have the time to do

it that last day, either.

He would have liked to give the boy more advice, but he had no breath left, and didn't utter another word. Together with the other sailors, he operated the device opening the cap of the launching tube.

SHHHHHH....

The human torpedo shot away from the hull amidst bubbles and sprays.

Giuseppe thanked the few boys who were still alive with his warm smile. He then fell, lifeless, lifting enough water to create waves inside the compartment.

His face, with its soft and golden beard, resurfaced a few moments later. His body was floating gently, with his arms spread out, and he looked like an angel about to fly to Heaven.

CHAPTER TWELVE

INFINITE DARKNESS

∼

The Good Giant had used the boy's suspenders to tie the two buoys under his arms. He had anchored them just above his underwear with a waxed cord, the kind used by submarines to hang T-shirts above their bunks. Giuseppe used it to hang up hams and sausages, expanding his pantry wherever he saw an inch of extra space.

With the force of desperation, he had tied onto Sergio a kind of life jacket. It would help him reach the surface. As he was no torpedo and, therefore, had no propellers, nor any self-propelled movement, the boy would not have been able to travel very far, despite the initial push of compressed air.

He knew that the boy's chances of survival were minimal, infinitesimal. Yet he had wanted to give him those, at least. The giant had died with a smile of hope.

In his violent exit from the torpedo-launching tube, Sergio got scratched all over: his back, arms, and legs. But he didn't feel it because of the pressure crushing his head and body.

The water was cold; it was like a slab of ice being perforated by his body as he went through it. He felt frozen down to the roots of his hair.

He was so thin that he felt as if water were seeping through his ribs. He pushed with his arms in ways he never knew he could, and he accompanied those wild movements with those of his legs and trunk.

He did not know how to swim. He had never learned.

Like him, many other boys who went to sea did so without ever testing it or attempting to dominate its force. At most, they might have dipped their toes or hands in the water before boarding. The sea was "bought" as a total package: glory and terror, angel and demon.

Water and darkness. A black mass of water began to surround Sergio: blackness under him, blackness on every side. But especially above him. Everywhere. He couldn't even tell whether his eyes were open or shut. They, too, were frozen. His lungs opened up well beyond his naked and bony chest. He felt them giving in; sooner or later, they would deflate completely. It had been only a few seconds. He knew he was alive. He was still alive.

That darkness was like a blade: it cut through his brain, it was disorienting, it paralyzed his muscles, and it shattered his hopes. Yet, at the same time, it sustained him. It was as if he were suspended in a void. He let himself go, with no strength left, overcome by the cold.

He tried to breathe inside his body, trying to find any breath of air he might have left within. He was floating in nothingness; he felt like a part of infinity.

There were no horizons. No point of departure, no landing place. Only a dispersion of energy, that energy Sergio wasn't able to hold onto. He would have liked to use it to float back up to life, but he couldn't.

A water barrier, one too thick to measure, blocked his ascent.

The submarine had been hit not too far from the Greek coastline near Patras, where the Supernavy had one of its bases. Sergio's crewmates were by now many meters underwater, lying underneath him, at the bottom of the sea.

He managed to open his eyes one last time, almost hoping to see a glimmer of light, a hope to hold on to until finally bursting into tears of freedom. But darkness was still the master of his existence. He saw nothing; there was nothing he could see.

In the nuns' books, he had often read about the struggle between good and evil, between smiling little fairies and a life of misfortune, presaged by dark shadows and ghosts, sometimes by enormous tentacled octopuses. Black was the color of death. When dark forces ordered someone to follow them, it was impossible to resist. Death grabbed Sergio by the hand and began to drag him through the darkest waves of the sea.

***

It was unsettling to see how desperately that frail young man had to struggle to survive, but I understood that it was all for good. My father made me aware of the angels that were protecting him and prepared me for the fight that soon would ensue between them and the dark forces.

***

Death was making fun of this little sparrow. It made him roll around. His lifeless body swayed gently from one side to the other. His head dangled, his legs and arms twirled, drawing sinuous movements as a school of fish would do, frequently bending to one way and the other following their leader and the currents.

Sergio felt he was dying and being reborn. He did not resist that state of mind. He thought of his mother and imagined that he was still a part of her. He thought he heard her heartbeat, in tune with his own. The dark forces kept tossing him about as he lay in a fetal position, safe in his mother's womb. He was waiting to escape that nightmare.

He thought of his first sixteen years, soon to be also his

last. Before this forced, resigned relaxation, his life hadn't been that boring, after all.

"It was worth it," he thought to himself.

He had navigated in his own *Nautilus* for days, maybe forever. The life he had lived, together with the other sailors, was one that only those with a special destiny could savor. Each gesture, each word, was marked by glory, emphasis, and triumph. Fear had turned into new and heroic enthusiasm.

Sergio was a boy with a positive attitude, never overcome by hardships. He was convinced that his mother was waiting for him upon his return from this mission. He had promised himself to find her, to let her know that he was okay, that he had grown up, that he wore a uniform, and that he had even been decorated with medals and honors. But, most importantly, that he loved her.

The pressure he felt on his chest was unbearable; the Black Death was advancing, suffocating him. It threw him like a rag into the pit of lost souls. The sea had decided to swallow up that boy, too, after having feasted on his crewmates.

Sergio ran to meet his mother. The sailors were all lined up on deck; the entrance to the port was a festival of colors and fanfares. The anthem resounded along the columns of the pier; the hands of the heroic submariners were pressed against their hearts, their gaze raised towards the flying flag on the turret. With a grand and authoritative gesture, the Commander saluted the units lined up for the welcoming ceremony and the mothers and families who were throwing confetti and streamers.

Disembarkation was orderly; despite the boys' eagerness to embrace their families, discipline always held a high place in their behavior. Nobody pushed. As soon as he landed, Sergio walked ahead, receiving pats on his shoulders from his crewmates.

"See you next time around!"

"Don't get drunk right away!"

"...and stay away from whore houses!"

Everyone was giving him advice, while his eyes were drawn only to one beautiful woman, wrapped in a white cape, who was following him from behind the barriers, drying her tears with a white veil. She looked like an angel.

She was trying to make her way through a group of cheering mothers, trying to reach her boy. She had with her a sign, on which was written in large letters:

SERGIO DAL BONI

She had reconstructed the path of her son's journey by forcing her uncle Aldo, who was moved to mercy by the despair of this mother, his much-beloved niece, to reveal where the boy had been kept from the earliest days of his life. Kneeling in front of him in tears, time after time, she had finally succeeded in making him tell her about his escape from the orphanage, his joining the Navy, and his being assigned to la Spezia, first, then to Taranto.

Aldo had then stopped following his moves, as guilty feelings weighed on him day and night, and as he hoped that his niece might build a new life for herself with the good husband, he had found her.

On the other hand, Adele had spent the previous three years knocking at the doors of any military installation that might have some information. She had gone to the Ministry of the Navy in Rome, the Arsenal in Taranto, and La Spezia. She had traveled to the naval bases in Messina, Trapani, Cagliari, Naples, and Brindisi. She finally even went to the Naval Academy in Livorno, although with a heavy heart at the thought of her Giorgio.

The visit to the Academy had been decisive. The officer in charge of the administrative office had taken pity on her, faced with her shiny eyes, so sunken and full of sorrow.

"Madam, I will do whatever I can to give you the information you are looking for. Please wait here for a moment."

He returned about an hour later with a broad smile. Adele felt the blood begin to circulate anew in her veins.

"We have a Sergio in the navy with the surname N.N.; he is in a submarine unit."

"He might be the one: there are no other N.N.s by the name of Sergio."

Adele fell at his feet, thanking him with utter devotion. The officer helped her up, full of embarrassment.

"Could you please tell me where he has embarked? I beg of you."

"Madam, I can't. I really cannot."

"… I would be court-martialed. It is a military secret."

"I beg of you…" Adele had continued to implore him, but the officer had looked down and bitten his lip to avoid saying what he would have liked to say.

The young woman suddenly hugged him.

"Thank you. Thanks anyway." Her embrace had lasted long enough to dampen the collar of the officer's jacket with her tears. He was touched, and while pushing her back gently and looking at her, he said,

"Goodbye…and…happy return to Sicily."

Adele left the Academy with an unexpected prize. She ran home, packed a couple of changes of clothes, took a piece of bread from the kitchen, and said goodbye to her "good husband" as she crossed the doorstep.

"I must go…"

She went to the station and took the first available train traveling south. When she reached Reggio Calabria, she took a ferry to Messina. She barely made it, as navigation had been suspended because of the outbreak of the war. The fleet of ferryboats had been almost entirely sunk. To cross the Straits of Messina, she had to rely on fishing boats.

As soon as Adele reached the island, she began her pilgrimage from one military post to another. She had joined other mothers who were traveling from base to base searching for news of their sons in the Navy.

Sergio had received some indications from Giuseppe, and he knew what to expect from an exploratory encounter with his parents. He knew the meaning of the note he had brought away from the Catholic Institute for Orphaned Children.

Sergio N.N.
Date of Birth – March 6, 1926
Mother: Adele Dal Boni
Father: Unknown
Born of an adulterous relationship. The mother's family opted to give custody of the child to a Religious Institution for Orphans.

He had analyzed those words together with the "Good Giant."

"Do you see here? It says that your father is unknown, and you were born of adultery," the cook had commented one day to Sergio during navigation.

"This doesn't mean that your mother was a loose woman," he had tried to hearten him. However, he had no specific reason to exclude the possibility that his mother Adele might have been a practitioner of the world's oldest profession in some protected house or even on the streets.

He didn't think so, and he had a reason for hope, as the note said, "the mother's family opted to give custody…" This, in itself, showed that the girl had someone behind her, someone with influence if they could "opt." Having a family in a position to choose was alone enough to elevate the boy above the level of the streets.

The fact that he was born of adultery and that his father had not recognized him was a hint that his father's family was of a high enough social class that he would not have been allowed to separate from his first wife. Or that he was prevented from doing so by other authorities, such as military.

"My boy, the day you meet your mother, you should hold her tight and never let her go again!"

"She, too, has suffered as you have. Someone else decided for her, and she could not object," said Giuseppe, who had lost his mother in that tidal wave and had always felt guilty about it, although it was not his fault.

"If only I had held her tighter..." remorse pounded on his brain, as when he pounded basil leaves in the wooden mortar to make a good pesto.

Adele had witnessed a dozen landings and at least as many missed returns. In the former cases, if her son was not among the sailors, she would pull herself together, take a deep breath, gather up her courage, and set off again with other mothers towards the next port where a docking was expected. In the latter cases, she would rush to the office of the Harbor Command to ask for the names of the boys left at the bottom of the sea, trusting that she wouldn't find Sergio N.N. on that list.

She had already hoisted that sign with his name in about twenty ports before witnessing the docking of the submarine that came from a mission in Crete. The poster was a little wrinkled but still legible. Sergio saw it as soon as the line of boys disembarking scattered away from the pier.

"MAMMA!" he shouted, with a voice full of surprise and happiness.

"SERGIO!!!" his mother screamed, even more forcefully, as she ran towards him.

The two stopped when there were just a few steps between them. They stared into each other's eyes, studied each other for a few seconds. She covered that last short distance. She enveloped him in a long maternal embrace. She ran her fingers through his hair. She took his face in her hands to admire him and gaze at him, over and over, and each time, she embraced him again.

"You are so handsome!"

"My love, you are so beautiful!"

"And what a big boy you have grown into!"

He was only sixteen, and his mother had missed out on all of his childhood growth, even though he was still very skinny and just a bit taller than her. Sergio recognized her voice, he had heard it many times when he was in her womb, and he knew its vibrations, the alterations in its rhythm when she was worried, if she was drifting off to sleep. The relationship between mother and child is so strong, so extreme, that sensations are twice as intense. If she is awake, he is, too; if she is hurt, he, too, feels pain.

The desire to hug each other was like a fire that devoured them from within and that finally could transform itself into vital energy so as to project them into the center of an impenetrable circle. The rest of the world disappeared, letting their emotions expand to infinity.

They walked silently along the harbor, following along the silhouette of the submarine tight in its moorings and as still as a sleeping whale. The sea breeze caressed their faces and the salt beaded the air. They held hands, their thoughts crossed, postponing questions and answers. They sat on a bench on the wharf, staring at a torpedo boat waiting to take on its crew.

"Mother," said Sergino, "I have thought of you every moment..."

"You are even more beautiful than I ever painted you in my dreams."

She listened to him without interrupting. She was completely enchanted with his eyes and enraptured by his smile, his dark and thick eyelashes, his heart-shaped lips, and his little button nose.

"How is my father?" He did not ask who he was, only how to idealize him. A brilliant man, a politician, a banker, a sailor... Yes, indeed, he must be a sailor, just like him. Was he tall, short, plump, thin, blond, brown-haired? And, most importantly, good or evil?

"Your father was a hero!"

She was not lying. In all those years, she had never laid on him the blame for taking his own life and compromising hers. Her love for Giorgio had not diminished by a single comma; on the contrary. That night had been worth a life, both of their lives.

"His life belonged to the Royal Navy!"

When Sergio heard about the sea and a man dedicated to sacrifice, he felt confident that he had always carried his father's genes within himself.

"You said he was a hero."

The boy also understood that he would never see him, that he could not do anything to erase that N.N. and convince his father to recognize him. But deep down, he already knew this, too.

"Mamma, I am sailing again at the end of the month..."

"...The enemy gives us no respite, but we rule the sea."

"I am proud of you, my son."

In her heart, Adele did not want to let him go to war anymore. She couldn't possibly risk losing him again. But she held back.

"You were born to be a hero, my son."

"I will wait for you here on the pier, in the front row, to greet you as soon as you get back to port..."

"Mamma," Sergio said while wrapping an arm around her back and drawing her close.

"You must not be afraid."

"You know, we had a close call the other day…"

Adele let herself be squeezed by her son while running her fingers through his hair. She couldn't stop doing it, and the lightness of that gesture was like sweet music to the boy. A fairy was caressing him, and that fairy was his mother. What more could he wish?

"The Captain ordered a rapid immersion, as we unexpectedly encountered a British ship, right there in front of us, in the middle of nowhere."

Adele didn't interrupt him as he spoke in a heated yet easy manner. He was not just pretending to be tough; he wanted his mother to free herself from the anguish of never seeing him reemerge from the deep waters.

"They dropped depth bombs all around us. They all exploded around us: starboard and port, stem and stern. The hull started spinning like a top."

Adele admired him with tenderness.

"I am so proud of you. Did you carry out your duties? Did you honor your crewmates? I am sure you did."

"Well, Mamma, the boys were dying. All of them."

"But I was in the torpedo-launching room, they opened the hatch, and I slipped out like an anchovy."

Sergino hugged his mother even tighter.

He could feel her heartbeat alongside his own. But her face was flickering, like a blurry film.

He held her hand tight, just as Giuseppe had told him to do. And the tighter he held onto her, the colder the water felt.

His mother's eyes started to dissolve, as did her hair, arms, and legs.

Adele was still calling him.

"Sergio."

"My little Sergio, stay awake. Please, wake up!"

"I'll wait for you here, at the pier. I am here."

Her voice lulled him; her smile accompanied him as

he plunged in the infinite darkness. The white luminosity of his mother gave way to that scary, icy-cold black ghost that suddenly swallowed him up.

The base in Patras received news of the sinking of the submarine from a support and supply ship.

Per required procedure, before sinking, the crew had launched a round buoy, resembling a small circular dingy and large enough to be noticed. The identifying plate on the buoy contained the name of the vessel that had been shot down. In a watertight compartment inside the buoy, there was a paper listing the sub's division, the mission assigned, the Commander's name, the number of men on board, divided by rank: officers, petty officers, sailors, support personnel.

That sheet of paper contained the essential information for the dramatic count of war heroes and the future awarding of medals for valor.

The regime would never have divulged the number of vessels lost in battle, nor of those remaining, nor certainly, would it ever have revealed how many men had thus far been sacrificed in the name of the Fatherland.

Istituto Luce broadcast news received from official sources in its newsreels. Nobody would have reported another submarine sunk by the enemy. Mussolini was soon to be deposed, and the propaganda machine was intensifying its efforts. There was no way to express opposition to it.

The film of the torpedo boats active in the Atlantic was part of the standard fare.

Shrill celebratory music accompanied the prescribed text as it was dictated. The dictatorship was increasingly eroded by internal treason.

"The assailants are attacking."

"The British are retreating."

The images of the bow of an enemy vessel as it sank

confirmed who ruled the seas.

"New Zealanders, Canadians, Indians, Africans. As usual, the British use others to cover their retreat."

Such messages were spread in order to light a patriotic fire in more young human beings, asking them to kill other human beings at the cost, if necessary, of their own lives.

No one, at that time, was in a position to reveal the size of that sacrifice. But those who lived at sea did keep a tally.

It was the summer of 1943, a few weeks before the Armistice and the dramatic transfer of the entire fleet under German Command.

The support vessel communicated the number of the new war heroes by radio. Altogether 67 men. No survivors.

The number of submarines lying at the bottom of the sea had grown noticeably; the war was lost. The Supernavy was in charge of informing the families and this was one of its most difficult tasks, given that many sailors were boys who had come out of institutes such as the one that had sheltered Sergino.

The Reverend Mother would have cried and prayed for him. She would then have informed uncle Aldo, who, in turn, would have had to decide whether to inform Adele or to allow her to live with the dream of her boy far from the battlefield, healthy, happy, and lucky.

The war went on for another two years. Nobody could tend to those heroes, nor to the many more thousands added to their numbers at that time. Medals for military valor would only be awarded in 1947, after the paperwork containing the lists of assignments, detachments, and combat units had been sorted.

Sergio, my father, was awarded the "Cross for Military Merit," for having "carried out his duties with bravery, abnegation, and sense of duty."

CHAPTER THIRTEEN

AN INANIMATE BODY

~

F atmira was a beautiful girl. She was sixteen years old and had lived her entire life in the poverty and dignity of a nomadic family that had set up its encampment along the Ionian coast, between Albania and Greece, just behind the island of Corfu. That territory had been occupied first by the Italians and later by the Germans, who had devastated entire communities by deporting their populations to extermination camps.

She had dozens of brothers and sisters: some were blood relatives, others had been gathered here and there during the family's wanderings to keep away and safe from battlefields and military torture. Most often, to better hide and blend into the surrounding landscape, nomads kept away from the sea.

They would get just close enough to the coastline to collect water from the streams flowing into the sea while at the same time being ready to start moving again in case of danger. They always traveled by land with their wagons.

Some of those kids had been found under the rubble, next to the bodies of their parents, who had died from air raids.

Fatmira loved to run on the sand with her siblings. The arena gave relief to their feet, never covered by fabrics or shoes of any kind. From an early age, the soles of their feet, hardened by time, served as footwear.

Irna, her mother, held the reins of an extended family

of at least thirty members, from the elderly and sick to malnourished infants. They did not build; they left nothing behind.

They had no documents, nor any records of the places where they had lived. As the years went by, their age became more and more indefinite. The older ones could be 50 or 80 years old, and it was impossible to establish a definite date of birth for each of them. Their faces filled with wrinkles not so much because of advancing age, as because of the elements they were exposed to, without a stable roof over their head.

The younger ones had dark splotches and striations on their olive skin. Even by observing them closely, it was impossible to distinguish whether it was a natural tan, thus not homogeneous, rather than the result of long-sedimented layers of dirt. In any case, their faces were palette knife portraits made with a unique technique perfected by Mother Nature. Their skin was a breeding ground for antibodies, and contact with all kinds of germs and infections made them practically immune.

The dazzling green-orange color of Fatmira's eyes was like a bright beacon for ships adrift at sea. She loved the sea, and, whenever she could, she would run to the beach to carve out a little piece of paradise for herself. She dreamt of being kidnapped by the sun's rays and led into a never-ending fairy tale, where she could meet her prince, a brave and smiling, impetuous and protective man.

That morning, Fatmira ran to watch the sunrise. In the camp, old men were still asleep. She tried not to wake her siblings, who usually caught up with her as soon as they felt the loss of heat and the void left on the straw mattress where they slept together at night. The light of day surprised her as it came up behind her shoulders, lengthening her shadow over the water until it rippled towards the horizon. She stood with her legs apart and her arms outstretched, letting the morning breeze blow through her hair, making it fly where the wind chose. She felt free from chains and light as a feather.

The sound of the lapping waves seemed different. Something was preventing the normal ebbing of the tides and the usual overlapping of the sprays along the shoreline. Fatmira snapped as if she had to dodge a large log coming at her. In front of her, a boy's body was being pushed about by the waves as they overturned onto each other.

She knelt down instantly, allowing the water to dig a small sand barrier between her and that young man. Two strange objects were tied around his chest. The boy's head was resting on the sand as his arms followed the movements of the water that seemed to be helping his body reach the driest part of the shore. His legs were almost entirely buried in the sand.

Fatmira sat near that body and studied it carefully. She lingered on the boy's profile, his nose, his curls, and his hands. She didn't get too close; she was waiting for him to open his eyes so she could smile at him. He was a fallen angel from Heaven, and she didn't want to scare him.

The sun was already high in the sky when her brothers joined her. They gathered close to Fatmira to admire that figure still being rocked by the water. One of them ran to call Irna. With branches, they built a rudimentary stretcher and carried the boy to their encampment. They then placed him on a pallet made of wood and leaves. They covered him with a heavy blanket.

In silence, she looked at him. And the more she looked at him, the more she fell in love with him.

"Mother, do you think he will open his eyes one day?" asked Fatmira.

"Yes," answered Irna. "He is breathing, but he isn't

here quite yet."

"What do you mean?" Fatmira asked again.

"That he is not among the living, nor he is not among the dead." Replied Irna as she read the palms of his hands with expert gestures.

Fatmira caressed his forehead, as she had done many times over many weeks, in fact, months now. He had become part of her family. Every time they moved, his lifeless body also traveled with that group of nomads.

Irna took the boy's hand again and brought it close to that of her daughter.

"This boy has suffered, ever since he was born. Do you see? Look here, look at the curve of his line," said Irna.

"Mother, may I keep him with me? Forever?"

"No, my dear daughter."

"Why?" said Fatmira with a start.

"I am sure he will fall in love with me; we will have loads of children. We will be happy; we will live together forever!" she added, trying to hold the severe gaze of her mother. She was seeking a sign of her final permission while her eyes rested on the boy's face, relaxed in that serene coma.

"No, Fatmira…"

"I am sorry, my dear daughter."

"Why?" the girl insisted.

The girl recognized that tone in her mother's voice. She had heard it many times before when it came to making important decisions or moving the encampment. She, and all the other family members, attributed to Irna the authority that is due to people who know how to interpret the past, survive in the present, read the future, and above all, guide their people through the three phases of life, without wavering.

"This boy will make his woman happy, he will have many children with her, and will live a life full of love…"

Palm reading, among the nomads, has been passed down from mother to daughter for hundreds of years. Chiromancy, according to some interpretations, was already practiced in the days of the Old Testament. The union of the Greek words *keir* (hand) and *manteia* (divination) has led the art of interpreting tomorrow, through palm reading, to be considered close to science, philosophy, astrology. It resisted religious persecutions and overcame the barriers of skepticism. Sometimes, due to bad-faith practitioners, it has slipped into the swamp of underhanded deception.

Irna, as she had learned from her mother and, even more so, from her grandmother, and as she would, in turn, teach Fatmira, followed a slow and methodical path when reading someone's palm. Her concentration made her seem in total synergy with the stars, with the heavenly vault. She would lay her fingertips on the hand she was reading, and she would follow its lines, trying to absorb the messages that were transmitted to her.

With slow and intense movements, her eyes moved from the boy's hand to his face to capture an overview of the past, the present, and the future.

Her credibility was beyond discussion among members of her clan. She understood that the boy would wake up but would not regain his memory right away. He would remain suspended in a world that did not belong to him and from which he would withdraw. He would have a short but intense romance with her daughter.

The world of nomads, however, was not in his future. Irna clearly saw that, for no apparent reason, he would go away. Just as he had appeared on the shore that morning, so, suddenly, he would disappear.

Irna tried to measure her words. She didn't want to hurt her daughter, but she had to warn her. She had no doubts that someday her daughter would have to give up her prince and suffer tremendously.

"My dear daughter... your futures do not coincide. It is written in your hands. You are not to be that woman..."

The girl's disappointment was great, and she sank into a deep dark mood. She ran off with her eyes full of tears, following the path of the moon as it receded from their encampment.

War was rumbling in the air. Sinister noises kept the gypsies awake and alert as they moved from one place to another, carrying along their belongings and that inert body. They rearmed the camp and moved again, dozens and dozens of times, until the fighting became less frequent, and they met more civilians than soldiers on their path. More rubble than houses. More people armed with shovels than with rifles and bayonets.

Fatmira had grown up. In the eyes of others, she had become an adult; she was at the right age to become a wife and a mother. Nomadic families met while traveling, some joined the group, and others left it to follow or form new families. Irna took her daughter aside.

"I think that young man is just right for you," she said, pointing at one of the sons of a clan that had recently joined them from the north. They exchanged information on which places to avoid, where to stock up on food, the town squares in which to carry out a bit of business. Among them were merchants and beggars; some were horse traders, others begged by dancing or simply sitting on the side of the road.

"No, I don't want to elope with him." Elopement was the way marriage most often took place among the nomads: the two betrothed would run away from the encampment while their families pretended to stop them. The girl would give herself to the young man, and he would bring her back to the encampment for the official recognition of the new couple.

"I will wait for him to wake up." She wanted that young man found on the shore.

Irna had tried several other times to dissuade her, but her answer had always been the same. Her daughter was so determined and insistent that, in the end, she had to capitulate.

"My boy," said Irna in a soft voice, holding Sergio's hands tightly in hers.

"You died at sea. The sea kept you alive, it protected you, and it didn't allow you to die. It gave you back to the earth…"

"I give you my daughter Fatmira as your bride."

"She will take care of you."

She took the girl's hands and joined them with those of the sleeping prince. She muttered something incomprehensible, even to her daughter, according to an ancient ritual repeated from generation to generation to ward off misfortune and the evil eye and attract well-being and prosperity.

Together, the two women lay their hands on Sergio's face and chest to transmit warmth and energy to him.

Sergio did not react.

***

Suddenly everything made sense to me. I felt as if I had always known it, and I exclaimed: "Babbo, you were in another dimension! He was pleased and patted me on my head as he used to do when, as a child, I would surprise him with my creative inventions. I felt my mind filled with knowledge, and new truths were revealed.

***

Sergio was in that unexplored place where the life one

has lived rushes by in an instant while bringing to the surface memories long buried in the most recondite corners of the brain, composing a mosaic of emotions, fragments of sentences, scents, sounds, and colors.

The body is separate from the soul but not detached from it. Not yet detached. It was the place, to quote Irna, where Sergio was not among the living nor among the dead.

He was awaiting his turn, the verdict to be given him at the entrance separating life from the Afterlife. That entrance that dissolves into eternal light or infinite darkness. It marks the ascent to Heaven or the fall into the dark.

It is the path towards our final destiny, the main road with a thousand and one paths that unfold. In some cases, there is a way back, in others not. The choices that we make during our life make us divert or take the right path. Mistakes and exploits, sins and generosity trace the pivot points through which we will be seen, judged and remembered.

***

"Dear Babbo, I have always been fascinated by set theory," I said.

He knew it, I didn't doubt it. But I continued.

"It is a language between mathematics and philosophy that has often helped me to understand or, at least, approximate your approach to life. It is mine, too. It has to do with the measure of infinity, with various classes of infinity."

Finally, I understood his thought clearly.

"You've told me many times of the darkness you went through once you were ejected into the sea, of the positive thinking that kept you afloat, of the faith that allowed you to breathe. Of your faith in something higher, in God, in the angels. You never wanted to consider life as a finite set, that is, one that is determined, complete, numbered, limited in its moments."

"That's right, my son," he picked up where I had left off.

"Such moments - he said - are all the more eloquent in the journey we make, the more we can shape them in the integrity of thought, action, and, last but not least, nor less valuable, reaction. The more we live them with respect for ourselves and others, in consideration that life is a marvelous gift and, as such, must be nourished, awaited, defended, and shared in a positive way."

"You have to believe it, always!" my father advised me.

"I do, you can count on it." I promised.

Indeed, at least in words, this may appear easy. But it is harder, much harder, to implement if you are overwhelmed by disappointments, fears, negative situations of all kinds. Yet, it works. If you want to look at things this way, and sorry if I try with numbers again: the difference between positive thinking and self-torture through negative thinking is the same as between zero and nothing.

They only appear to have the same meaning, but zero is a number, and therefore it is something. Nothing is nothing.

Zero is a glass half full; nothing is the half-empty one. Zero is the bottom from which you can climb up, while nothing is the darkness that grips you. Zero can become one, two, one thousand, ten thousand, and can continue to grow, or descend into the negative, below zero, like the temperature. It moves, it does not sit still. The void is a physical and mental emptiness, it is a trap in which one remains prisoner, crying, complaining, and not reacting.

***

Fatmira kept hoping, even though that body had not moved voluntarily since the day it was picked up on the beach. She was sure that, sooner or later, the boy would regain consciousness.

And, even if her mother's vision turned out to be accurate, she would have what she had been dreaming. She would give that boy a new hope for life; she would kiss him, she would caress him again, she would see the color of his eyes and join them with hers. She desired him with all her soul, and this occupied her every thought, day and night.

The nomads moved again. Fatmira rearranged her wagon and covered the boy with a blanket so that he might travel comfortably, without jerks and jolts.

She looked at him intently, trying to infuse him with energy, warmth, and hope. She thought she saw a smile take shape on his lips. Maybe it wasn't just her imagination.

Sergio opened his eyes.

The girl, who hadn't lifted her eyes from him for a second, took his hands, started to kiss them, and placed them against her cheeks to give him immediate warmth.

"My prince!" she whispered.

"I have been waiting for you all this time..." she couldn't stop caressing his hands and face and stroking his hair while he tried to understand where he was, why he was there, who was that beautiful girl who was showering such love upon him.

Sergio tried to pull himself up, levering his hands against the side of the wagon. She held him up gently.

She was talking to him in an unfamiliar language, but she never stopped smiling. The words uttered by Fatmira were incomprehensible, but they had the sound and the colors of happiness. They were a pure melody. He didn't understand, but he smiled at her with his eyes, holding on to her in an attempt to sit up.

Sergio managed to get up on his legs and, pulling himself up with difficulty, still supported by Fatmira, he tried to climb off the wagon.

Sergio had returned to life.

The two of them turned towards that lifeless body still on the stretcher. On their faces glowed a smile of peacefulness and serenity.

***

"But!? Then, whose dead body is that on the stretcher?" I asked my father. The white glow that radiated from him enveloped me; his expression of love canceled all my fears. I felt at peace, I had understood, and I was not frightened.

It was not Sergio's body.

It was mine!

CHAPTER FOURTEEN

SHARKS

~

A lexa is a wonderful woman. I am lucky, very lucky. I am deeply in love with her, as she is with me. Even when she is not there physically, she is always with me, and I smile at her as if she were in front of me.

She didn't have an easy childhood. Germana, her mother, would have loved me, I am sure. And I would have loved her, too. I didn't get to know her, as she died of cancer when Alexa was only eight years old.

I remember Germana's face perfectly, her delicacy, her intelligent eyes. I had seen her many times in a slightly yellowed photograph, in which she is holding in her arms that little pest that entered my life when I was almost 46 years old. Since then, Alexa has been my inseparable half, and she was nearly 38 years old.

Alexa has always been highly competitive. We have challenged each other at every moment, in every context, in a perennial competition, as she has constantly moved onto new playing fields: surprise vacations to celebrate her birthday or mine, the knowledge of people and things. All of these competitions have ended in smiles, in hugs above everything and everyone.

Each new challenge has always been better than the previous one, and the outcome has always been the same: another excuse to kiss and love each other.

We have played soccer, obviously on opposite teams. Each time Alexa has turned into a sort of bulldozer regardless of the hard kicks to her shins by opponents who were quite ruthless towards the gentle sex.

In tennis, I have almost always lost with her; perhaps because being one against the other and no one else in the middle or next to her, she could go all out with me. She has never gifted me one single point, and a hilarious ballet accompanied by funny war cries has always underlined her winners.

That time, too, I came close to winning but ended up losing again. We were living in Tampa, Florida overlooking the Gulf of Mexico, across from Miami. The year 2015, three days before Christmas, five more months, and I would have celebrated my 60th birthday.

After the game, I collapsed on a chair, out of the sun. Something was wrong. I felt a terrible, sharp pain in my chest. I was out of breath. I couldn't breathe.

"Love, I can't breathe…"

Alexa saw me slide out of my chair like jelly and slump to the ground. I was staring at the sky and gasping for air through my open mouth and nose, trying to open up my chest. But to no avail.

Alexa didn't utter a word. She knelt next to me and began rhythmically compressing my chest, one hand over the other. Once, twice, ten times, with increasing intensity. She tried to perform mouth-to-mouth resuscitation; she held my nose while breathing into my mouth.

On other occasions, I had spent all my energies in a tennis match, but my good physical shape had lulled me into the idea of being a superman, almost supernatural. Nothing could harm me.

I have never drunk alcohol, except for sparkling wine or champagne on birthdays or an occasional toast. A bottle to celebrate has always been in the refrigerator, perhaps out of a habit acquired over the years in Latin America, where the saying "*Que sea un motivo,*" is widespread, meaning that any occasion is a good one to drink and be merry, even at funerals.

I did not choose to abstain from alcohol because of some vow. I just don't like it. It may seem absurd, yet not even good wine interests me.

***

For the first time, I was remembering what had happened that terrible day. I re-experienced the growing pain that was then pervading my body, and I felt how agitated Alexa was becoming. But I couldn't push back a fun wine memory that had come to my mind, and I shared it with my father. He laughed with affection.

One day, we went to a trattoria in Tuscany together. The innkeeper discovered that I was disdaining his Chianti, and came out of the kitchen with a shotgun used for hunting wild boar.

"Either you shoot him or I will! - he said dead serious. - If he doesn't drink, he doesn't deserve to live!" On that occasion, I had to accept his kind offer.

***

I have never smoked, except for one cigarette that my older brother Claudio, an avid smoker until his last breath, stuck in my mouth when I was 13 or 14 years old, so as not to be the only one punished for violating our father's absolute prohibition on smoking. We were discovered, and we spent a really bad quarter of an hour!

In addition, a nasty taste of charred paper and nicotine remained in my mouth and throat, and I asked Claudio about this in the following years.

"But doesn't it make you sick?"

"No!" he would answer, blowing smoke rings, while his wife, Anna, would look at me, wringing her face in a grimace of disgust, mixed with the knowledge that she could not do anything to stop him.

My father lived long enough to meet Alexa and to fall in love with her. When he left us on a cold February afternoon in 2006, I am sure he was serene because he knew that I was finally happy.

Our life has always been illuminated by love, even when we have encountered difficulties and stressful times. There were many of those, but never between the two of us, never.

Playing with Alexa has been like playing chess with my father, but with the roles reversed. She always won, even when I didn't throw the game. But I have never backed down. I have always accepted her challenges, like that time on the top of the highest mountain I could possibly have imagined.

We were in the Pennine Alps, at the border between Italy and Switzerland. The Cervino or Matterhorn, depending on the country from which you face it, is a mountain carved by ice and continental drift hundreds of millions of years ago. Its peak is above the perpetual snow line, its sides are steep, its slopes treacherous, especially for amateur skiers like myself. Not like her.

I was happy to prove, first of all to myself, that I was not possessed by a reverential fear of that peak crowned by creamy white clouds.

We went up, up to the last station of the chairlifts and then the cable car, ready to ski back down to the valley, drawing serpentines on the fresh snow.

I did not have that typical question mark on my face, "Now how do I get back down?"

No, I didn't ask myself. Nor did Alexa, as she knew that, being always positive by nature and habit, I would somehow find a way.

She is elegant with skis on her feet; she dances along

the slopes caressing the profiles of the mountain, and she paints soft lines like a brush does on a canvas.

"Honey, this is a black run, for super experienced skiers, just like you," she told me, with a sly air.

"I would have bet!" I replied, gritting my teeth. I was not complaining; I was taking up the challenge.

Alexa smiled mischievously as she pushed off with her arms and legs to attack that steep slope of blinding snow.

As she started down, she yelled in amusement: "Let's see how long it takes you to get to the shelter that's halfway!" Which was like saying, "You have no chance to win!"

I did not wait: I took off my skis and, holding them in my hand, I threw myself into the void. Sitting!

When I was a child with my brothers, I remembered that we hurled ourselves down towering hills of sand, clay, grass, or cement with cars made of cardboard. We found them everywhere, in Cuba, in Colombia, Panama, Venezuela, as we followed our father, who constantly moved with the whole family in search of greater fortune.

One of those times, my brothers and I built a decent vehicle out of cardboard, complete with openings for windows. We were laughing like crazy, but we hadn't considered the laws of physics.

We were like bullets out of control. Instead of just sliding down the hill, our cardboard vehicle started somersaulting with us inside. We got to the bottom full of scratches and bruised, but still laughing.

My ski pants were like the cardboard I used as a child, and the snow was softer than sand or concrete and very slick because semi-frozen. I slid down effortlessly.

Expert skiers passed me and stared at me as if I were a fish out of water, a fool who would show up (as an adult!) on a black run with no clue as to what to do and how to keep his skis on.

It made me smile all the more as I definitely knew about skis and skiing.

I was just aiming at getting beyond that first part, a stretch that was particularly narrow and steep, to show those arrogant fools and my beloved on the run, who they were making fun of.

When I finally reached where the mountain opened up in its entire splendor, leaving immense space to the imagination on the track to choose for the descent, then I put my skis back on.

Obviously, there was a problem, which for me meant a solution. I was a good skier, but only on water. A zero on snow, and I said zero, not nothing. The alpine ski techniques involved balancing one's weight on the downhill ski when turning, or perhaps the other way around, I don't remember. In any case, it was too complicated to put into practice in that situation. So, I decided to repeat what I had learned as a child, something that could be cheerfully translated as "a little here and a little there" movement. In short, the classic zigzag.

I started zigzagging extremely fast, without any kind of brake. Snow sprayed all around me as I created irregular swirls, and my speed reached frightening heights.

Alexa was almost at the shelter and enjoying the fresh air on her face; she seemed figure skating rather than skiing. I passed her, laughing, just like in the days of my cardboard slides.

She started chasing me, but it was too late, and to add insult to injury, I raised my left leg as I used to do when water-skiing, a scene she had already seen during our first vacation in the Caribbean. With the right ski on the snow and the left one up, I covered the last few meters, but I was having too much fun just to stop there and act the great champion. I smashed into a snowbank just a few meters from the finish line. Alexa took off her skis and ran towards me, covering me with snowballs and warm kisses.

"You did it again! I'll beat you up!" She remembered the Caribbean holiday I've just mentioned.

She was on the speedboat, and I wanted to show off. I asked the guy piloting the boat to accelerate to the maximum, and I was flying over the water.

I took off my left ski, and it floated away in the boat's wake. I rested my bare left foot behind my right one on the only ski left.

The rope was so taut that, when I jumped over the high column of water raised by the boat's engine, I flew sideways with such force that I tilted the speedboat, with Alexa on board.

In one of those feats of bravado, I pulled up alongside the boat and thumbed my nose at her with my left hand. All of a sudden, I began rolling wildly on that sheet of water like a stone thrown with strength and dexterity that skips time and again on the surface.

When they pulled me back on board, Alexa was nothing short of excited. "Love, but where did you learn to ski like this? You're incredible!"

The reward was one for the books.

We left our room many hours later. Music was still playing on the beach. While we were dancing, I confessed. It was not to take away her admiration for my athletic performance; it was rather a way to allow her to punch me gently, as she did at the end of competitions lost due to some subterfuge of mine.

Over the years, my ability to keep such amusing secrets has decreased considerably, or rather, she now knows me better, and my tricks are sooner unveiled. Such surprises last less.

"I fell, my love."

"What?"

"I fell; I lost the only ski I had left!"

As I no longer had skies under my feet and having pulled the rope so taut it was at the breaking point, I had become a spinning top. I was swirling on my back and rolling and bouncing like a ball thrown down the stairs.

I got away with some light contusions, but I came home triumphant, even though I had never taken water-skiing lessons, nor of any other sport.

***

More memories came to me. I felt my mind expand and could see in great detail my previous life. This time, I was with my father in Venezuela.

***

"Come one, take your skis! I want to take you for a spin," my father had told me one day.

I love the Caribbean Sea, and it reminds me of everything about him. I wonder why? I sense him to be in symbiosis with this sea more than any other. Maybe it is because it is the place where my father "made a man" out of me, as he used to say.

His bond with the sea was so strong that often his life lessons took place among the waves. Whenever possible, he would take me out by boat. He sunbathed; I was his crew. Then it was time for a *spin on your skis*, and he would take the helm and turn on the engine, and I would dive into the water after throwing my skis and the rope overboard.

Once, we were at a club in Catia La Mar, on the coast near Caracas. It was the only one in Venezuela well equipped for nautical sports. Most importantly, it was the only one with a *malecón*, a breakwater made of huge stones and concrete, a barrier against rough seas. Inside the malecón was a very wide bay, with calm and reassuring waters, where you could swim, fish, go sailing, do water-skiing. On the outside was *the outside*, the open sea with all of its inhabitants!

My father always loved me very much. Sometimes I think he saw a special kind of light in me as if he could communicate with me through thought alone. He waited for me to put on my skis, and he checked to make sure that the rope was good and taut before he revved up the engine to pull me out of the water at the right time, without any jolts.

He went around the bay twice, and on the third lap, usually the last, he surprised me by going straight and heading for the open sea!

"Babbo! Babbo!" I wanted to scream, thinking that he might have gotten distracted, but I knew it would not make any difference. He had decided to do it, and he was doing it.

I saw the malecón as we speeded away from it, and as we reached the first wave, the motorboat my father was piloting climbed up to the crest before immediately disappearing into thin air, leaving me alone with that monster. In front of me, there was a mountain of water that rushed towards me, and I saw the darkest blue I had ever seen, only interrupted by the rope linking me to the speedboat.

Luckily, I could still see that rope cutting through the water, which meant I was still tied to the speedboat!

I managed to get to the top, and it was my turn to come down on the other side of the monster while my father and his little boat, which seemed to grow smaller and smaller in that immensity, began to climb the next wave.

My head was full of tales by the sailors of Catia La Mar and the signs at the exit of the malecón. *Peligro. Tiburones!* These were no fantasies nor baseless warnings against the danger of sharks. Underwater power grids protected the entrance to the bay. Along the beaches outside of the club area, it was hazardous, often fatal, to swim even close to the shore.

Five, ten, twenty waves. They seemed more than a thousand to me until my father made a wide circle to catch the waves in the opposite direction and return to the bay. I was holding the handlebar so tightly that my hands were practically glued to that rubber tube. I didn't stray from the boat's wake. My eyes were fixed on the water as it was being carved by the speedboat and on the spray that came out from the engine.

In my mind, I have a clear and well-defined image of a shark's fin disappearing under the waves and reappearing just beyond the crest. Little does it matter if it was the result of adrenaline or if, together with the fin, there was a fierce beast ready to devour me with one snap of its jaw.

When the boat found its way back into the bay, I understood the message my father was sending me. He had never turned around to check if I was still attached to the rope or if an enormous shark had swallowed me.

I cannot say for sure because I had been staring at the engine and the stern of the boat, but I think I would have noticed if he had turned around, even just for a moment. He trusted me more than I trusted myself.

"Fabino, you are now 14 years old, and now you are a man!" he said endearingly, as I pulled the boat ashore and tied it to the mooring post in the marina.

It was no reminder that he had gone off to war at my age. Nor did he want to bring up his submarine story and the fact that he was saved from death by crossing first through the infinite darkness of the sea and then the darkness of coma from hypothermia.

"Life must be faced head-on, with an open mind and an open heart. Always remember that."

I listened to him in silence. I would have liked to tell him that I hadn't been afraid. Over my fourteen years, he had already conveyed to me that mixture of serenity and madness that he called inner balance many times, and it had allowed me to move from a state of danger and difficulty to one of strength and hope.

"Do not rebel against the greatness of the universe; rather, build your own path by fighting against the weaknesses of men who have no conscience. Never let yourself be infected by superficiality. Open yourself to the ideas of others. Reach for dreams, and grab them. If you don't succeed, start all over again."

Thank you, Babbo, for teaching me all this. I am happy that you could share this with Alexa, too; her life is made of dreams that coincide with mine, and many of them we have achieved together.

Alexa understood that she wouldn't succeed. My body was shutting down. I saw her disappear inside the tennis clubhouse, a large and elegant building on the other side of the courts.

"GO! GO! GO!" I yelled, hoping she would hear me.

I no longer felt my feet; it was as if they had been amputated.

As the minutes went by, probably not all that many, maybe just a couple, that terrible feeling of paralysis became more and more insistent; it kept creeping up, crawling along my ankles and up towards my knees.

I felt my legs go numb and then gradually freeze as if paralyzed.

Inside my head, I was screaming in a way I'd never done before, and as I had never heard anyone do. But not a sound came out of my mouth. Alexa would certainly have forgiven me if she had heard me say all those swear words.

Something unknown and swift was separating me

from her, from our life together. I was screaming at an invisible enemy that was consuming me from within.

Alexa ran back with Allegra, the director of the tennis club. I saw her terrified expression, but also her determination in making me take a couple of aspirins.

"Take them, my love; they will make you better," Alexa told me while Allegra opened my mouth.

I wasn't crying, but I was despairing.

"I am completely paralyzed from the waist down. I can't get up…"

I was speaking, but I did not know whether my words were, in fact, just staying in my mind.

Alexa tried to pull me up.

"Oh my God! My hands are paralyzed, too!

'No. No, NO!"

"I won't die here, I promise you!"

"I am not ready!"

The ambulance arrived in no time and made its way through the tennis courts to reach me.

I could only move my eyes. I felt as if I could no longer breathe. I could no longer recognize my voice, not even inside me. The words I was putting together were confused, uncoordinated. I kept railing somehow against a fate that was taking me away.

They loaded me onto a gurney, and very shortly after that, I found myself inside the ambulance.

I did not understand what the EMT people were saying. They moved around, attached me to wires, and waved syringes. I thought they wanted to sedate me, and I started struggling and wriggling, or at least that's what I was trying to do to keep myself from falling into a permanent sleep.

"Sir, Sir, calm down!"

"No, NO, I AM NOT GOING TO CALM DOWN!"

They forced an oxygen mask onto my face. I no longer

could see Alexa, and I kept awake by trying to figure out whether she had succeeded in getting onto the ambulance or whether she was following us by car.

We quickly reached the Florida Hospital Pepin Heart Institute in Tampa, now called AdventHealth Pepin Heart Institute. I felt as if I had traveled the whole time in apnea; it felt like an eternity!

I remembered having been in a similar situation at least a couple of times before, if not three or four. They were not direct memories; they were more like glimpses of memory captured by my subconscious. They had not been as serious as this, but I took them as models to convince myself that I would get through this one, as well.

The first time I was, more or less, three years old. One of my siblings, as a prank, pushed me into a swimming pool. I didn't know how to swim and, however frantically, I flailed about, I was sinking like a stone.

While the siren accompanied the run from the tennis courts to the hospital, I saw myself there, sitting at the bottom of the pool, with my face surrounded by bubbles, with my eyes wide open, and a skyscraper of water above me.

No, my time had not come so soon - it was too early! I saw that child push off from the pool floor with his legs and move his arms like a frog to float up and reach the edge, where someone immediately pulled him out of the water.

I smiled and held my breath under the oxygen mask.

I had another close call in a swimming pool. I had gotten into the habit of competing against myself to see how deep I could go to try and touch the bottom. I was seven or eight years old. With great effort, I reached the bottom of the deep end, where lay the grid that trapped objects lost by swimmers and where I often found coins and other lovely treasures.

I touched the grid, but just at that moment, the suction pump turned on, pulling those trophies away, and along with them, the baptism chain that was around my neck. Its medal got caught in the screen. I had barely enough breath to float back to the surface, and I wasn't able to unhook it. I remained at the bottom of the pool like a dead weight.

As the ambulance began to slow down, I saw that boy scratch his hands and his neck in a desperate attempt to tear off that thin little chain and its medal, then suddenly turn around and push away with a powerful kick to return to the surface.

I smiled again, and again I held my breath, even though I had precious little to breathe. None of my muscles responded to my commands any longer. I don't even know if I could still move my eyes, but I desperately wanted to look around and find Alexa.

The ambulance came to a complete stop. Immediately, white, green, and blue scrubs surrounded me. My thoughts were keeping me alive. I fought against the terrifying idea of entirely separating from my body and seeing my soul fly away.

I thought back to the children in the swimming pool and their last-minute rescue.

I saw the big shark swimming around my water skis and the next wave that pushed it back.

I saw the devastating Caracas earthquake of 1967, with the accordion-like collapse of the thirty-story building where we lived and our miraculous move to another neighborhood just the day before.

Each of these images, and the many dozens going through my head, threw me into panic as I felt that they anticipated the arrival of death and announced a clean break with Alexa, our children, and our dreams.

Yet, at the same time, each of these images offered me an unhoped-for way out and intervention from above, a protective shield. And to them, I clung with all my strength.

I did not see Alexa. But I did see a team of doctors and nurses ready to take charge of me.

I don't know their names, at least not all of them, but I do remember their faces and their words.

"We are losing him! Quick, QUICK!"

***

I couldn't believe it.

I had no logical explanation for why this was happening to me, why it was my body on that gurney and not my father's.

I didn't understand why, seventy years after those tragic wartime moments, which had, luckily, not been part of my own life, why I was living through, in a lightening-fast sequence, the dreams, the ravings, the disappointments, the hopes of two generations before mine -- that of my father, Sergio, and of his parents, Adele and Giorgio.

I knew their stories which my father and mother had told time and time again. I thought they were over; I didn't expect to be reliving them myself. My father's awakening in the arms of Fatmira, and their farewell. His meeting his mother Adele, just as he had imagined it while in the deepest darkness. His travels to Latin America and his embracing my sweet mother, Erika, in Brazil. My father's death in 2006, that of my mother nine years later, just six months before that terrible day in my life.

It was like a novel I did not wish to read, and I had kept it on my bedside table without ever opening it.

***

The nurses rushed the gurney along the corridor of the

Emergency Department carrying my paralyzed body, my eyes desperately seeking Alexa, my empty lungs, and my heart now at rest.

I wasn't able to tear that thin little chain and medal, nor to push off one last time with my legs. Forgive me, Alexa, forgive me, Babbo. I will take care of you.

At that very moment, I died.

CHAPTER FIFTEEN

ANGELS

~

Alexa had entered with me into the unpredictable path of memories. Perhaps she was traveling through it in a parallel world, with fragments of her childhood, desolation in her heart before a future that we would no longer spend together. The meaning of life had vaporized, dematerialized. She let it flow away, unable to resist what was happening.

The feeling of helplessness is most devastating for a human being; it is like falling into a hole from which it is impossible to get out, and where, after a thousand, a hundred thousand attempts, that have gone wrong, there is no longer the strength nor the will to continue to try. It is worse than surrendering; it is even worse than giving up without a trace of hope and, much worse, than losing the last glimmer of faith.

Alexa's eyes were full of tears, fixed on that flat line that she could make out through the half-open door of the Emergency Room. When the monitor had started ringing and no longer registered a heartbeat, she had been hurried out. It was flat far too long. She watched in a stupor all the movement taking place around the inert body of her husband, her best friend, her soul mate, the love of her life.

"I warn you; I'm for total love!" I had told her when we first met. It was, in part, as a warning to her and, in part, to remind me that I had had enough unfortunate loves.

It meant, in broad terms: no shortcuts concerning the truth, zero tolerance of romantic escapades, total dedication to the family we would create.

She had found that warning very amusing. It was, in fact, a rather childish request on my part for a promissory note, knowing full well that no woman would be willing to sign it just like that, a priori, without double-checking. What was I asking for, after all? Eternal love? What madness!

With tears filling her eyes, Alexa smiled at the thought of that request. She smiled not because she thought it unfair or unjustified, quite the opposite. She would have asked me the same herself, hadn't I done it first. "I couldn't ask for anything better, my love!"

Alexa tried to summon all the inner strength she had learned to master over 11 years in a Catholic boarding school, where she had been left after the death of her mother by her father, a general, who was unable to manage three young children.

She sought within herself the courage that had shielded her while reporting from areas ruled by armed rebels during the dissolution of the Soviet Union, long before she met me. She was part of the New York Times team of reporters in the Moscow Bureau in the very years of the collapse of a system of power that had lost its grip over entire populations.

I had just left behind me the invisible entrance that Irna had described when looking at my father's motionless body. My life had detached itself from that middle station, between the living and the dead. A great light lit up my eyes, warmed me, and filled me with peace.

The whiteness was absolute.

The light came towards me. It wasn't I who was advancing towards infinity; it was infinity that was enveloping me. The immense was taking over my senses -- hearing, sight, and touch. I was free from all my worries, my most secret passions, and my most persistent desires.

Or perhaps it was my soul that was expanding beyond measure, free of my body, without boundaries. I was weightless; not a single bond prevented me from blissfully levitating while, in fact, never moving.

Everyone, at some time, has sought happiness – and nobody will ever convince me of the contrary, however hard they may try, and with all due respect – everyone has wished it on someone else, has wished to build it and defend it at all costs. To share it.

It is a primordial state that evolves with billions of facets, as in an extraordinary kaleidoscope. We seek happiness in a vacation when we associate it with fun, and a refuge from our daily concerns. We seek it in love when it is linked to the sense of wellbeing drawn from the smile of the person who means the world to us, life itself. In studying, when we realize that the sky is the limit and that we can go even beyond that because our mind is capable of anything and its opposite. In sports, in work, in writing a book, in giving alms, in begging.

We try to measure it with the dimension of a space, an area, and a perimeter. We try to measure it in time, with the passing of hours, minutes, and years. We want it for our children, for our loved ones. In many cases, it is what we most wish for them, and we take on problems and responsibilities to try and ensure it for them. We take their doubts and fears on our shoulders.

And we never, ever regret it. Should the sky fall, we would do it again, probably with even greater dedication, if not obstinacy. And who cares if there is no gratitude or if, after all our efforts, it turns out that we were mistaken because, after all, it was not what our beloved really wanted.

I don't know about you, but for me, the meaning of happiness has always been, first and foremost, *giving*. Giving happiness to others. Then, also, receiving it, even though it may have been induced. If you are happy, I am more than happy. I am happy because of your happiness, first, and consequently, of mine as well. I am not saying that I have never been able to be happy on my own. But if you are, too, I'm twice as happy.

Happiness, contentment, cheer, bliss, joy, ecstasy, wellbeing. They are all branches of the same tree, one on which we climb every day trying to touch the air, and we continue to climb to seek fresher air above.

Once beyond that entrance and as I gradually grew into pure spirit and became part of infinity, or, if you prefer, once I entered Heaven, those branches became the stage, united to form a great, total bliss.

Bliss. I said before that I was flying, blissfully, without ties. I had assumed the essence of angels -- a complete, perfect state of constant happiness; celestial, entirely supernatural, and eternal.

I felt no guilt, no remorse, and no regrets. I had been freed of all the treasures and burdens of a beautiful life, one that had been, at times, also difficult, with accumulated sorrows set aside so as not to suffer but to continue to look ahead, with moments of extreme adrenaline and extreme enjoyment. A life like any other, but unique because it was mine. And it was gone.

I was in Heaven, literally. The place for the just, and I didn't ask myself whether I, too, was one of them. Or whether I had always been among them. I was a chosen one, predestined for glory and eternal grace. The light of salvation that surrounded me made me aware of what I am telling you now. The whiteness was absolute.

Never, during my earthly life, have I had the chance to witness such clear, crystalline refraction. As a student, during a physics course, I carried out the classic experiment of the stick half immersed in a glass of water so that it would appear, depending on the point of observation, as either broken or just bent at the line of demarcation between the liquid and the air. The stick is split in two or deformed by the deflection of light rays.

All around me was completely white and at the same time extremely colored. I have never seen so many colors altogether and all so brilliant. The light was not like that of the sun, which burns your eyes if you look at its source, even if just for an instant.

The light was white. White was its source, white its rays, white the whiteness that emanated, white and sincere the blade of light that penetrated my spirit. But its dispersion was extremely colorful: red with infinite reds, blue with unimaginable blues, green with incredible greens, and billions of purple, yellow, orange rays. Greys with majestic shades, yes. But not even a thread of black.

An unparalleled, beautiful prism!

Everything was white. And at the same time had sharp but no cutting edges. The outlines were delicate, the curves were soft, and the horizon line was within reach. Although everything I saw was white, I could distinguish my shape and my natural colors. My skin was white, as was my hair. I had no clothes on, no shoes, nothing extraneous to my body, although it no longer existed. It was as if I had stepped out of a purifying bath. But I did not feel naked. Colors and shapes were part of my mental refraction, but the whiteness was overwhelming. It came straight from the Almighty.

I saw myself from behind as if I were filming the scene with a camera positioned a few meters away behind me.

The silence was absolute, respectfully absolute. No sound broke that immaculate, marvelous purity. The sky was white and radiant. No sound was resonating between the ground and the horizon. The light blue of clear seawater, the green and golden reflections of hills full of blossoms, all the colors of the universe converged into a white mirror that reminded me of pure, extremely pure milk. It was peaceful, reassuring.

I felt like in a cloud of cotton that covers you without suffocating, supports you without your noticing, lights up your eyes, and regenerates your lungs. It was mystically familiar, and I felt at home as if I had never left from there. It had no walls, no windows; it was infinite, as vast as the desire to discover new galaxies, comfortable beyond any discomfort.

I was holding my sweet Alexa by the hand, whom I saw a little blurred as if she were not really there. She wasn't there. I sensed her aura; it was inside me.

I saw angels dancing lightly. They were figures expressing goodness and generosity. I admired their features; they conveyed positive energy.

"My adored Babbo. I am so happy to see you again..."

My father was there, in a long white robe; his green, deep and clear eyes were part of the prism that transformed everything into eternal light.

No voice broke the silence in the air. There was no air. No one breathed. Emotions floated lightly, like the contented and quiet sleep of a newborn on its mother's breast.

My words did not cause my lips to move or any musical reverberations. Nor did my father's.

Words and thoughts flowed through our minds; they flowed without any sudden fluctuation in vibrations or changes of tone.

My father smiled at me. He never stopped smiling at me. He smiled with his eyes, his face, his hands, and his shoulders, without moving any of them.

He communicated understanding, tolerance, and peace to me.

He was in front of me. But he wasn't alone. With his left hand, he held Germana gently and protectively. Germana was in front of Alexa; it was a natural reflection between mother and daughter. There was no communication between them; they couldn't see each other. Germana was only in my sphere.

I didn't ask myself why Alexa's mother was there and not my own. No doubt or fear crossed me. She, too, smiled at me with the same intensity.

The love between Giorgio and Adele, the child of that love, that restless boy, the young Balilla, the bombs, the darkness of the sea closing in around my father until he lost consciousness... The novel I didn't want to read was scrolling before my eyes, emanating from my father's smile; it belonged to me from the very moment I was conceived. It was part of me.

"There are angels everywhere, my Fabino."

He wasn't giving me any explanation or advice; he was only allowing my mind to open up to memories, even those that had been buried. Everything was coming back to the surface with clear outlines.

I felt the caresses of the angels through my father's retelling of things -- those stories blended with my own memories.

Small and big misadventures I encountered, terrible moments I escaped, serious situations I had to confront. I had thanked my good luck and marched on. There were angels behind that good luck!

Alexa sat motionless in the waiting room as she awaited the cardiac surgeon's verdict. The dramatic situation threw her mind into confusion. She wondered what would happen if I didn't survive, what would she tell our young children.

She was beside herself with grief, petrified, helpless, lost. She let herself relive the many beautiful moments we had shared, which now intertwined wildly with the unacceptable reality of my death.

The flat line she had glimpsed on the monitor continued to carve within her a terrible furrow between panic and reason. She wished she had died with me, right there, alongside me on that gurney. To leave everything behind. But she felt immediately ashamed and scornfully dismissed the thought of causing her children the same pain she had suffered when her mother had died. Her intellect and her sense of responsibility had engaged in a ruthless battle against the impulse and denial of life itself. She was crying; and at the same time, trying to pull herself out of the hole where she had ended up. She was trying to press the reset button to start over. She didn't want to give up.

She remembered when she was 13 years old, and she had fallen into a deep ravine while skiing in low visibility. She had come down that slope countless times, and as the pacesetter, she was skiing ahead of a group of friends. She knew she had to turn left, but at that spot, the safety cord had been ripped up by the blizzard of the night before.

She plunged into the frozen mountain ravine. She tried to call for help. It was still not *our* Matterhorn, it was *her* Matterhorn.

"HELP!"

"HELP!" she yelled at the top of her lungs, but there was not a living soul around. They had all gone back to their mountain shelters. There was no visibility.

She started crying, and when her tears froze on her cheeks, she began praying. She understood that no one could come looking for her, and the small chocolate bar she had in her pocket would not be of much use. She prepared to freeze to death.

"Help, help." She heard another voice calling for help, and it was her sister Eugenia, a couple of years older than her.

It was all in her head, but Alexa found the strength to get up. Her sister was in danger.

She took off her skis and planted them into the wall of

frozen snow. She pushed them in deeply as if they were pickaxes. She pulled herself up inch by inch, using all her strength. She repeated the maneuver time and time again to climb higher and still higher. Holding on to that smooth and frozen mountainside, she finally reached the top, where the fog hid the ski run. Eugenia was still calling her.

"Help me, help me." Exhausted, Alexa put her skis back on just as she saw the snowmobile lights with the rescue team who had come looking for her.

"Doctor, do you want the time of death?" asked the nurse, who wasn't the only one feeling defeated.

"The patient, 59 years old, male, showed up at the Emergency Department..." she started reading the medical report.

"...With coronary artery disease to one single vessel, and with the left descending artery 100 percent occluded..."

"Another victim of the *widow-maker*," echoed in a subdued voice another medical assistant, commenting on the very low chances of surviving this type of heart attack, the one sadly known as the widow-maker.

"Fabino, often we don't see them because they are women, men, living beings whom we encounter along our path..." My father had become more and more mystical over the years.

He had been a Reiki Master and many of the people to whom he had brought relief saw him as a beacon, even a source of life. He had taken me to a Reiki seminar and had tried to encourage me along the path to becoming a Reiki Master myself.

He didn't succeed because I insisted on not taking him too seriously about it. Logic prevented me from seeing the spirituality of this Japanese-born doctrine. My incredulity didn't allow for the encounter between primordial energy and universal vital energy, the key to understanding Rei and Ki.

"Babbo, tell me how you learned to lay your hands, to heal with them." For the first time, I was not irritating him, as would have happened when we were alive, and I was visibly skeptical.

"Soon, very soon, you will learn it yourself. You don't need me. You have more energy than I ever had. I've always said it to your mother."

"…Fabio has inside him the strength of the universe; one day, he will discover it, and he will be able to concentrate it in himself to give full happiness to others, beginning with those he truly loves…"

His words gave me an almost childlike pleasure. I thought of my mother, and I saw her delight in those words. She was proud to have brought me into the world, even though she kept reminding me that it had been a miracle.

"You clung to life, and you never let it go," my mother would tell me as she recounted how she had fallen during her pregnancy and had seriously risked losing me.

"An angel brought you back," would add my mother, who had always been in perfect harmony with my father.

"No, not yet," exclaimed the surgeon, calm but determined, stopping his assistants who were sadly recording the data for the final report.

"Doctor, it has been almost eight minutes now…" a member of the medical team pointed out.

"I want to try; I want to get him back on his feet…"

"Quickly! Set up a discharge…" ordered the doctor, pointing at the defibrillator, which had now been set aside like a blunt weapon.

He was half bent over that body, preparing to place a kind of electrical bomb on his chest, and was studying the exact points where to intervene. He clasped his hands together to warm them and gather all his strength.

"Here, Doctor…" They handed him the two metal plates by the handles, and he gripped them tightly as if he wanted to lift a concrete pillar.

"GO!" he ordered the electric shock on that lifeless chest.

My father's smile vibrated with magic, even more full of life and warmth.

"Fabino, I never went beyond the entrance you left behind. My heart was frozen, but it still worked…"

I listened to his words with great devotion.

"In the infinite darkness of the sea, angels brought me back; they didn't allow me to enter here. It was not my time."

"They guided me toward your mother."

The energy conveyed to me by my father was infinite. It reached every single cell, even the most remote and depleted.

"Let the balance flow within you, rediscover the integrity that belongs to you, expand your senses. There are angels with you. Help them…"

His words had become mystical, insistent, not less loving.

"When I said that you could learn the path to healing, this is precisely what I meant, this precise moment."

The smiles of my father and Germana merged into one.

I felt immensity pour over me, with a force I had never felt.

"Babbo, I am not ready!" I said abruptly.

"I know. Now, go back to Alexa!" said my father, with the serenity of someone who knew how to guide you through the light.

His embrace was powerful; his goodness was explosive. We looked at each other one last time until I saw him expand into white; until it disappeared.

The flat, mute line on the monitor gave a jolt.

"Doctor, we got him back. We got him back!"

"My God, my God!" exclaimed an assistant who tried to check if other signs of life accompanied the heartbeat.

The radiant and pleasant whiteness suddenly thinned out, leaving me with a sense of uneasiness. For a couple of seconds, I was annoyed at how I had been snatched from Heaven. But that strange feeling vanished immediately.

A yellowish-whiter dot replaced the absolute white, like a tiny dull sun. It was the flashlight that a doctor was waving before my eyes.

"What is your name, Sir?"

"Fabio," I answered immediately.

"Repeat it, and spell it," he urged me.

"F_A_B_I_O," I said without hesitation.

The operating room was a party choir. I could see the agitation of the medical team, but now it was light and radiant.

"Quick! Let's proceed with the stent!" The operating room was readied quickly. The surgeon was ready to insert the microscopic tube into my femoral artery to reach my heart and eliminate the blockage.

The procedure lasted about twenty minutes.

The cardiologist left the operating room and walked over to Alexa, who was still holding her face in her hands.

"Ma'am, everything went well!"

Alexa felt herself sway as her body filled with warmth, new energy. Her color came back to her face; her blood was bubbling up. Her hands had reached the edge of that cursed black hole, and she was coming out of it!

She began breathing freely again. And she quickly gave in to liberating tears. She hugged the surgeon; crying turned to sobs.

"His heart has started racing again, like that of a child!" The doctor breathed in profoundly while deciding how to describe what he had just witnessed.

"His vital signs are healthy. All normal."

Alexa hugged him again, and he returned her embrace with sincere emotion while trying to explain that return from a death that had seem inevitable.

"It's the first time that something like this has happened to me. The heart that starts beating again after such a long time, and vital signs returning to what they were before…no necrosis as if nothing had happened…"

He was a man of science. He would have liked to say the word "miracle." Alexa read it clearly in his eyes as he let go of her embrace. The surgeon had work to complete.

He went back to the operating room, where I was fully awake and looking around me, trying to understand.

"I am Doctor G, that's what everybody calls me…"

He was young, did not reach the age of 35, and had more than a familiar smile. It gave me peace.

"It's an Indian last name; nobody knows how to pronounce it," he said in a friendly way.

"He is the best plumber in the world," joked a doctor on his team.

"You chanced on the right doctor at the right time," added another one.

My father's words about the existence of angels resonated with clarity; I could still hear them.

"My angels. I see them all around here!" I thought to myself as Doctor G held my hand and his team rearranged the machines, ready to save more lives.

"Fabio, your wife is waiting for you. Soon you will be able to see her."

"What happened, Doctor?" I asked, turning towards him.

"…What happened is that you died!" He answered without hesitation, in an affectionate tone.

"… And what happened is that you came back to life!" he didn't take any credit, even though he had continued to believe that he could do it until the very last moment, despite everything, despite the medical textbooks.

I looked at him as one looks at a holy image, a product of the unconscious, of hope.

"Thank you, Doctor G!" I said, with tears in my eyes.

"Fabio..." said that angel, taking my right hand between his.

"...I didn't do it..."

"...Someone has given you an extra life."

"Enjoy it!"

NOTES

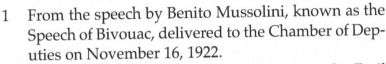

1 From the speech by Benito Mussolini, known as the Speech of Bivouac, delivered to the Chamber of Deputies on November 16, 1922.

2 From the book *Talks with Mussolini*, written by Emil Ludwig during his meetings with Benito Mussolini in the Hall of the Globe of Palazzo Venezia, in Rome, between 1929 and 1932.

3 From the *Speech of the Ascension (The Fascist Regime for the Greatness of Italy)* delivered to the Chamber of Deputies on 26 May 1927.

4 From the preface by Benito Mussolini to the Italian translation of Riccardo Korherr's book, *Regret of Births, Death of Peoples*, published by Unione Editoriale d'Italia. September 1928.

5 From the *Program of the National Fascist Party*, November 1921.

6 From the *Italian Football Yearbook 1932 - 1930/31* - File: Vol.3

7 From *Il Balilla*, number 17 - Year X - 28 April 1932

8 From *Twenty Thousand Leagues Under the Sea* (Jules Verne) - 1870

9 From *Decalogue of the Fascist Soldier* (1935)

10 *From the Royal Decree, 5 September 1938, n. 1483*

11 The Song of the Submarines (Guglielmo Giannini-Mario Ruccione, 1941)

12 From *Il Cinema - Myths, Experiences and Reality of a Totalitarian Regime* by Luigi Freddi (L'Arnia - 1949)

13 From *Newsreels* of the Luce Archive (Istituto Luce, Rome)

14 From *Newsreels* of the Luce Archive (Istituto Luce, Rome)

15 From *Newsreels* of the Luce Archive (Istituto Luce, Rome)

ACKNOWLEDGEMENTS

~

As I said at the beginning, I wrote this book to leave a testimony of the beauty of life and of the existence of Heaven and Angels, which allowed me to come back to life and return as a child who looks at the world with a huge and happy smile.

I could not have written this book without the indefatigable help of Alexa. Thank you, my love -- I love you so much!!

And certainly, I wouldn't be here to tell you my story if it wasn't for Venkataramanan Gangadharan, also known as Doctor G. I can say that he is not only a phenomenal cardiologist, he is an angel who has the gift of making the heart of people like me beat. Thank you, Doctor G.!

If at Hunter's Green Country Club, the Director of Raquet Sports, Allegra Campos, hadn't intervened immediately with those two aspirins, I wouldn't have made it. Another angel! Thank you, Allegra, you scored the match point of my life!

When the ambulance entered the hospital, I was practically dead. At that time, I didn't know the name of the hospital. Well, it's the AdventHealth Pepin Heart Institute in Tampa.

Behind this name is a man, another angel, named Tom

-- Tom Pepin. When his father Art died from heart disease, Tom decided to put his entrepreneurial skills at the service of cardiovascular research, donating to the hospital an entire facility dedicated to the heart. Thanks to the help of Jan Berry and Crisha Scolaro, who have always supported me, I met Tom. I hugged him and thanked him. I was so moved that I almost couldn't speak when WFLA News Channel 8's Stacie Schaible interviewed us together. Thanks, Tom! Thanks, Jan! Thanks, Crisha! Thanks, Stacie!

I also met Tom's daughter Tina, who leads the Pepin Family Foundation. I told her about the book I was writing and, ever since, she has always encouraged and supported me. And she too, today, is by my side. Thanks, Tina!!

Behind the hospital name are thousands of people, who are part of the Adventist Health System or AdventHealth with hospitals in every corner of Florida. They are angels, heroes who, every day, dedicate their lives to saving other people. Many thanks to each of you!!

I wrote in Italian, as I would surely have made many mistakes in English or Spanish. I have a thick Italian accent when I speak English and most people in the US put up with me with sympathy! I know Ughetta Fitzgerald Lubin worked hard and with dedication to translate my story from the Italian. A special thanks to her and to my wife who reviewed the manuscript with acuity. Amy Cianci, my awesome editor, was invaluable; likewise Isa Crosta who formatted this book with infinite patience.

Finally, I want to thank all those people who, like me, love life and believe in goodness and generosity. They are many and I don't know them all. How do I recognize them when I meet them? Simple: they return my smile!